To Howa

Read this book and spread the message.

Karen C. Diehr
10/22/96

770.593.4798

or

770.417.5542 (pager)

THE TIME HAS COME

THE TIME HAS COME

A Social Murder Mystery

XAVIER C. DICKS

FARRY BELL PRESS

Farry Bell Books, Inc., 100 Peachtree Street, Suite 200, Atlanta, GA. 30303

Printed in the United States of America
First Farry Bell Book Printing: September 1995

ISBN: 0-9647003-0-1
LC: 95-90487

FOR
ROBERTA AND C.J.

♥

And he answered and said unto them, *Have ye no read,*
that he which made them at the beginning made them male and female,
And said, For this cause shall a man leave his father and mother,
and shall cleave to his wife: and they shall twain to be one flesh?
Wherefore they are no more twain, but one flesh.
What therefore God hath goined together, let no man put asunder.

MATTHEW 19:4-6

ACKNOWLEDGMENTS

To all the people who influenced this book, I say thanks to you
from the bottom of my heart. Without you, this book would not have been
possible. It was only with your suggestions, encouragement, and prayers
that I was able to complete this book. While I can't mention everyone, I
would like to give special thanks to my mother, Leola, who taught me how
to write speeches, Pat Jones, Shirley Fay White, Josephine Smiley, my aunt,
Kevin Stewart, Sherry Churchill Nolan, Christie Davis, Robert Mckie Sr,
Rev. George McCalep, Michael Woods, author of the book, "Afromation,"
Xavier C. Dicks Jr., my wonderful son, and most of all, to my wife, Roberta,
who had faith and believed that I would successfully complete this book.

AUTHOR'S NOTE

There is perhaps no topic that is more hotly debated than how best for Blacks to achieve racial equality in America. Over the years, there have been a number of strategies tried such as affirmative action and other entitlement programs to try to help the plight of Blacks in this country.

Still most Blacks would argue that the condition of Blacks is as bad in the mid-90's as it was in the mid-60's. There is high unemployment, ever increasing instances of violence, lack of education, children born out of wedlock, alcoholism, drug addiction, and blatant racism.

There is an emerging belief that the only way for Blacks to better themselves is to do it themselves. This self-help philosophy is being pushed by everyone except the current crop of civil rights leaders.

The following story is offered to both entertain and to cause anyone who reads it to think very deeply about what Blacks need to do to solve their dilemma. No one person nor group has the answer, but perhaps by reading this story, some person may gain just a little more insight that may assist in solving this puzzle.

Chapter 1

It was almost 5:00 a.m. The janitor was sleeping soundly in the broom closet. He was stretched out on the floor with his feet just barely touching the door that led out into the hallway. He had slept during most of his 10:00 p.m. to 6:00 a.m. shift.

Suddenly he lifted his head, sat up, then got to his feet. He stretched, shook his head and turned on the light switch. He had gone through this ritual for the last 15 years and got up each morning like clockwork.

"Ah, it's 5:00 a.m., time to turn on the lights, unlock the doors and make sure all of my cleaning equipment is put away." The janitor had worked for so long in this part of the Capitol Building that he had his job down to a science. Clean and mop for three hours, sleep for four, put on the finishing touches for one hour and go home.

He turned on the lights, and there it was: the famous floor of the U.S. Senate. Everything was squeaky clean. After all of these years, the janitor was still in awe. He walked over to the main entrance
doors and took his key and unlocked them. He noticed the large agenda board, "Reverend Johnnie Benson on School Desegregation, 9:00."

*   *   *   *   *   *

The hotel room was marvelous. It was larger than most three bedroom apartments. In the center of the room near the wall opposite the large king size bed set a big screen TV.

It was 6:00 a.m. Mr. Benson was up, already shaven, dressed in a very expensive dark brown suit and reading <u>The Washington Post</u>. He turned on the big screen TV. Immediately the familiar face of a national newscaster appeared. The newscaster ran down the daily list of our national pastimes: overnight murders, burglaries, arson fires, trade deficit, sports and the usual I-don't-give-a-damn-what's-happening political updates.

After about twenty minutes, Mr. Benson began to review his notes for his speech on the Senate Floor. He felt that he was going to be especially good today.

He thought to himself, "It's time for the members of Congress to take this school busing issue seriously, get off of their asses and do something about it. My brethren and I have worked on this issue too long, and I will not let it be forgotten. The Supreme Court has done its part, but it can only interpret existing laws. It's up to these legislators to pass laws and penalties to make sure that busing is carried out. It is utterly ridiculous that some small county named DeKalb in Georgia is still not complying with court-ordered busing. Here it is 1993 and segregation in those schools continues to exist. It's time for Black and White kids to receive equal education and thus equal access to the job market and the American dream."

Mr. Benson walked into the bathroom and looked into the full length mirror. He smiled. There was fire in his eyes. He had not felt this energized in months.

There was a knock on the door. He thought to himself, "Breakfast." But it was too early; too early by about 30 minutes. Then again, this was the best hotel in Washington, D.C. As a matter of fact, only the elite could afford to stay here, and they started their days very early while all the wanna-be's were still fast asleep, futilely dreaming about how they were going to be somebody.

Reverend Benson opened the door without looking to see who it was. Who else could it be this time of morning? He turned his back to the open door and headed back to the desk near the window to retrieve his notes.

A good looking man in an Armani suit stepped in. "Good morning, Reverend Benson. How are you? I want to thank you for all of your contributions to society, especially those to the Black race. You will long be remembered."

Reverend Benson spun around just in time to see the flight of the switchblade in mid-air. It was too late. There was not enough time to move out of the way or to get his arm up to block the blow. The cut was surgeon-smooth. There was very little blood. Mr. Benson's world went black and silent.

$$* \quad * \quad * \quad * \quad * \quad *$$

People were beginning to get impatient. It was 9:30 and all of the preliminaries were over. The Senators were having their second cups of coffee knowing that they needed to be alert to confront the barrage that the Reverend Benson was sure to bring upon them. Besides that, this meeting was being televised. No need to have the stigma of having fallen asleep on national television for your local constituency to see.

The Majority Leader signaled one of the aides closest to him and instructed him to contact the hotel where the Reverend Johnnie Benson was staying and see if he had left yet.

The maid couldn't figure out what it was lying by the door to room number 1002. "What are those pieces of paper lying on the floor? How could anyone in their right mind put torn up pieces of paper in the hallway of our hotel?"

She stopped her cleaning cart, hobbled around it and headed down the hall to pick up those pieces of paper. It was only 9:30 and her ankles and feet already hurt. Perhaps she should have taken her doctor's advice and gone on a diet to lose the extra 150 pounds her poor legs had to carry around. What did the doctor know? He was fat himself.

The maid saw it but did not believe her eyes. "My lawd! Look a here! Some heathen has torn up the do not disturb sign!"

As she bent over to get the debris, gravity did not let her forget the extra 150 pounds she carried, and she pushed on the door to room 1002 to get her balance. The door, which was not fully closed, burst open and the maid fell into the room, stumbled, and with a loud spill, landed on the floor. Shaken, she got to her knees and saw the unbelievable. Five feet in front of her lay the lifeless body of Johnnie Benson. She screamed, "My lawd! My lawd! Oh, my lawd!"

Chapter 2

The dining room was simply extravagant. The chandelier sparkled high above. The waiter inquired, "Sir, can I get you anything else?"

Reginald Johnson, Attorney at Law, answered, "No, thank-you. I have to leave to attend a seminar shortly."

The seminar on "Violent Crime in America" was one of many such seminars held all around the Country. This one just happened to be in Washington, D.C., the legislative and judicial heart of our beloved United States. Ironically, also the very heart of violent crime in the U.S.

After the seminar, Reginald returned the car to the airport rental car company. The Cadillac was okay, but quite a step below what he was used to. His flight to the West Coast left on time. The meal was exquisite. There was nothing to satiate the palate like lobster tails served with the proper wine.

The stewardess asked the passenger in one of the first class window seats if there was anything that he needed.

"No", replied Attorney Johnson, "Everything is just fine."

Of course, Mr. Johnson knew that it would be, which was why he flew this airline to begin with. He always went first class, not only when flying, but in everything in life. After all, that was why he became a lawyer in the first place. And he was not just a lawyer, he was widely recognized as one of the best personal injury lawyers in the Nation.

The stewardess brought the afternoon paper. The headlines read, "PROMINENT CIVIL RIGHTS LEADER MURDERED !!!"

Reginald sat back in his seat and proceeded to read the paper. He had time, since the flight from D.C. to San Francisco was roughly five hours.

"Stewardess, I changed my mind. Please bring me a Bacardi and Coke. Bring the dark rum, please."

"I don't believe we have the dark rum, sir."

"I'll take the light if that's all you have."

Reginald finished the paper in about thirty minutes. He closed his eyes and began to reminisce about his favorite city, San Francisco.

It was beautiful this time of year. October and November were traditionally the hottest months of the year. When one looked out over the City, it seemed to shimmer. It was magical.

Many people you met always talked about the "Big Apple" and that was Reginald's second favorite city. But no place on earth could match San Francisco's culture, scenery and, most of all, its lifestyle. One visit there and like the song said, "You left your heart."

*   *   *   *   *   *

Denise McMillian was a beautiful young woman. She was as smart was she was pretty. As she drove along Highway 101, she blew her horn back at the two young Black men who had honked at her as she sped alongside them.

She knew she looked inviting. Her blouse was low cut, revealing cleavage that begged to be touched. The black leather mini skirt she was wearing showed off her shapely legs. If one looked close enough, he could just catch a tiny glimpse of her white panties covering her crotch. She shifted her new red BMW 325i convertible into fifth gear as she sped along the Golden Gate Bridge.

Denise was the daughter of Representative George McMillian. She, like so many other young affluent Black kids, had been spoiled rotten. George McMillian had accumulated quite a bit of wealth from the businesses that he owned. Add to that the political bribes and kickbacks he took, and one could understand how he had amassed quite a fortune.

Representative McMillian was not known for his money. Rather, it was his record on Civil Rights that readily came to mind when his name was mentioned. He had singlehandedly taken on the big corporations in the Bay Area and demanded that they hire more Blacks to positions that mattered. As a result of his efforts, many of the more notable corporations had given yearly scholarships to minority students and sponsored all sorts of events for minorities.

Denise was George's child from his first marriage. He and his first wife had divorced when Denise was only seven. His wife had accused George of being money hungry. Even though they had struggled for ten years and the bill collectors had called and bothered them relentlessly, all she wanted when George finally made his fortune was time and affection.

But George, like most people who had struggled for years and then made some money, never wanted to be poor again. All he wanted to do was make more money. He liked making money more than he liked having sex.

He wanted his daughter, Denise, to share in the wealth. He did not want her to grow up poor like he did. He wanted her to enjoy all that life had to offer.

And enjoy life was exactly what Denise did. Her grades in the 11th and 12th grades reflected just how much she did enjoy life. Her G.P.A. fell from 3.5 down to 2.9.

Of course, Denise did not care about her G.P.A. since she had no intention of going to college. She felt that she already had all that life could offer her. She drove a beautiful car. She lived in a 20-room Victorian house that overlooked the San Francisco Bay, and she could shop in all the exclusive stores on Union Square.

Who could tell George McMillian that his daughter was not going to college and that she would never realize her full potential? Even more importantly, who could tell him that it was his fault that she would live most of her adult life in mediocrity?

Representative McMillian had given Denise the finest things that money could buy. Her weekly allowance was more than most professionals made; however, he had not given her what really counted. He failed to instill any of the basic values that Black children needed to make it in this world. Denise had not been taught the value of hard work and discipline. She did not understand that she lived well because someone else had gone out and earned the money.

George did not understand that parents were supposed to provide children with a roof over their heads and put food on the table. The ultimate responsibility of a parent was to teach a child how to survive on their own. George had failed as a parent. He had equated the ability to provide an abundance of material wealth as the barometer for being a successful parent. Denise, as a result, was spoiled, lazy and arrogant. She could not perform the simplest of household chores. Without her father's money, she would starve within a week.

The line at the toll plaza on the Golden Gate Bridge was not long because it was in the middle of the day. Denise was glad since she had to meet her dad in ten minutes down in the City at a little exclusive restaurant on Lombard Street. They often met somewhere in the City for lunch. It was something of a ritual for them.

George McMillian hurried toward his car in the public parking garage on Geary Street. He had just spoken at his monthly meeting with the members of the "50 Black Men of the Bay Area." George had founded this group of Black professional men in response to the growing crime and poverty of the young Blacks in the Bay Area. He never missed this meeting.

Level three was just up the next set of stairs. He came out of the exit door with his keys in-hand. He pushed the little button on the key and the infrared signal unlocked the driver side door to the Mercedes SL 500. George got in and within a few minutes exited the garage and headed down Geary Street. He was only five minutes late. His daughter would wait.

He never noticed the rental car that followed him. It made every turn that George made. When he parked at the restaurant, the rental car parked four spaces away from him.

Denise was seated at a table by the window. They hugged and kissed each other. George and his daughter laughed and joked and caught up on the latest gossip. As usual, Denise asked her father if there was a woman in his life. The answer was always the same, "I'm working on it. Why do you ask?"

Just as George was going to take the first bite of his steak, his pager buzzed. It was his answering service. George asked his waiter where the phones were located, and he waiter directed him down the stairs and to the right.

George inserted a quarter into the phone and began to dial. As he did so, someone tapped him on the shoulder.

"Aren't you Representative George McMillian?"

"Why yes, I am. I'm pleased to meet you. What can I do for you?"

"Nothing, I just thought it was you."

The gentleman in the expensive suit and shoes turned his back to George. George did the same to him.

As George was re-dialing his office number, he felt an arm grab him around the neck. It was a very powerful arm. He could not move. When he saw the shiny blade of the razor, he knew his life was at an end. He knew this was not a robbery because the gentleman was dressed more expensively than he. Like the prey in the predator's grasp, he was frozen with fear and did not struggle.

He thought to himself, "Who had the audacity to kill Representative McMillian?" If he had to be killed, at least it could have been out in the public eye and not in the downstairs of some little restaurant. This was the last thought that Representative McMillian had.

Denise began to get impatient. Her food was getting cold, but she would not eat until her dad had returned. It was not like him to be gone this long. The Governor of the State of California himself could not cause such an interruption of their lunch meeting.

Jimmy the waiter punched the time clock. His shift was over and it had been a profitable day. He had made over one hundred dollars on tips. Today he would take a taxicab home instead of the usual ten block walk. All he had to do was use the phone downstairs.

When Jimmy got to the bottom of the stairs, he saw the middle-aged Black man leaning over the phone. Something was not quite right though. He was not leaning; rather, he was propped up.

Jimmy walked over and touched him. He fell to the floor with a hard thud.

Jimmy said, "Mister, are you okay?"

Then he saw the tiny trickle of blood on his throat.

"My God! His throat has been cut! His throat has been cut!"

He ran up the stairs to get help all the while yelling, "Somebody help! There's a man downstairs! His throat is cut! Call an ambulance, somebody!"

The owner of the restaurant called for an ambulance.

Denise panicked. She ran to the stairs and hurried down to the bottom. There he was. Her father. Her friend. He was dead.

What would she do now? She had no one to take care of her. No one to look out for her. Her mother had died of cancer two years ago. She was all alone. She fainted.

Chapter 3

Looking out the window, he just caught a glimpse of it, then more of it, until he could finally make it out. There it was, the Atlanta skyline. That's right, Atlanta, the so-called land of milk and honey to so many Blacks in the early '90s. Nothing could be further from the truth.

Reginald remembered when he first came to Atlanta from the West Coast. Born and raised in the South, he, like so many other Blacks, had migrated to the West or the North to get away from the racism and lack of opportunity that the South was known for.

He remembered his first few months exploring the Metro Atlanta area. He was shocked to discover that the image Atlanta projected to the rest of the world was not the Atlanta that actually existed. It did not take long to discover that the Atlanta Metro area was laid out like a wagon wheel. The wheel was called I-285 with a diameter of roughly 50 miles.

Most of the companies' headquarters that had relocated to the Metro Atlanta area had moved to the outer perimeter of I-285. With the exception of Midtown and Buckhead, the inner part of I-285, which includes Downtown, was desolate, poor and filled with violent crime.

The only bright spots Downtown were the State Capitol Building, the Fulton County Government Complex, the Justice Center, the Federal

Government Buildings and the two stadiums, the Fulton County Stadium for the Atlanta Braves and the Georgia Dome for the Atlanta Falcons.

Atlanta was one of the few cities in the Nation where one could not shop Downtown. There was simply no where to go. The stores were located out in the numerous large shopping malls spread all around the perimeter.

After about 6:00 p.m. the City was dead. The only reason one had to be Downtown was either because there was a sporting event going on at one of the stadiums or arenas, you were staying at a hotel for a convention or you were homeless.

Aside from the fact that Atlanta was chosen as the site for the 1996 Olympics, Atlanta was perhaps best known as the home of Dr. Martin Luther King. He pastored Ebenezer Baptist Church located on Auburn Avenue. Not far from the Church was the King Center, founded in his memory.

What had made Reginald sad was the fact that Atlantans seemed to be frozen in time. They were proud to have been a part of Dr. King's legacy, but had done very little to accomplish his dream. They had talked about and celebrated the dream for so long that the dream had turned into a nightmare.

The areas immediately adjacent to the famous King Center and Ebenezer Baptist Church were slums. The areas were run down, desolate and wrought with crime and poverty.

While Blacks were out parading and shouting, Whites had quietly and efficiently moved the things that counted out of the City.

The landing was butter smooth. Reginald enjoyed traveling through the Atlanta Airport. It was very modern and efficient, like himself.

The car started immediately. The fan from the automatic temperature control, set at 72 degrees, was barely perceptible as it quickly brought down the temperature to what it was set for. The smell of new leather filled the cabin. Reginald put the car in gear and the car lunged forward with the vigor of a thoroughbred.

He felt the sense of invincibility as he soared past all the lesser cars heading up I-75/85 North. None of the freeway imperfections could be detected as the Mercedes S 600 loped along at 70 miles per hour, 100 more miles per hour in reserve.

Forty-five minutes later Reginald entered his driveway. The 22-room house stood majestic as he pushed the garage door opener and one of the doors to the six-car garage opened.

None of the neighbors saw that Reginald had returned home. No one cared. In this neighborhood, everyone minded their own business. This was true of most of the Alpharetta neighborhoods. People who lived in estates in the two million dollar range tended to be that way.

Reginald filled the bathtub with bubble bath and sat down in the foaming water. He thought to himself, "Ah, what a successful trip! But I don't have much time. The elections are six months away and I have only just begun my task. I have a lot of work to do and very little time to do it."

"They loved me at the seminar in D.C. on `Violent Crime in America', but I have to become more familiar to the people that will be casting the votes and to those that wield the power.

"While I'm not running for Governor of a state or for a Congressional Seat, getting elected to a meaningful position in the NAACP is no piece of cake.

"Oh well, better get some sleep; it's 1:00 a.m."

*   *   *   *   *   *

It was 5:00 a.m. The weights were very heavy. "Just three more reps", Reginald said out loud. His arms were burning and felt like lead. His biceps and triceps were bulging. He curled the barbell from the top of his thighs to just below his chin. He felt his biceps burn as he continued his upper body workout, getting the most out of the barbell curl.   He exercised four days a week with Mondays and Thursdays being upper body days, and Tuesdays and Fridays being lower body days. He had exercised for years with weights and attributed his olympic build and youthful appearance directly to weight training. The workouts lasted for 45 minutes each. In 15 minutes he could shower, shave and dress for work.

At 6:00 a.m., he read <u>The Wall Street Journal</u> and <u>The Atlanta Journal-Constitution</u> while having his morning meal consisting of cereal, fruit and orange juice. This completed his morning ritual when he would head out to the office by 6:30 a.m.

The skimpily-clad receptionist burst into the office. "Mr. Johnson, Mr. Johnson, did you hear the news? Reverend Benson was murdered yesterday in a hotel room in Washington D.C. They say it was the work of White extremists. Reverend Benson has worked in the Civil Rights movement for as long as I have been alive."

Reginald answered, "Yes, it is a terrible tragedy. I don't know what to say. He will be surely missed. This is sure to have an effect on the Civil Rights movement. I only hope that they catch whoever did it."

He took his first phone call of the morning. The claims adjuster was sweating, but you could not see this on the telephone. He said, "Mr. Johnson, we are prepared to offer your client $75,000.00 to settle this claim."

The adjuster knew that Mr. Johnson would never accept this offer. Reginald would not accept anything less than $250,000.00, but the adjuster had to try to pay substantially less. It was company policy: charge high premiums, pay low claims.

Reginald replied, "Thank you very much for your offer. I appreciate your prompt and courteous attention to this matter. I will relay it to my client and send you a written reply."

The claims adjuster knew that the worst had happened. When Reginald Johnson said that he would send you a written reply, it usually meant that he was sending you a copy of his complaint, complete with interrogatories. If the company had to pay out that kind of money, it meant huge layoffs, starting with this adjuster.

*   *   *   *   *   *

The elevator was filled as it descended from the 35th floor. The marbled walls and thick piled carpeted floors reflected the wealth of the people who worked at 191 Peachtree Street. The elevator door opened and it was as if one had walked right into a large cathedral. This was appropriate since that was exactly the effect that the architects were seeking when they designed the building.

Reginald Johnson, Attorney at Law, exited the building onto Peachtree Street. He was heading west on Peachtree Street in the direction of the Fulton County Superior Courthouse. He was going to file the complaint in the matter that he had discussed an hour ago with the claims adjuster. It had been quite a while since he had actually been down to the Superior Court and he had informed his paralegal that he would file the complaint himself while he was there.

The light changed at the corner of Peachtree and Auburn. Reginald headed through Woodruff Park. A young man in dirty dark green clothes approached him.

"Hey, brother, man, you sho looks good. You'se must be a minister. Well, Reverend, can you lend me fifteen cents to catch the bus?"

The smell of the young man was almost unbearable, but Reginald never flinched. Instead, he reached inside his pants pocket and pulled out a bundle of dollar bills.

"Here young man, take a dollar and have a nice day."

"Thank ya, sir. Thank ya. God bless ya."

Midway through the park Reginald paused. He listened to the sounds in the park and took in the scenery. Seated on the park benches along the walkway were about 80 young homeless Black men, their clothing tattered and worn. They were totally unkempt. A few of them were talking to themselves. Others were listening to a street preacher.

"God hates the White man. A rich man can't make it to heaven. You can't take it with you. You see, you ain't happy. Hey you, sister, God ain't pleased with you. Man is the head of the household, but you won't let him be. You supposed to be home and the man working, but you out here with your short skirts, pressed hair and perfume. You won't even support the Black man."

The air wreaked of body odor. The stench was sickening. Reginald thought to himself, "How could this be? How could so many young Black men turn out to be beggars?"

Reginald continued his journey to the Courthouse noticing the many young Black women that passed by him. Most were in groups of three or four. They were well dressed. Their shoes matched their purses. They smelled perfumy. Their hairdos were flawless.

Black women, for the most part, always seemed to get a job in the end. They bought small economy cars and starter homes. They worked on their appearances constantly.

What was sad was that there were few brothers who had anything at all on the ball. The brothers, for the most part, were not even trying. They had become expert at living off of the women.

The gap between Black women and Black men was widening more each day. The women were on an upward, self-improvement trend. The men were on a downward spiral to death and destruction.

Chapter 4

Judge Hall was a young, tall, very light-skinned Black man. He had graduated in the top five percent of his class at Emory University. Upon graduation, he accepted a job as a Federal Prosecutor. Three years later, he was appointed to the Traffic Court of Fulton County. Two years later, he was appointed to the State Court of Fulton County. One year later, he was chosen to serve as a Superior Court Judge in Fulton County.

He was very proud of his accomplishments. Judge Hall had grown up in one of the projects in Atlanta known as "Carver Homes". His mother, who worked as a cook at the Varsity Restaurant, had stressed education. Every night when she got home, she checked his homework. Even though she herself could not read, she still could discern if all the blanks were filled in.

Judge Hall's courtroom was one of the larger ones at Superior Court. He was rocking back and forth in his chair, administering justice in his usual form: harsh and swift. He stared down the defendant standing in front of him. The young man had been found guilty of possession of cocaine with intent to distribute.

"Do you have anything to say before I pronounce sentence?"

The young man, looking down at the floor and rocking back and forth on his heels said, "Well, sir, I's just standing on the corner and the cop came up and arrested me. I's not doing anything. I's not have anything on me. The police foundt dem drugs in the bushes and said they wuz mine."

Judge Hall scanned the defendant's record in front of him. He noticed that there were three previous drug arrests, one which resulted in a conviction.

He thought, "It's the same old story. These Blacks coming in here lying, and I'm sick of them. They all should be in jail. After all, I wasn't born rich. I went to school and worked while I went. I'm from the projects and look at me! They could do it too. I don't feel sorry for them. I'm tired of them embarrassing me day after day."

The bailiffs in the courtroom knew what was to come next. They knew that the young man would be lucky to get anything less than 15 years to serve. On a weekly basis, the bailiffs in this courtroom saw about 40 young Black men between the ages of 18 and 30 get at least 10 years to serve. As far as the bailiffs could remember, they had not seen a white male come through the system in Fulton County for about two years.

Judge Hall published his sentence to the courtroom.

"I sentence the defendant to 20 years to serve. It is time that young men, such as you, learn that the system will no longer tolerate drugs in our community. I will continue to send the message out that if you come before Judge Hall, you will not commit any more crimes because you will spend your growing years in jail".

The defendant's mother burst into tears. Her knees gave way and had it not been for her nephew standing next to her, she would have fallen to the hard tile floor.

She yelled to Judge Hall, "He is a good boy, Judge!! Why couldn't you give him another chance? I did the best that I could! Don't take my boy away from me!"

Judge Hall did not even respond to her. He simply said, "Next case."

Attorney Johnson entered the Civil Clerk's office for the Superior Court of Fulton County. Seated directly behind the counter were two young Black women. In the area behind them, there were approximately ten other young Black women carrying out the various filing tasks that never ended in the clerk's office. The two young women at the desk appeared as though they had just swallowed an overdose of lemon juice. They had that "I dare you to ask me anything look" in their eyes.

Attorney Johnson spoke up, "I need to file these documents, please."

Without looking up, one of the two women said in a very harsh tone, "I hope you have all the proper documents, otherwise what you file will be returned to you. I'm tired of having to tell you lawyers what to file."

Attorney Johnson smiled and replied, "Thank you very much for your help. I can appreciate the difficulty that you face in your job. You have a lot to do. I'm not sure I could handle the stress and strain myself."

"All the more reason I hope you have your stuff together so I don't have to do double work."

While the clerk was date stamping the documents, a very clean cut white attorney approached the counter. Immediately, the other clerk behind the desk jumped to her feet.

"Hello, sir, how can I help you?"

The attorney answered, "I have a complaint that I need to file, and I'm not sure that I have everything that I need."

The clerk reached out and took the documents. She scanned them as meticulously as a surgeon would during a tedious operation.

"Sir, you are missing three forms that you need. I'll be glad to put them in for you. I just need you to sign them for me."

He signed them and replied, "I appreciate that very much. Have a nice day."

Judge Hall finished court for the day and informed his secretary that he was leaving. He took the judges' elevator to the parking lot. He exited on level D. He walked to the spot reserved with his name on it and placed the key in the door of his red Porsche 928. He heard footsteps and turned to see who it was.

"Oh, it's just you. How are you? What are you doing down at the courthouse today? I thought only judges were allowed to park on this level."

The person responded, "Nice car, judge. I'll bet she's fast."

"That she is, that she is."

Judge Hall opened the door and sat down. As he turned back to look at the person, he felt a stinging sensation on his throat. He placed his hand on his throat to loosen his tie. When he looked down at his hand he saw it was covered with blood. He noticed that he was having difficulty breathing. In fact, he was beginning to gasp for air. Then everything was black. His head fell forward and rested on the steering wheel. The horn began to sound.

It was early the next morning and sweat was pouring down Reginald's forehead profusely now. He thought to himself, "How can it be that these weights never get lighter? Six, seven, eight. That's the last set of dead lifts. Oh, well, I guess 300 pounds is nothing to sneeze at."

Reginald walked over to the full-length mirror that hung on the wall of his exercise room. "Ah, not too bad a bod there."

He noticed how defined his muscles had become. He was indeed a hunk. Add to that his striking resemblance to Denzel Washington, and you had a package that women found hard to resist.

Reginald heard a thud at the door. "It's about time the paper got here." He opened the door and grabbed The Atlanta Journal-Constitution. The headline read: "PROMINENT BLACK JUDGE FOUND SLAIN IN COURTHOUSE PARKING GARAGE."

The Journal-Constitution dedicated half of the front page to the story. It detailed how the judge had left word with his secretary that he was leaving the courthouse to attend an NAACP meeting. Judge Hall was to have officially been named National Spokesperson for the NAACP at that meeting.

The judge had been found by a janitor in the parking lot after the janitor had heard the sounds of a horn for about ten minutes. The judge's throat had been cut. The police had no leads. What was puzzling was the fact that the parking garage where all of the judges parked was secure. It could only be accessed by an elevator to which only judges and a couple of senior bailiffs had the key.

This was the third murder of a prominent Black leader in as many weeks. All were very active in the civil rights movement, and two of them were very active in the NAACP.

The Reverend Johnnie Benson had been brutally murdered in Washington D.C. three weeks ago and the police still did not have any leads. The local Black leaders were calling the police efforts unenthusiastic and shoddy. They were outraged that after three weeks, there were no leads, no suspects, nothing.

Representative George McMillian had also been murdered in San Francisco, California. He had been found downstairs in an expensive little Italian restaurant one day after the Benson murder. Again the police had no leads nor suspects.

Black people all over the Nation were beginning to wonder if these killings had something to do with a government coverup or if White racists were just getting bolder. They wondered if the racists and the government were one and the same.

Reginald opened the door to his black and palomino Range Rover. He loved this vehicle more than any of the others. It was roomy, quiet, and comfortable. He could pack his camping gear, fishing supplies, cooler and blankets, yet still have room to carry five people in Mercedes-class style. When the going got rough off-road or there was snow and ice on the road, the Range Rover came through.

The traffic heading down I-75 was already heavy. It seemed that everyone in the Metro Atlanta area had a car.

Reginald thought to himself, "How could it be that a City with nothing Downtown and so many ways into it have so much traffic on all the major roads? After all, Atlanta, unlike New York and San Francisco, is not surrounded by water." Nevertheless, by 6:45 a.m., Atlanta's freeways were always packed to capacity. There were at least 15 wrecks during rush hour.

At last he was there. The Black valet at the Marriott on Peachtree wore the usual attire consisting of a tuxedo with tails and a top hat. If you didn't know better, from the way he acted, you would think that he was part owner in the hotel. He was so proud to be there.

He quickly informed Reginald that he could not park in front of the doors, that this area was reserved for patrons of the hotel. If he wanted to pick up someone, he had to park down the street and then walk back to the hotel entrance to get them.

Reginald smiled and informed him that he was there for the NAACP meeting. The valet said, "Of course, sir, I'm sorry sir. Please forgive me, sir. May I park our car, sir?" Reginald handed him the keys and went inside.

The NAACP meeting was in the Plaza Suite, the finest suite the hotel had to offer. The NAACP meetings were always done in style. More that two-thirds of the budget went to cover the cost of such meetings. This meeting was classified as an emergency
meeting in response to the death of Judge Hall.

Attorney Johnson entered the suite. Seated around a conference table were 21 men ranging in ages from 35 to 75. The Moderator introduced Attorney Johnson to the rest of the group.

Reginald had become quite well-known in the NAACP over the last year. He had attended all of their meetings and conferences and paid his dues for a lifetime membership. Members of the group had actually began to rely on him since he was always in attendance. One of the major problems of the organization was attendance. Those with the highest attendance tended to be those who held positions of power.

The Executive Director, who most referred to as the Moderator, continued, "My brethren, as you know, something terrible has happened. Another one of us has been struck down by the White devils. The powers that be are not doing anything about it because the victims were Black people who most likely were killed by White racists.

"I have called this emergency meeting for us to discuss what type of response we should give in order to get the attention of the media and rally our people around a common cause. Otherwise, I fear that this murderous activity may continue."

"Brother Moderator," a man jumped up at the corner of the table three seats down from where Reginald was sitting "I feel that we should discuss how much money is in the treasury first, so that we can decide how many meetings we can have to formulate our discussions on the matter."

Another man interrupted, "Mr. Moderator, I am prepared to organize a march on Washington right now!"

The Moderator looked at everyone in the room. His eyes had an almost hypnotic stare to them. He said very calmly, "Gentlemen, there are always sub-issues involved when trying to deal with any problem. I hope that today we can at least formulate what our response to the media will be. This does not require any money or expenditures of any resources other than time."

The first man that had started the initial interruption of the Moderator jumped up. "Mr. Moderator, I think that we should put it to a vote about what we should do. I move that we decide how much money we have and when the next meeting will be."

Another man jumped in, "Also, who is going to be our National Spokesperson for the NAACP? I don't see how we can give a response without a spokesperson."

"Gentlemen, you are quite right. I have overlooked the fact that we don't have a National Spokesperson. The late Judge Hall was to have been our spokesperson. This position must be filled in order for us to deliver a consistent message throughout." The Moderator continued "I believe that this must be done today even if we don't accomplish anything else.

"I also believe that the Lord has blessed us because he has sent us Attorney Reginald Johnson, who is widely-known and well-respected all over the Country. I move that Mr. Johnson be our interim national spokesperson until we have our annual meeting in January, at which time his appointment can be ratified."

The room was silent. One could hear the proverbial pin drop. Suddenly, an elderly gentlemen struggled to his feet, "I second the motion."

After attempting to follow the procedures outlined in <u>Robert's Rules</u>, the motion carried.

Attorney Johnson looked overjoyed. "My fellow associates, I am thankful that you are willing to put your trust in me for such an important task. I will do my best to communicate this organization's wishes to the rest of the world."

After about three more hours of debate, the group was able to decide that they would place the blame on White supremacists. They intended to put pressure on Washington to get something done in terms of stepping up the investigation; and, ultimately, arrests being made.

A press conference was to be scheduled in five days with the national television networks to accomplish their goals. The details of the actual content of the communications were left up to the discretion of Attorney Johnson.

The next meeting of the NAACP was to be held two days after the press conference. The site selected was the Fairmont Hotel in Chicago, Illinois.

At that meeting, discussions were to be held to determine what, if anything, the FBI and state agencies had accomplished regarding the murders of three prominent Black leaders. It was also time for nominations regarding the election of officers for the next three years, especially for the positions of Executive Director and Treasurer.

Many in the NAACP felt that the current Executive Director was losing the fire and drive that one needed to head such an organization. He was simply becoming too passive and too much a part of the system. The glory days of marches, sit-ins, and boycotts were almost nonexistent and the White establishment was beginning to ignore the NAACP and what it stood for. Even Black people were discounting the validity of its existence.

Everybody liked Mr. Harrison Weeks, the current Executive Director, well enough. He had become what everyone referred to him as, a moderator. Even Mr. Weeks himself suspected that he had been the Executive Director two terms too long. He would not seek another term.

The Executive Directorship needed new blood. Someone dynamic and outspoken, not afraid to take on the establishment. There were several viable candidates on the horizon. They would receive serious consideration for nomination at the meeting in Chicago. Then, at the annual meeting in January, someone other than the Moderator would be chosen.

Attorney Johnson would stay in Atlanta tonight. He would treat himself to a good meal complete with expensive wine. He was starting to feel very good inside. The meeting turned out even better than he had thought possible.

Now, he would be the voice of the NAACP. He could control the tone of the organization. Slowly, subtlety, but surely, he was going to move the organization in the direction that he wanted it to go. The only thing that he had to really be careful about was not to move too fast.

Black people tended to worry most of all when a newcomer in either an organization or town came along and got too much attention or power too quickly, relative to the current regimes. Reginald resolved to be low-key and non-threatening. He would play along and pretend to believe wholeheartedly in what the organization was doing. He would befriend the people that counted. He would not have a harsh word to say about anyone. By the time they figured out what was happening, it would be too late. He would be in control.

Reginald knew that he had four months left in order to complete his plans. He had to be finished before the meeting in January in Atlanta to elect new officers for the NAACP. If he was not ready, he would have to wait another year, perhaps even begin all over again in order to carry out his plans.

Timing was everything. The January meeting was always held to coincide with Martin Luther King's birthday and to set the stage for the entire year. More importantly, it was around the time that the nation celebrated Dr.

King's birth, held Black History awareness month in February and generally focused on Black people in general.

Chapter 5

The media room at the NAACP headquarters was filled with wires. There seemed to be no rhyme or reason to where they were going or to what they were connected. There were red ones, blue ones, and white ones. It looked like one large electrical generator coil had been unraveled and left in the middle of the floor, though technicians did not seem to have any apprehensions as to what went where. They were scurrying about like ants, each with an apparent function.

All at once the camera lights came on. They were as bright as sunshine. Nowhere in the room could a shadow be seen.

A man dressed in khaki pants and a sweatshirt said, "Mr. Johnson, we will be ready to broadcast live in ten minutes. Please be prepared to address the cameras at that time."

Attorney Johnson scanned the room. There was a platform with a podium where he was to speak from. There appeared to be at least 25 microphones, all positioned within a foot from the podium.

Fifteen feet behind the microphones were twenty chairs with reporters all equipped with pad and pen. They reminded Reginald of a pack of wolves, waiting to devour anything that happened to wander their way.

Seated in the far left-hand corner of the room were Mr. Weeks and several other members of the NAACP inner-circle. They were staring directly at Attorney Johnson.

Reginald was ready. The years of preparing for trial had taught him to always know what you were going to say and anticipate every question from your opponents. He had spent two days preparing for this press conference.

Today he would be the proverbial actor. He would play a role that he knew he disapproved of in the worst way. He would publicly blame Whites for the ills of Blacks. He would try to make Whites feel guilty for what was happening to Black people and hopefully get them to take some action on behalf of Black people. It had to be done. All of his plans depended on it.

Reginald stepped up onto the platform and approached the podium. The camera lights were dazzling. Fortunately, they were strung along the ceiling and one could look directly into the cameras without being blinded.

The man in the khaki pants was wearing a set of headphones now. He motioned to Attorney Johnson, "Five, four, three, two, one, go!"

"Good afternoon to all the viewers out there. My name is Reginald Johnson, Attorney at Law. I am the acting National Spokesperson for the NAACP. On behalf of the Executive Director, members of the Executive Counsel, and friends everywhere, I am prepared to deliver to you the NAACP's position regarding the recent deaths of two of our prominent members.

"Let me begin by saying that any death is tragic, but what makes these deaths unique are that they all were Black and two of them were prominent members of the NAACP. Representative McMillian was not a member.

"We believe that this was not mere coincidence. It is our belief that one of the violent White supremacists groups was responsible for these deaths. We further hold that these deaths may be just the tip of the iceberg for other deaths to follow.

"We demand that something be done by the appropriate federal and state agencies of this Nation to ensure that both the perpetrators of these heinous crimes are brought to justice and that these acts are not allowed to repeat themselves.

"The action that we feel is needed is for those agencies to begin questioning members of well known racists groups such as the Ku Klux Klan, the Aryan Nation, and the Neo Nazi Party.

"We ask the President of the United States to personally get involved in this matter to ensure that Black people, the people that helped get him elected, are protected from this murderous and senseless violence.

"We advise all Black leaders everywhere to be very careful. Don't go anywhere without being escorted. There is every reason to believe that any one of you could be targeted at any time. As far as the general Black population, please be calm. Don't take matters into your own hands. Allow the government time to do its job.

"I say to anyone out there listening: if you have any information regarding these deaths, please call the authorities."

Reginald thought to himself, "Brilliant! This speech was short, concise, and right along the lines that the NAACP would position itself." Now he would continue his assault on Whites during the questioning session.

"Gentlemen, at this time, I will answer any questions you may have."

"Mr. Spokesperson, I am Walter Jenson with National News Network. Do you have any evidence that these killings are the work of White supremacists groups?"

"We, the members of the NAACP, believe the killings to be at the hands of White supremacists because they were directed solely at Black people. It is White people who stand to gain the most by silencing outspoken Black voices in this Nation."

"Sir, Jessica Beatty, Washington Post. What will the NAACP advise the Black population to do if the law enforcement agencies of this Nation do not pursue this matter as quickly as you would like?"

"At the present time, we are urging both our members and the public at large to act with restraint and to allow law enforcement officials time to do their job. If after thirty days nothing has happened, we will look at other alternatives."

"Can you tell us what these alternatives are?"

"Not at this time, but we would like make it very clear that we are a nonviolent organization"

"Barry Moore, New York Daily News. Why do you think that Blacks affiliated specifically with the NAACP are being targeted?"

"Well, you see, the NAACP has always been an outspoken advocate for freedom, justice and equality for Blacks in this Country. During recent years, especially during the Reagan/Bush era, there has been a pattern of trying to reverse all trends relating to improving the quality of life for Blacks in particular and minorities in general. Apparently, doing this by political means was not enough to satisfy the White supremacists, so they are merely trying to speed up the process. I would like to reiterate, though, that Representative McMillian was not a member of the NAACP."

The Moderator looked on from the corner of the room. He was extremely pleased at the way Attorney Johnson handled the questioning. He liked the fact that Attorney Johnson spoke for the NAACP and didn't use language such as "I" and "my" when addressing questions about the NAACP. Attorney Johnson was a very fine spokesperson indeed. He was cool under pressure and didn't let people pin him down to specifics.

The press conference was broadcast all over the Country on both television and radio. People watched and listened with anticipation.

The mood of the Country was one of tension. Just when it seemed that racial tensions were about to ease, there was always something that happened that upset the status quo.

Now the distrust between Blacks and Whites was once again heightened. Friends were looking at each other in the workplace with a cautioned eye. The more radical Blacks were beginning to talk among themselves.

Many Whites who worked in the downtown metropolitan areas were beginning to leave home for the suburbs by 3:30 p.m. They did not want to be caught in any kind of panic just in case the Blacks took to the streets, as they always did when they believed that they had been wronged.

The cost to repair broken windows in expensive sedans had become prohibitive, not to mention what might happen to a White person who was unlucky enough to be caught alone in a group of Blacks once the rampage started. Look what happened to Reginald Denny.

At last the press conference was over. The media people dissipated as fast as a pack of hyenas once the carcass had been devoured.

The members of the NAACP had finally finished congratulating Attorney Johnson on the fine job he had done at the press conference. The accolades were endless.

By 10:00 that night, Reginald was back in the sanctity of his Alpharetta home. He was enjoying one of life's little pleasures, soaking in the hot tub while drinking wine and munching on cheese, caviar and crackers.

Reginald smiled. "Everything is going according to plan."

Chapter 6

It was still dark. The pre-dawn air was crisp, fresh and invigorating. It was so quiet — so peaceful. Most everything that lived and breathed was still fast asleep.

Reginald picked up the pace just a bit. He was into the third mile of his ten mile run. He had warmed up now. His breathing was aerobic. His strides were even and regular.

He loved these mornings. These were the mornings of his long runs. These runs comprised most of his aerobic workouts.

One of the less publicized benefits of running was that it was extremely relaxing and allowed one to think. Think was exactly what Reginald did.

He thought to himself, "Black people are so stupid! They never worry about the things that really count like making money and self-improvement. Just provide them with a way to blame the White man for all of their troubles, and they will wallow in the cause until the cows come home.

"Blacks are always so one-dimensional and weak. Of course, the weak are always easily led, and Blacks have been led since the beginning of time with the exception of the period of the Egyptians and Pharaohs, if you believe that nonsense.

"I for one do not believe that a race of people that allegedly possessed the technology and discipline to build the great pyramids, to begin civilization as we know it, could have become the walking mat for every other race today."

Reginald heard footsteps up ahead. They became louder and louder. He could see a figure running in front of him. It was a young white female running at a pace not that much slower than his.

"Good morning. Have a nice day," Reginald said has he passed her by.

He began to reflect on the days when he had practiced criminal law. He had practiced criminal law for the first two and a half years of his practice. He had been very good at it. Few of his clients ever went to jail.

In just two years, he had grown tired of criminal law. Everyone associated with crime seemed to lie. The defendants lied, the police lied, the victims lied, the witnesses lied, the lawyers lied, and yes, even the judges lied.

There was never a truer saying than "Birds of a feather flock together." The more defense lawyers hung around their clients, the more like criminals they became. Criminal lawyers even dressed tacky like the defendants, wearing polyester suits most of the time.

People did not respect criminal lawyers. Oftentimes, people felt that the criminal lawyer was as bad or guilty as the defendants.

After defending murderers, rapists, drug dealers, thieves, child molesters, and wife beaters for two years, Reginald became fed-up. He stopped accepting new criminal cases and took the next six months to close out the existing ones. He then entered the silk stocking world of civil law.

A dog barked in the distance. It was probably pissed off that some crazy human had the nerve to disturb its sleep by pounding the pavement at 5:30 in the morning. After all, its hearing was supersensitive and what could take the constant sound of feet striking the pavement time and time again?

Reginald continued to reflect on his early days as a criminal lawyer. During those days, he would be down at the courthouse by 8:30 a.m. It looked like a dance hall. There were Black men everywhere. They lined the halls and filled the courtroom. They were defendants. It seemed as though most Black men between the ages of 18 and 35 accepted being arrested and serving jail time as part of life.

Always seated at the front of the courtroom on the front benches were about 25 lawyers waiting to be appointed to one of the criminal defendants on the court calendar that day. Sometimes it was difficult to tell the difference between the lawyers and the defendants.

After the Judge called the calendar at 9:00 a.m., the prosecutors and defense lawyers went to work, negotiating the fate of the hapless Black criminal defendants. Sometimes the negotiating would go on until 1:00 p.m. In the end, the results were the same. Most of the Black defendants would be given jail time. If not jail time, then a huge fine and probation.

When defendants were put on probation and received a fine, everybody got paid. The fines included fees that went to the defense lawyers, the sheriffs fund, the jail construction fund, and anyone else hidden under the guise of surcharges. Crime was big business and, like other businesses, Blacks were the consumers.

It had gotten to the point that there probably were more Black men going to the courthouse for criminal matters than there were going to school and to work. Something had to be done. Something had to be done now. If the current trend was allowed to continue, there wouldn't be any productive Blacks left.

Reginald began to wonder what to do about all of this. While it was true that this whole situation that Blacks found themselves in was created by design, dating back to slavery and segregation, it was the results now that had to be dealt with.

Blacks simply had no purpose, no direction, and no place in the society of the 90s other than as someone to be exploited and hated. What was sad was that the situation that Blacks were in was much worse than Black people were willing to admit.

Blacks have never really had to face the truth. Every time someone tried to point it out, they were silenced.

If the person was White and told the truth about how he or she really felt about Blacks being lazy and violent, they were labeled as racists and supremacists. He or she would be asked to publicly apologize and then be asked to resign. Many times they would be forced to resign.

If the person was Black and telling the truth about Blacks being lazy, violent, and looking for handouts from Whites, he or she would be ostracized by other Blacks. When the pressure became too great for Blacks who had the nerve to preach self-help and self-reliance, they would fade into the woodwork, never to be heard from again.

To make matters worse, the current Black leadership was actually helping the march to destruction accelerate. They helped create the climate where if anyone said anything about Blacks which was different from their own agendas, they would be met by an immediate response of media scrutiny and possible boycotts.

As well-intentioned as the current Black leaders were, they still believed in the mistaken premise that through racial integration, Black peoples' problems would be solved. These leaders just could not see or refused to accept reality.

The result of years of trying to integrate had led to Black slums, Black-on-Black violence, unemployment, guns in the schools, teenage pregnancy, widespread use of cocaine, uneducated youths and a basic lack of Black pride.

The current Black leaders were upper-middle class preachers for the most part. They still promoted becoming part of the establishment. These leaders enjoyed being asked to be on television talk shows, appearing at legislative policy sessions and attending well-publicized social gatherings. Other than being Black, the current leaders had nothing in common with the average Black person who was unemployed and frustrated.

These Black leaders were still living and exploiting the accomplishments of past civil rights leaders. They had become rich and comfortable by promoting the movement. They failed to understand that civil rights meant basic human rights.

The civil rights movement was not designed to encourage individual achievement and self-improvement. It was the lack of individual achievement and self-improvement that was the root cause of so much of the current social and moral decay of the Black race.

It was very clear: Someone had to do something and someone had to do something now. That someone was going to be Reginald Johnson.

Reginald began saying to himself, "In every era of a people's history, there was always one man or woman who turned the tide. There was always one person who came forth and saved that particular race of people from destruction.

"The tide had always been changed the fastest and most efficient when that person had used violence. Even the Creator himself had used violence against pharaohs in Egypt when he had had enough of the status quo and decided to effect change.

"Another notable example was Adolph Hitler with the Nazi Movement. Through the use of violence, he led a down and out race of people to greatness.

"Actually, if people were really honest with themselves, they would have to admit that the very foundation of this Country was built on violence. How else did America get the land from the Indians, break free from British rule, stop the South from enjoying free slave labor and conquer most of the desirable tropical places in the free world? In fact, one of America's crowing achievements was the attack on Hiroshima. It does not get anymore violent than that.

"But why me? Why must Reginald Johnson be the one to change history? The answer is simple. God chose me! He chose me the same way that he chose Adolph Hitler, Abraham Lincoln, George Washington, and a host of famous and infamous men and women, all of whom used violence as a tool to promote change. Just like in the case of all those other famous violent people, when it is all said and done, the end justifies the means.

"The only difference between those people and me is that I am liberating a race from itself. That liberation will come by providing a new direction. This new direction cannot happen with the current Black leadership in place. They must be excised the same way you excise cancer from an infected body."

The cars were passing Reginald more frequently now. The world was waking up and people were beginning their daily ritual of going to work.

Reginald sprinted the last four hundred yards of his run. Once back inside his house, he showered and read the paper. He would spend today and tomorrow catching up on paperwork, and then he would fly off to Chicago for the NAACP meeting.

Chapter 7

The ceiling of Mt. Bethel was thirty feet high. It was laden with gold leaf inset. The large stained-glass windows that surrounded the 10,000 seat sanctuary were breathtaking. When you walked down the aisles in the sanctuary, your feet left imprints in the thick cut-piled carpeting. The pews were made of solid oak and stained to such perfection that even the great furniture builders of Europe would envy them. In the center of the pulpit was the minister's chair, which in reality was nothing short of a throne. It was lined with red velvet and wide enough that it could hold even two people comfortably. The other 40 chairs that made up the pulpit were themselves larger than the minister's chairs in most churches.

In addition to the sanctuary, the Worship Center contained a fellowship hall complete with a kitchen, five meeting rooms, a gymnasium and an infirmary.

Mt. Bethel's Community Center consisted of a day care center, a fully accredited elementary school and a senior center.

Reverend Althea Ranson was proud of what her congregation had accomplished. She had accepted the pastorship of Mt. Bethel just three years ago. At that time she was the ripe old age of 29, the youngest minister to head a church of this size in the Country. The accomplishments made at Mt. Bethel over the past three years were truly remarkable.

Under her leadership, the annual collections had gone from a meager seven hundred thousand dollars to a whopping five million dollars. It was this increase in collections that allowed the construction of the new Church Complex. The attendance for the Sunday worship services had increased by forty percent to the current level of 7,500.

The accomplishments of both the Church and Reverend Ranson had not gone unnoticed. Mt. Bethel was the envy of the of the other churches in the National Baptist Convention.

Reverend Ranson was well-known both locally and nationally. People liked and respected her. She was outspoken and radical, yet effective. She had become quite a power broker in a number of Black organizations, especially the NAACP.

The general consensus was that she could possibly get elected to the presidency of the NAACP when the elections were held in the Spring. The primary reason for this was that Reverend Ranson was one of the Nation's most outspoken proponents of affirmative action and school desegregation. She had been asked to participate in numerous debates, most of which by general consensus, she won.

Church services this Sunday were to include a ceremony in which Reverend Ranson was to be honored for her accomplishments at Mt. Bethel and to celebrate the completion of the Worship Center.

Reginald's flight from Atlanta to Chicago arrived on time. Getting a rental car out of Chicago's O'Hare Airport was a zoo, to say the least. There were cars going in every direction, and the line to get to the entrance to the freeway was mind-boggling. Attorney Johnson did not get upset. He turned up the volume a bit in the superb sound system in the Lexus LS400. The acoustics were excellent. This was helped by the silent running of the car's sewing machine like engine. Reginald liked the Lexus almost as much as he did his Mercedes. In fact, he often referred to the Lexus as the poor man's Mercedes, even though no poor man would quite be able to come up with the fifty thousand dollars or so needed to drive one off the showroom floor.

Reginald loved Chicago. This was the "Windy City", referred to as such because it had been labeled this by the bragging Chicago boosters when the city hosted the 1883 World's Fair. However, it was now often understood to refer to the fierce winds that blow off of Lake Michigan.

Oftentimes when he visited the City and had the time, he would drive all over Downtown and the Metro area. His favorite buildings were the 100-story John Hancock Center and the 110-story Sears Tower, the tallest building in the world.

The area of Chicago that he liked most was the Gold Coast on Chicago's Near Northside, a luxurious residential area containing expensive high-rise apartment buildings along Lake Michigan. Most of the apartment buildings overlooked Oak Street Beach where Reginald had spent countless hours sunning and relaxing, just to get away from it all. Reginald had maintained a condominium on nearby Milwaukee Avenue for the last five years.

Reginald would not visit his condo today. He only had time to attend church services at the Mt. Bethel Church and then the NAACP meeting at the Fairmont Hotel. After that, he had to head back to Atlanta and begin preparing for a trial scheduled on Tuesday.

Mt. Bethel was located on the Southside. This was Chicago's largest section in both area and population. About sixty percent of the Southsiders were Blacks. The rest of the population was made up of Whites who were either of German, Hispanic, Irish or Polish descent.

The Southside had very few integrated communities. Most of the Blacks who resided there lived in poverty, living in public housing projects. The largest of these projects was the Robert Taylor Homes, which covered about 15 blocks along South State Street. Assault and robbery were the order for the day in these projects which housed about 20,000 residents.

The services at Mt. Bethel began promptly at 10:00 a.m. The pews were filled to capacity with people adorned in their Sunday best. The sermon was to be preached by Reverend Ranson, after which ceremonies would be held to honor her and to celebrate the completion of the Worship Center.

Reverend Ranson began, "My friends and fellow Christians, to say that I am happy to be here today is like saying I am happy to be breathing. Serving God at Mt. Bethel is as necessary to me as breathing.

"But today is not about me, it is about you, the congregation. It was you who saw in your infinite wisdom to allow me to serve you. It was you, the congregation, that supported me and all my efforts to help Mt. Bethel blossom into the wondrous place of worship that it is today. We not only serve ourselves, but also our community."

Reginald thought to himself, "If only Black people could use this same enthusiasm and commitment that they use to build churches and use it to construct businesses in the Black community such as laundries, restaurants, and retail stores, we would not have to depend upon other races to provide our basic services to us.

"Instead, Mt. Bethel, like so many other Black churches all around this Nation constructed a beautiful, multimillion dollar structure, even though just five blocks down the street was another multimillion dollar Black church complex. Neither of these two churches were filled to capacity.

"Why don't Blacks consolidate their churches like the Catholics do? They could pool their money, build a beautiful spacious place of worship, and use the remaining monies to build Black businesses. Rather, Blacks have built a church literally on every corner."

The congregation was constantly applauding. Reverend Ranson was giving one of her patented sermons. As always, her sermon was sophisticated in content, but simplistic in the delivery.

Reverend Ranson continued, "God uses ordinary people to do extraordinary tasks. For you see, he has used me, plain old me, to guide this Church along its remarkable path to glory and to take its rightful place among the great places of worship of this great Nation. And speaking of rightful places and extraordinary tasks, I would like to inform you that I have been told that my name will be among those that may be voted on to become the next Executive Director of the NAACP. If I am chosen, I promise that many of you here at Mt. Bethel will be called upon to assist me in carrying out various tasks."

The applause was deafening. The members of the congregation stood and clapped for over five minutes. They were overjoyed.

Reginald thought to himself, "Oh boy! Some white restaurant owner is going to make a killing today. It is a well-known fact that when Black folks enjoy their church services, they rush out and eat after the services. And today these members were very happy indeed!"

No one paid any attention when a gentleman in an expensive dark suit exited through the back door of the sanctuary. He walked down the stairs that led to the bowels of the massive Worship Center. The basement had been constructed with a circular design. If one were willing to walk the distance, he would eventually come back to the spot that he had started from.

The gentleman walked along the long corridor. He read door sign after door sign until he came upon the one he had been looking for: "Pastor's Office".

He put on his leather driving gloves and tried the door. It was unlocked, which was the usual practice for most church offices. After all, if you can't trust Christians, who can you trust?

He walked inside. The room was large. A reception desk was in the center of the room. Behind it were two large double doors that had a name plate above them that read, "Minister". Located in front of the reception desk was a leather sofa and several leather arm chairs.

He pushed against the double doors and they sprang open, revealing a lavishly decorated office. The mahogany roll-top desk was a sight to behold. There was a refrigerator, a microwave, and a big screen TV, all brand names that commanded premium prices. The carpeting was even thicker than in the sanctuary. On the walls was expensive artwork. There was a small TV screen on the desk that showed the entire reception area, no doubt coming from a hidden camera somewhere in the waiting area.

Reverend Ranson's hands hurt. They were almost numb from shaking hands with hundreds of members of the congregation. She headed down the stairs from the sanctuary, hoping that there were no more hands to shake along the corridor that led to her office.

Several members were waiting outside of the Church to escort her to one of Chicago's finest restaurants. They were going to have a feast before attending the NAACP meeting at 4:00 p.m. Reverend Ranson had intended to leave with them directly from the sanctuary, but she had to go to her office to retrieve her purse which she always left there during services.

Reverend Ranson opened the door to the reception area and walked quickly to the door of her office. She entered her office, unsnapped her robe and placed it on the brass coat rack behind her desk. She had on a red two-piece linen suit. The skirt was just above her knees.

The gentleman, who was hiding in the coat closet, could see Reverend Ranson clearly through the slightly open door to the closet. She was beautiful. She had shoulder length hair and her body was in excellent condition, obviously from working out. Her buttocks and legs would have made Tina Turner proud.

The gentleman wanted to reach out and touch her butt. How could such a beautiful woman be a minister? The gentleman in the closet felt that even he would have wanted to join Mt. Bethel, just to be close to her on a regular basis. Still, there was a job to be done. And this job meant killing a goddess.

He wondered to himself, "Did this woman have sex? Was she celibate? Oh, how he would like to make her scream in ecstasy!"

As the gentleman opened the closet door, it made a creaking sound. Reverend Ranson spun around. She looked scared, but still in control.

"Oh, why could I have not met this woman before today," thought the gentleman.

"I would certainly have liked to have sex with her followed by some long inspirational conversations. But now it is too late."
Reverend Ranson screamed, "What are you doing there? Who are you? What do you want?"

The gentleman did not answer. He walked closer to her. He gave her a look that told her that he could have loved her or at least made love to her. He reached into his pocket and pulled out something that Reverend Ranson could not identify.

Reverend Ranson suddenly turned and picked up a paper weight in the shape of a cross. She flung it at him. It struck him in the chest. He felt sharp pain, but only for a moment. His chest was like steel.

For an instant, the image of the huge Oriental man in James Bond's "Goldfinger" movie flashed across his mind. In that scene, James Bond threw a bar of gold bullion into the Oriental man's chest and it just bounced off.

The gentleman grabbed Reverend Ranson from behind and held her by the neck to steady her. Her body was pressing against his. He felt warm. He pulled her in closer to him. His manhood suddenly sprang to life. It pressed against her butt. The sensation was overwhelming. He now understood how rape murders occurred. Had he not been so disciplined, he might have succumbed to the temptation to bend her over her desk doggie style, pull her panties down, and put his swollen, aching penis into the warm, moist folds of her womanhood from behind. After a few minutes of long deep strokes and feeling and seeing the cheeks of her naked butt against his stomach, he would have squirted his thick white nectar deep inside her moist pussy.

"This is not going to happen," thought the gentlemen as he cut Reverend Ranson's throat. The blood gushed out of her throat as she fell to the floor. She squirmed and twitched for about a minute. Then she was still.

The Church custodian was going about his usual after-service ritual. He was a middle-aged White man who, along with his three sons, had acquired the cleaning contracts for most of the Black churches on the Southside.

This White cleaning company had gotten the contracts to clean the churches even though many qualified Black cleaning companies had bid for the contracts. Blacks could always find a way to give their money to Whites. The more financially successful Blacks became, the easier it was for them to give their money to Whites. It made them feel as though they had arrived.

Today the custodian would clean the aisles and the pulpit area, and tomorrow he would clean between the pews and downstairs. He thought he had heard a noise downstairs. Probably some Church group meeting after service which many of them did. But he was sure that he had heard screams. He decided to check it out. He walked down the stairs and headed down the long corridor.

The gentleman came out of the Church office as though nothing had happened. He closed the door and headed up the corridor.

Their eyes met. The expression on the custodian's face said it all. "I don't know you, you have no business being down here. I am going to check the office when you leave, and I am going to remember what you look like."

The gentleman spoke up, "How are you today? I was just looking for a telephone and apparently I got lost."

"Well, that sure is easy to do in this big ole place," replied the custodian. "I clean here two days a week and I still sometimes lose my way. Did you find a phone in the office?"

"Yes, sir, I found what I was looking for."

The custodian began to walk past the gentleman who began to smile so sincerely that even the shrewdest of poker players would have been fooled. Just as he was side by side with the gentleman, he saw the gentleman pull out a shiny object. That was the last thing that he saw.

The members who were waiting outside for Reverend Ranson decided that it was taking her a long time just to get her purse. The young man whose car they were to take to the restaurant got out and walked to the main doors. When he pulled on them, he discovered that they were locked. He beat on the door with his fists. After waiting five minutes, he and the other members decided that Reverend Ranson may have gotten involved in a call of some kind and simply would meet them at the restaurant.

*   *   *   *   *   *

Reginald attended the NAACP meeting at the Fairmont Hotel. The usual faithful were there along with quite a contingent from Mt. Bethel. Notably absent from the meeting was Reverend Ranson. The members of her congregation in attendance could not offer any explanation. As far as they knew, she had every intention of being there.   Nevertheless, her name was submitted along with three others to the nomination committee to be placed on the ballot for the position of Executive Director.

There was a lot of discussion about how well Attorney Johnson had conducted the press conference a week earlier. If all went well, he was sure to become the permanent National spokesperson when the NAACP met in January.

For the next two hours, a heated debate ensued regarding the murders of the Black leaders. Many theories were put forth as to who was doing the killings and why. In the end, no one was sure of anything. All they knew was that three prominent Blacks leaders had been killed, and no one had taken responsibility. The next scheduled meeting would be the National Meeting in January, notwithstanding emergency meetings that might be needed in the event of more murders.

High-ranking members were advised to be extremely careful at all times.   They were told not to go anywhere unescorted and to be aware of strangers or even people that they were just slightly familiar with.

Mr. Weeks, The Executive Director, also instructed the members to advocate nonviolence. They were not to participate or encourage any member or non-member to do any act or say anything which might later suggest that the NAACP promoted violence.

When the meeting adjourned, Reginald quickly headed for the airport and turned in the rental car.

On the plane flying back to Atlanta, he reflected on the upcoming week. He knew that he had quite a busy week ahead of him. He had to prepare for the upcoming trial on Tuesday which was predicted to last through Wednesday. On Thursday at noon, he had to attend the monthly meeting of the Black Lawyers' Bar Association and a luncheon that followed. Thursday night at 6:00 p.m there was the Black Professionals Network Conference. Friday would mean heading to New York City on some important business.

Reginald knew he would have to be very careful in the remaining three months. The FBI, the police and only God knew who else would soon be involved in trying to solve the murders. He had to be sure that he got as much rest as possible. The likelihood of making a mistake increased exponentially when one was tired.

Chapter 8

The intercom to the floor sounded again, "Agents Kelly and Stone, please report to the briefing room ASAP. The Supervisor is waiting to see you." The message repeated itself.

Agent Kelly was a short, stocky White male, 45 years old. He had spent his entire professional life in the Federal Bureau of Investigation, Eastern Regional Office.

His specialty was serial killers. He had solved some of the Country's worst serial murders. When the Bureau needed something done, and done fast and efficiently, Agent Kelly was called upon.

Agent Stone was a tall, very muscular Black male in his early thirties. He had joined the FBI three years ago. While he never confirmed it, many in the Bureau felt that he had joined simply to have a place where he could escape national scrutiny.

Agent Stone had been a running back with the New York Giants. During a regular season game, Stone had gotten into a fight with one of the opposing team's defensive tackler. During the fight, Stone hit the player in the back, fracturing his spine. The player never walked again. Everywhere Stone went, the fans booed him. They called him "Tombstone". Stone retired when the season ended. Two months later, he joined the FBI.

Supervisor Thompson and Agent Stone were seated at the conference table when Agent Kelly walked in. Supervisor Thompson handed agent Kelly a copy of The Washington Post. The headlines read, "ANOTHER WELL-KNOWN BLACK LEADER SLAIN".

Supervisor Thompson began, "Guys, I don't know what is going on here. Early this morning in Chicago, the Reverend Althea Ranson was found dead in her office along with the Church custodian. Both of their throats had been cut.

"You tell me why a well-respected Church minister would be lying dead in her office, nude from the waist down, with the Church custodian, also dead and nude, lying between her legs. It does not make any sense.

"We have to do something. I am getting tremendous pressure from the top, if you know what I mean.

"There has been some sporadic violence literally in every city in America in response to the killings.

"People, especially Black people, want some answers. They want something done.

"The Director of the Bureau has had several meetings with his senior advisors. He told me that the consensus was that we have about one month to solve these murders. After that, there could be riots, burnings, and killings that will make the violence in Los Angeles after the Rodney King verdict look like a food fight.

"So, gentlemen, I want your opinion, your suggestions, whatever you got."

Agent Kelly spoke first. "My experience tells me that what we are dealing with here is a well-organized White supremacist group. Their goal is to escalate the level of racial hatred in this country."

Agent Stone spoke up. "But why haven't they taken responsibility for the murders? It is not their usual style to keep quiet and not take credit."

"Well, Agent Stone, they probably are planning to come forward soon, most likely with some type of demand. And you can be sure it will be for a large amount of money."

"I don't know, Agent Kelly, these killings don't fit the patterns of some crazy hate group. They seem well thought out. There are no witnesses, no evidence, nothing. It is almost as though whoever killed these people knew the victims."

"I would remind you, Agent Stone, that serial killings are my specialty. Look at what we have here. We have five dead bodies. Four of them prominent Black leaders. The fifth person who was killed was White. I would guess that he was killed because he saw something. Maybe he witnessed the actual killing itself.

"Agent Stone, who else would want to kill well-known and successful Blacks except White supremacists?"

"I just think that we should explore all probable theories as to who killed these people and why."

"Apparently you were not listening, Stone. So let me say it again and this time very slowly. Maybe that way it will sink in. My specialty is serial killings. What we have here is merely similar killings. These killings are not the work of a serial killer. Rather, they are the result of one of the White supremacists groups, conspiring to eradicate successful Blacks as part of some superior race doctrine and to make money.

"Whatever group was responsible for these killings, they have gone to great lengths to make it look like the work of one killer. Each of the victims had their throats cut with a sharp instrument. The murder weapons probably were very sharp, either knives or razors."

"Agent Kelly, what you have described are, by definition, serial killings."

Supervisor Thompson interrupted, "But why were these particular Blacks killed?"

"Well sir, they probably figured out that by killing these well-known Blacks first, they would get a lot of media attention quickly. That is exactly what happened. I believe that now they will kill any notable Black person. They are on a roll. When they have killed enough Blacks, they figure the government will be willing to pay anything to stop the killings and restore law and order."

Agent Stone got up and began to pace around the room. "I just don't get the sense that these killings are the result of hate violence. They just seem too obvious. Any hate group in this Country knows that if they were to even attempt something such as these killings, the FBI would be on them like white on rice. They simply would not risk having the full force and fury of the FBI brought down upon them.

"I think what we are dealing with here is far more sinister than some mere garden variety White supremacist group. I have seen death many times, but when I think of these killings, it causes a chill to run down my spine. I am telling both of you that this case cannot be solved focusing on the obvious theories. By the time we change our thinking, I believe it will be too late."

"Well, Agent Stone, I trust Agent Kelly's judgment. I say we operate on the theory that we are dealing with some White supremacist group. We can fine tune what the motivation is later.

"Agents Stone and Kelly, I suggest that we step up our monitoring of the well-known hate groups immediately. We should shakedown some of their leaders and see what falls out. You know the drill guys, get to it. Let's put a lid on this one before it blows up in our faces."

Supervisor Thompson left the room and headed down the long corridor to his office.

Stone and Kelly remained in the room. Stone said, "Look, Kelly, I know you have all this experience and all, but think about this for a moment. Most of the Blacks were members of the NAACP. They either held or were going to get elected to important positions in that organization. I for one believe that these killings are limited to the NAACP."

"Well, Stone, I guess you are going to suggest that we place all of the prominent members of the NAACP under surveillance. In fact, why not all of the members?

"Look, Stone, these victims were prominent Blacks. As you know, most prominent Blacks are members of the NAACP. Your theory does not make any sense.

"Now, why don't you do what you get paid for? You know, to assist me? While I know you are well intentioned, please leave the planning up to me. What do you say? Let's go and grab a bite to eat. Then we can pull the files on these groups and get busy."

After lunch, the file clerk delivered three large cartons of files to Agent Kelly's room as ordered. There were four hundred and eighty-two files.

"How in the world will we be able to investigate all of these groups?"

"Well, Stone, it looks like we better call our families and tell them that we are on an assignment. I suspect that we will be putting in a lot of overtime."

"Ordinarily, that wouldn't be bad except that we don't get paid for it."

"Well, who said life was fair, buddy?"

Agents Stone and Kelly worked through the night. They put the files into three groups.

The first group consisted of those organizations that operated nationally. These groups would have the financial and manpower resources to kill people on a national scale.

The second group was chosen on the basis of having highly-visible and vocal leaders, leaders who were constantly causing unrest. Leaders who were skilled at inciting the kind of racial hatred that is buried way down deep in each of us, just waiting for the right moment to be unleashed.

The third group was chosen solely on the basis of activity. That is, activity that occurred within the last twelve months. Activity was defined as state or national level rallies, marches or civil unrest staged at major televised events on college campuses.

The two agents then took ten files from each of these three groups. They would concentrate on these thirty files for two weeks. Then take ten more from each group and work on then for two weeks. They would repeat the process until either they solved the case or ran out of files.

It was decided that either Agent Kelly or Agent Stone or one of the ten agents they would enlist full-time on this case, would approach the leader of a particular organization and at least two of the known members. These people would be rigorously questioned.

They would follow-up on the ones that showed promise by placing them under 24-hour surveillance. This surveillance was to come from local authorities. Once the local authorities saw something significant such as the leader calling large meetings, they were to contact the Bureau immediately. Agent Stone or Kelly would drop whatever they were doing and concentrate on that group. They would pick up the group's leader for questioning.

While down at whatever police station or precinct being interrogated, the suspect would be given a glass of water containing a mild sedative. Then he would be injected with a specially developed truth serum. He would be interrogated regarding the current murders. While under the effects of the serum, questions would be asked about the group's present and future plans. The beauty of this serum was that it was undetectable in the blood stream after two hours. When it wore off, the suspect would not even be able to remember that he or she had ever been questioned.

Agent Stone hoped that this plan would work. He did not agree with Agent Kelly's more drastic methods of getting information. He had seen Agent Kelly go into an area, find the local snitch and beat the hell out of him until he was glad to spill his guts. Agent Kelly always got results. The means were not important to him, just the results.

On more than one occasion, Agent Kelly had beaten the snitch so badly that he died from internal injuries caused by the beatings. The local authorities had attributed these deaths to gang violence or robbery. In any case, they were unsolved murders.

Deep down, Stone knew that Kelly liked inflicting pain and looked for any opportunity to do so.

Chapter 9

Mary Dafney was getting concerned. It was four in the morning and her husband, Murray, had not come home yet.

He usually called her if he was going to be late. Why had he not called her? She had not spoken to him since Sunday afternoon at 1:00 and it was now Wednesday morning.

Mrs. Dafney had no idea where to start looking for Murray. All she knew was that he had the contract to clean about 40 local Black churches. Different churches were cleaned at different times. She never got involved into the day-to-day running of the business. Murray arranged every cleaning and Mary knew no specifics of his schedule. She was a dutiful housewife. Murray was not the type to stay out all night. He ran the business and she ran the household.

She had contacted the police station Sunday evening when he had not come home. They had told her that three days had to elapse before anyone could be considered a missing person.

Mary called the local hospitals and jails. No one matching Murray's description had been cared for or processed. All of this meant that she had to suffer extreme anxiety for another sixteen hours until the police would help her find her precious Murray.

Why did Murray have to be missing now? Why couldn't he be missing at some other time? Not now! Not now when his three sons were off together on a cruise in the Caribbean!

The three Dafney sons and their wives had gone on a cruise last Saturday to celebrate the younger Dafney's tenth wedding anniversary. The three sons often celebrated things together. They were a closely-knit family. Mary tried futilely to reach them on the ship, but couldn't.

The phone rang and Mary Dafney's heart pounded in her throat. She thought, "Oh my God! Who could that be? I know it is bad news. My Murray would never go away for three days and not let me know where he was."

Mary mustered all the courage that she could find. Her hand trembled as she reached for the phone. She picked it up on the third ring. The receiver felt as though it weighed a hundred pounds.

"Hello?" a strange voice on the phone said. "Is this the Dafney residence?"

"Yes, it is. Who is calling, please?"

"This is Agent Kelly with the FBI".

"Oh my God! No! No! My God, no!"

"Is this Mrs. Dafney?"

"Yes."

"Mrs. Dafney, I have some bad news for you. Early Monday morning, your husband, along with Reverend Ranson, was found dead in the Church office of Mt. Bethel. Both of their throats had been cut." Even Agent Stone did not have the heart to tell Mrs. Dafney that both her husband and Reverend Ranson were naked.

"The police were not able to locate you before now because we found no identification on Mr. Dafney. Mt. Bethel only had a phone number for Mr. Dafney. That number was to an answering service for his company, My Three Sons' Cleaning Service.

"It is my understanding that the folks at the Church called your husband, Mr. Murray. They had no idea how to contact him other than his answering service. You see, Mr. Murray received his compensation for cleaning the Church in cash. So the Church did not even have an address. It was only after we ran Mr. Dafney's fingerprints that we were able to determine his true identity and where he lived.

"I am truly sorry, Ms. Dafney. If there is anything that I can do, let me know."

Mrs. Dafney did not answer Agent Kelly. She simply hung up the phone. She knew her Murray was dead even before the call. In all of their 30 years of marriage, not once had Murray not called when he was going to be late.

She dropped down to her knees and thanked God for allowing she and her Murray to enjoy life together for this long. She had loved him and he had loved her. What more could anyone ask for than a relationship like Murray and Mary Dafney had?

Mary Dafney was tough. She would not faint or have a heart attack. She was the head Dafney now. She would fill the role that her husband performed. She would become the mentor and confidant of the Dafney family.

The news of Reverend Ranson's death spread quickly on the Southside. Facts quickly became rumors which eventually became gossip.

The word on the street was that Reverend Ranson had been attacked by White custodians in her office after service. She had been raped. She had managed to kill one of her attackers, but the others had gotten away.

In the days that followed, Blacks marched in the streets on the Southside. Each day, the crowds grew in size. Each day, they were more vocal.

On the Saturday night following Reverend Ranson's death, thousands of people filled the streets in and around Mt. Bethel. The crowd was tense. The people were like gas soaked rags, just waiting for anything to ignite them.

Suddenly, a young Black man picked up a bottle and threw it at a passing car. It struck the windshield, shattering it.

Other people picked up whatever they could find and began throwing objects at the windows in buildings and parked cars. Someone lit a match and set fire to a garbage dumpster. Others, upon seeing the flames, lit matches and started burning whatever looked flammable.

Within minutes, a whole city block was blazing. The sound of fire trucks could be heard in the distance. The sirens adding to the confusion that was ensuing.

People started running everywhere. It was pandemonium. Storefront windows were being shattered all over the Black neighborhoods. Cars were set on fire and some were overturned.

It started as a tiny spark. The flame began to grow bigger. In an instant the drapes were blazing. Someone had broken into the front door to Mt. Bethel and set the drapes on fire.

The rage inside of him over his pastor being murdered had engulfed him just as the flames were now beginning to engulf the sanctuary. He yelled, "Let this be a lesson to the White bastards! When they mess with Black folks, we will fight back! We will burn the whole damn city! When I finish, this whole damn church will be nothing but ashes!

"When I finish with this here Church, I'm going down the block and burn every business in the neighborhood."

The looters were out in full force. Appliances of all types could be seen in the arms of people who, just earlier in the day, were begging for quarters.

The police were trying unsuccessfully to restore order. They soon found themselves out manned and outgunned. They were caught completely by surprise. No one had foreseen the rioting and destruction that occurred this night on the Southside.

Daybreak finally came. The sun fought its way over the horizon, one ray at a time. What daylight revealed was horrifying. It looked as if a bombing raid had occurred. The landscape was charred. The few structures that were not burned all had the windows broken out. Glass was everywhere.

Bodies were lying all over the place. Some were people who had been trampled to death. Others had been shot by nervous police officers who had become frightened when the huge crowds headed in their direction.

By 8:00 a.m., all the major television networks were showing scenes from Chicago's battered and burned Southside. Viewers watched in horror all over the Nation as thoughts entered their minds that their beloved cities could be next.

Attorney Johnson listened on his car radio as he headed through Downtown Atlanta on I-75/85. He noticed that the Atlanta skyline had grown somewhat, despite the exodus of buildings out to the Perimeter.

Perhaps with the Olympics coming to Atlanta, there was some small glimmer of hope for the Downtown area. A lot of construction was planned in the remaining year and a half before the big event was to take place.

Of course, "no one" really lived Downtown except the homeless and the folks in public housing. They would never benefit from the construction. That was for certain.

Reginald exited off of I-85 onto Exit 18, the Airport/Camp Creek Parkway exit. In a mere 45 minutes he would be flying to the Big Apple. It gave him a break, considering his past week.

He had gone to court last Tuesday for a personal injury case. Both the client and the defendant had been a pain.

The client had been recommended to Attorney Johnson by a previous client who had received a large settlement.

His new client, Betty Mayberry, was a Black woman in her fifties. She worked for a clothing manufacturer in a textile mill in a small, jerk-water Georgia town.

Betty's job title was "Spinning Room Machine Operator". Her job was to run the machine in the mill that completed the last of a series of processes that made cotton into thread.

The machine that she operated pulled rope-like strands of cotton from containers in back of the machine and spun them down into thread. The thread was collected onto large spools. These spools of thread in turn would then be sent to the weaving room and woven into cloth.

The spools on the machine were held onto spindles by tiny clips. These clips kept the spools from working their way off of the spindles and flying into the air.

Betty was severely injured when the clips on her machine became unseated. Several of the spools went flying into the air, striking her in the face, head, and neck. She suffered a concussion, a broken nose, and a broken collar bone. She also lost some of her vision in her right eye.

Betty had been very excited the first time she and Attorney Johnson spoke on the telephone. She was happy that he had accepted her as his client. She indicated to him that she would be happy if he could get her anything above $20,000.00.

Her attitude changed considerably when she came into the office for her first appointment. It was then that she realized that Attorney Johnson was Black.

She indicated to Attorney Johnson that she just didn't believe that he would be able to get her a reasonable settlement. Black lawyers just were not that good. She believed that a White lawyer could get her more money.

Betty was like so many other Blacks. They put their faith in White people. The very people that enslaved them and abused them for generations were now the people the older Blacks practically worshiped.

Reginald understood this. With many older Blacks coming of age, there simply were not Black professionals. Most Blacks could not even receive a good education because they were barred from better institutions of learning.

The Blacks of the 50s and 60s discounted many of the fine Black colleges and universities. When many of the White colleges did not accept Blacks, rather than attend these Black institutions, some Blacks chose not to go.

There were other reasons, too: the lack of financial resources; the lack of preparation; and the lack of role models to combat generations of the belief that Blacks could never become doctors and lawyers.

Reginald had tolerated Betty Mayberry. She had been very demanding. She, like most Blacks that patronized Black businesses, wanted nothing short of perfection. It was almost as though they thought they were doing you a favor and, in return, you had to give them more than they deserved.

Three months before the trial came up, Betty threatened to take her case to a White lawyer. Attorney Johnson did everything that he could to appease her. In the end, all he was concerned about was getting a huge settlement which would ensure that he continued to live in style. Good business people never lose sight of this all important fact. It's about the business of making money, not changing people or getting your point across. Smile: the customer is always right.

As usual, Attorney Johnson came through with a hefty settlement. Betty Mayberry was overjoyed. Now she would be a walking advertisement for Reginald Johnson. Because he had been patient with her, even though she did not believe in Black lawyers, he felt sure that he would make even more money when she got the word out about how much she recovered in her case.

The defendant in Betty's case was just as much a pain. Southeastern Textile Corporation absolutely refused to accept any kind of an offer prior to trial. They had said that no sleazy lawyer, and a Black one at that, was going to blackmail them out of any money.

Southeastern Textile Corporation had hired the best insurance defense lawyers that money could buy. Attorneys for the defense sent over a mountain of standard but time-consuming discovery and notice to produce documents. They had deposed everyone on Betty's job the day the accident happened, including Betty herself. They filed every available motion, including summary judgment, a motion that alleged the claimant did not have a legally valid claim.

They hired a private investigator who followed Betty twenty-four hours a day to make sure that her injuries were legitimate. The private investigators videotaped Betty's every move. They were intimidating shadows just waiting for her to slip up and do anything that would show that her injuries were not serious.

Betty complained to Attorney Johnson that the constant surveillance was causing her tremendous stress. She felt she would have a nervous breakdown if it continued.

Betty called Attorney Johnson's office almost hourly. It got to be so bad that Attorney Johnson stopped taking her calls. After weeks of her constant calling, Reginald decided that he had to do something.

The first thing that Reginald did was turn up the heat on Southeastern Textile Corporation. He scheduled a deposition for the President of the Corporation. He questioned him for four hours on the company's safety practices, including employee safety training and compliance with all state and federal regulations.

Since the deposition was set for 4:00 p.m., Reginald said that he would have to continue it at another time. The President was furious because it interfered with his busy schedule.

The second thing that Attorney Johnson did was to amend his complaint. In the amended complaint, he alleged wanton and willful negligence on the part of the textile company. He alleged that they purposefully did not ensure that their employees had a safe environment within which to work because ninety-eight percent of their workers were minorities. The other two percent were managers who worked in plush offices located off-site and were not exposed to any material hazards. Reginald increased the amount of the damages requested from $700,000 to $4 million.

The third thing he did was to hire two private investigators of his own and have them follow the Southeastern Textile's president and the manager of operations. He instructed the investigators to follow them everywhere they went, 24 hours a day. They were to take photographs of anything that might be embarrassing to either of the two company officials and the officials were not to know they were being followed. There was a bonus in it if the investigators were not discovered.

Two weeks later, Southeastern Textile's President was seen going into a local Day's Inn Motel with a prostitute. Attorney Johnson's investigators promptly rented the room next to his. They skillfully drilled a hole in the wall and placed a specially-developed miniature camera into the hole which was designed to take wide angle shots.

The day of the trial was the previous Tuesday. The members of the defense team sat across from the plaintiff's table. The lawyers of the defense team looked as though they were statues. A chill could be felt in the courtroom.

The jury selection process began. The judge began by making some general statements about how the case was a personal injury matter, specifically a tort action. He proceeded to ask some general questions of the panel. He asked if any of them knew or were related to the judge, the defendants, or the plaintiffs. He asked if there were any infirmaries that any of them had that would prevent them from carrying out their duties as impartial jurors. He concluded by asking the jury if they had any biases that would influence the outcome of this trial.

The attorneys began the individual *voir dire* of the jury panel, asking questions on everything from the juror's employment, their families, and their hobbies and other interests.

After three and a half hours of boring and repetitive questions, a jury panel was selected. A hearing followed on the pre-trial motions filed by both sides. There were no fewer than 20 motions in all. None of the motions were granted.

The jury selection and the motions process took the entire day. The Court recessed until Wednesday morning at nine. The lawyers were to be ready for opening statements.

Attorney Johnson arrived at the courthouse at 8:30 the next morning. He had asked the President of Southeastern Textile to meet with him for about five minutes. This meeting was off the record. The President agreed over the objections of his defense counsel.

The two men met in the bathroom. Attorney Johnson took out nine pictures from a manila envelope. They were high quality 8 x 10 glossies.

Neither man said a word as Attorney Johnson held up each photograph. The photographs showed a middle-aged businessman in bed with a voluptuous young blond woman. They both were naked. The woman was tied to the bed railings. The man was on top of her, obviously having intercourse. There was no question as to who the man was.

The President of Southeastern Textile asked, "How much will it take to make both you and your client go away.?"

"Well, $500,000 for the client. For me, it will take 200,000 for my fees and a bonus of $100,000 for finding this envelope before someone else did."

"You have yourself a deal, Attorney Johnson. Would you consider working for me?"

"No, I like being on my own."

"Well, maybe we can have lunch sometime. I know I would like to hire you as a consultant someday."

"That may be possible. But I warn you, my retainer is $100,000 minimum."

"The best always cost, Mr. Johnson."

The President informed his defense team that he had decided to settle. The head lawyer was absolutely livid, but his protests made no difference.

Chapter 10

The pilot informed the passengers that they were about to experience some turbulence. Immediately, the clicking of seatbelts was heard all over the plane. The stewardesses continued to serve meals as though they had not heard the announcement.

The shaking was slight at first, yet became progressively worse. The noise level in the cabin diminished as people started paying attention to just how bad the turbulence was getting.

The plane began to really bounce. Then it shook furiously. A few doors to the upper compartment storage spaces popped open.

Reginald was a frequent flyer. He had flown on many flights that had experienced turbulence. But this turbulence was worse than most. It felt as though the plane was coming apart. The turbulence caused the plane to bounce up and down. With each air pocket, the passengers experienced the sensation of endless free-fall like being on a roller coaster when it was racing from the top crest to the bottom of the ride.

The passengers began to get uneasy. A little child started to cry. Suddenly, a small suitcase fell from a storage compartment and struck a lady in the head. It knocked her unconscious. Panic erupted throughout the plane!

"Oh my God, we are going to crash," a lady yelled up toward the front of the plane.

Reginald thought to himself, "This is what I get for flying business class! I should have taken the later flight. At least the people who fly first class have too much dignity to panic and show their fear."

The turbulence lasted for about 20 minutes. The passengers where terrified. Except for the occasional scream, you could hear a pin drop.

Finally the turbulence subsided. The rest of the flight was uneventful. Reginald continued to reflect on the rest of his week. The plane seemed to have held together, even though the maintenance people would discover later that it had sustained severe damage. Ten more minutes in the turbulence, and one of the engines would have fallen off because the rivets had come lose.

Last Thursday, he had attended the monthly meeting of the Black Lawyer's Bar Association. They always met in the second floor conference room of the Equitable Building located on Peachtree Street. As usual, there were only about ten lawyers in attendance. Like most Black organizations, it was not very well-organized. Most of the lawyers in attendance were just wanna-be's. They did not have any real money. Most were just bullshitters. Listening to them, you would think that they all made six figure salaries.

Reginald attended these meetings even though he knew that the Black Bar was not really serving the needs of the Black lawyers in the area. He figured that one day, perhaps soon, all Black organizations would be forced to take a hard look at themselves and focus on the things that counted. Perhaps they would eventually begin to bond together for the common good of all Black lawyers and figure out ways for themselves to make money and control the legal community.

For now, he would just attend the meetings. At least a lawyer of his stature lent some credibility to the meetings. It did not bother him that most of the people at the meeting were there to get something from him. That was the way is should be. This was supposed to be a way to network, to get to the inside track. Not enough successful Black professionals understood that once you became successful, you had a duty to ensure that others of your race enjoyed the fruits of your labor.

Reginald had helped at least 25 Black lawyers get established in the Atlanta area. He wished that he could do more.

On Thursday night, he went to the Black Professionals Network Conference. Again, this meeting was filled with pretenders and liars. The men were trying to impress the ladies by telling them how important a position they held, what type of car they drove, or shoes they wore. Throughout the evening, most of the men chased women. Not once did you see three or more Black men seriously discussing business.

Black males seem to have an aversion to each other. Perhaps because they all know that deep down, none of them have any real money or power. Yet, they can easily keep up the facade by not really talking to one another for any length of time nor discussing any specifics about their job or financial status.

Professional Black men don't really have a network of friends that they really know and can count on. Most Black men are trying to make a living by working alone. Appreciable wealth cannot be made by oneself. It can only be made by pooling the resources of at least 10 people to be able to invest or borrow or build.

Until Black men learn how to talk to each other, be honest with each other, trust one another and help each other, they will forever occupy the cellar in the business world.

The pilot came on the intercom, "Ladies and gentlemen, we are approaching Kennedy Airport, please fasten your seatbelts. We will be landing in about 15 minutes. The weather in Manhattan is a breezy 35 degrees. All of us at Delta Airlines hope that you enjoyed your flight."

Reginald looked out the window on the left. He marveled at the Empire State Building. He wondered how could such a building have been built back in the 1920's. He saw the twin towers of the World Trade Center. If he had time, he would have dinner at "Windows on the World" restaurant located at the trade center.

He continued to look at Manhattan, the Big Apple in all of its glory. No matter how many times you visited New York, you were still awed by its landscape. There were so many tall buildings. One could readily see that one block of Manhattan contained more tall buildings than were located in many states.

Reginald loved driving in Manhattan. The traffic was fast. People had no time to sightsee and mope along. Stay at a red light for two seconds after it changed and the car behind you sounded its horn. People seemed to have a sixth sense when driving in New York. They cut in on you if you left a third of a car length between you and the car in front of you. Sometimes they just cut in front of you anyway.

The yellow cabs down in the theater district were a nightmare to the novice New York driver. Most people would rather deal with an 18-wheeler bearing down on them than a yellow cab in Manhattan. The cabs test your nerves. They will literally run right into you. You have to stand your ground or wimp out of their way.

With all the darting in and out traffic; with all the fast pace driving and people cutting each other off, there were very few accidents in Manhattan. Actually, once you got used to driving in New York, you wish everybody in the nation drive like they do. You actually got impatient with the way people drove in other cities.

Reginald would spend the night in at a friends apartment in Brooklyn, one of the five boroughs of New York. The other four burroughs being Queens, Staten Island, Manhattan and the Bronx. He often stayed at this friends apartment when he came to New York. This friend was away on business a lot and would allow Reginald to use her apartment when he was in Brooklyn.

Traffic was not too bad heading out of town this time of night. Most of the traffic jams were over. Now at 10:00 p.m. on a Friday, most people were heading out to party or trickling home after happy hour. This was not to imply that there was no traffic. Quite the contrary. This was the Christmas shopping season. It's just that it was not the usual stop and go.

Reginald entered onto the Brooklyn Bridge. This bridge spanned the East River from Brooklyn to Manhattan. It had been designed by John Augustus Roebling and was built from 1869 to 1883. The Brooklyn Bridge was the first bridge to use steel for cable wire. During its construction, explosives were used inside a pneumatic caisson for the first time. The bridge's 1,595-foot main span was the longest in the world until the completion of the Firth of Forth cantilever bridge in Scotland in 1890. A distinctive feature of the bridge was the broad promenade above the roadway.

When Reginald came to New York, he always went to Brooklyn. He loved looking at the lovely brownstones and seeing a lot of middle-class Blacks.

Reginald unlocked the door to his friend's apartment and went in. He showered and changed clothing. He was going out tonight at his favorite hangout. But first he would have a steak dinner at a local restaurant.

He arrived at Michelle's at about midnight. The club was located at Bedford Street and Albemarle Road. It had been in existence for about 20 years. The waitresses and even the D.J. had been there for about 15 years. It was best described as a neighborhood bar. Everybody there pretty much knew each other. Most of the patrons were Caribbean. So if one wanted to dance all night to socca and reggae, this was the place.

When one danced to the point of hunger, all he had to do was go in the back room and there was a kitchen. The man that rented and ran the kitchen had likewise been there for years. The food he served was legendary. The menu included fried fish, peccadillo, puerto freta, carne guisada and pescado escobeche among other things.

Reginald partied until 4:00 a.m. He had a wonderful time. Besides strenuous exercise, there was nothing that cleared the head and relaxed one like partying. Reginald was indeed relaxed. He had drank himself into a coma. He didn't care because he did not have to get up until 10:00 a.m.

Reverend Allen Hampton stepped up to the podium. The crowd began to cheer. He raised his hands, egging them on for even more cheers. Reverend Hampton loved giving speeches. He, like many civil rights activists, had made a career giving speeches. Today he was giving a speech to a large gathering of about 20,000 people in Prospect Park. This was a large park on East Flatbush that was used by most Brooklyn residents as a place to experience nature, picnic, and walk the dog. Had this been a warm summer day, the park would have been filled with about 50,000 people.

Reginald had gotten up at 7:30 a.m. He simply could not stay in bed past 8:00 a.m. under any circumstances.

He went running along East Flatbush heading to Kings Plaza, the only shopping mall in Brooklyn. The streets were busy this Saturday. The section from the intersection of Clarendon Road and East Flatbush to the shopping mall was filled with middle class Whites. They comprised the bulk of the residents in this whole area. Very few Blacks lived on this part of East Flatbush.

One of the first things that you noticed was that the homes and the yards were very well maintained. This seemed to be true wherever Whites were in the majority, with the exception of the pockets of the southern rednecks.

When Blacks moved into an area and it passed the tipping point, roughly 35 percent, an area always went down. You started seeing Blacks hanging out on the patios, washing cars in the street, and playing loud music. The only time that this didn't happen was if the Blacks who moved into an area had a household income of $50,000 or more.

When Reginald got back, he put on jeans and pullover shirt with a hood. He wanted to be dressed casual when he went to the park. That way, he would blend in with the rest of the listeners.

Reginald walked from his friend's brownstone down President Street to New York Avenue. This area was inhabited mostly by the Hasidic Jews. They wore the traditional yarmulke and long robes. Most had long beards and hair. They looked unkempt.

The relationship between the Brooklyn Blacks and Jews was strained, to say the least. The general consensus was that Blacks were to stay in their areas and the Jews in theirs and never shall the two meet.

The perception a Black got when walking past one of these Jews was that they felt superior to you. They looked upon you as a nuisance, something to be taken out with the trash.

No matter how unkempt the Jews appeared on the outside, their bank accounts were always in order. There was no such thing as a poor Jew. Since the beginning of time, Jews made money and that was still true today.

As Reginald neared East Flatbush, he notice that he quickly entered an area where mostly Caribbean Blacks lived. The brownstones where they lived were pretty well cared for. Oddly enough, Blacks from other countries seemed to do better in America than native born Blacks. One notable difference was that Black immigrants seemed to own businesses and were more likely to purchase their own home.

Here we have a country where you are not destined to live in the class in which you were born; and yet, most American Blacks did. The reason probably was that Blacks from other countries never really got the brainwashing from both American Whites and Blacks that Blacks were inferior and poor. American Blacks were never really exposed to whole governments being ran by Blacks. The average American Black learned that the only people with land and money were White and that Blacks worked for them and bought services and supplies from Whites.

American Blacks somehow believed that the only way they could have something and achieve anything was by the way of the White man. Whites had to help you or at the very least, condone what you were doing.

It was time for this programming to be interrupted and for Blacks to build and have something of their own.

The crowd was large in Prospect Park. Still, the voice of Reverent Hampton could be heard clearly over the large speakers set up around the podium.

"My, brethren, they are trying to wipe us off the face of the earth. They are trying to silence us. But I will not be quiet. As long as I live and breathe, I will speak out against the evils that the White man has perpetrated and continues to perpetrate against the Black man."

The crowd began to cheer. The cheers got louder and louder, almost earth shattering. You could feel the electricity in the air. The crowd hung onto Reverend Hampton's every word.

"Now the White devils are trying once again to systematically exterminate us. This is not the first time. No, they tried it by refusing to let us attend institutions of higher learning. That way Blacks would remain illiterate and not be able to learn a trade and take care of our families. We would thus die a slow death from poverty and hopelessness. But praise God, that did not work.

"Even before that, they enslaved us, worked us into an early grave. They separated us from our families and loved ones. They told us that we were inferior, that our reason for being was to service them. But glory be to God, that did not work

"Now, I want you to understand that the number of instances of Whites trying to exterminate us are many, but I am only touching on a few of them. It would take a week for me to tell you all the ways in which they have tried it.

"The ways in which Whites have tried to exterminate us have not always been open. Sometimes it was very subtle. By that I mean that you don't even know what's happening until it is almost too late.

"I'll give you an example. In the late sixties and early seventies, White owned liquor and beer companies developed cheap booze. They sold these cheap beers and wines only to the Black communities. As a result we saw scores of winos and beer guts.

"But the most recent example is crack cocaine"

The crowd cheered in agreement. Some people clapped their hands, others stomped their feet.

Spread thinly among the crowd of Blacks were quite a number of Whites. There was no such thing as a completely Black rally. Anytime you had a substantial gathering of Blacks, be it in the church, at a dance hall or anywhere, there were always White onlookers. They were there to see what the Blacks were up to.

Black people were a strange breed indeed. They just were never able to plan anything behind closed doors. Everything that they intended to do was always broadcast to the world at the idea stage. This gave the rest of the world, Whites in particular, time to plan and diffuse the course of action even before it materialized.

Blacks seem to have a need to tell Whites what they are up to. They will call a press conference at the drop of a hat. They will stand there on national television and tell their oppressors what they are going to do.

There is no such thing as planning and thinking at an all Black retreat or on the golf course. There are no exclusive private clubs that Blacks own and can go to discuss matters that affect them.

Everything that Black people do is ultimately monitored and controlled by Whites.

Reginald started moving through the crowd. Slowly but surely he inched his way forward. People gave him dirty looks as he pushed and shoved his way toward the podium.

The Reverend Hampton was known for shaking hands with members of the crowd once he finished speaking to them. Today would be no different.

Members of the press would charge the podium right after he finished talking, but he would snub them and go right off into the crowd.

For years this technique had helped him to become known as the voice of the people. Wherever he went, Reverend Hampton was well liked. People felt they could identify with him. He dressed like them. He walked with them. He fought for them.

Reverend Hampton was fired up now. He had the crowd right where he wanted them.

"Crack cocaine is the greatest evil that Whites have ever unleased on the Black man. It is worse than slavery. Worse than segregation.

"Crack cocaine is destroying the very fabric of the Black race. Some might say, well, young Black men don't have to use crack. That's like saying, well, no one should take a social drink. The difference is, is that a hit of crack cocaine is cheaper than a bottle of booze. Also, one inhalation of crack cocaine and you are hooked.

"Listen to me, this is by design. Some White chemist figured out a way to make what was very expensive cocaine in such a way that it is now like being able to get the feeling of shopping at Bloomingdales by going to K-Mart. What used to cost $500 in powdered cocaine is now $25 in crack cocaine.

"How do we know that the Whites are behind this? Simple, how many Blacks do you know have airplanes that can fly down to Columbia, pick up a load of coca plants and bring them back to the United States. Then the coca plants are processed into crack cocaine in laboratories by White chemists.

"Black people don't have these kinds of resources."

People in the crowd began to cheer and clap their hands again. The applause of deafening.

"Whites have made crack cocaine plentiful in all of the predominately Black neighborhoods in America. By doing so, they have made sure that those who are less fortunate, who are down and out, who have the least amount of willpower, are addicted.

"But the Whites have gone one step further, they have enacted laws which make the use of crack cocaine a heinous crime. The way it is now, you could have 500 grams of powdered cocaine, you know, the White man's cocaine, and not face the mandatory jail sentences that Black's face from using crack cocaine.

"The justification that the system uses for this is that allegedly, where you have crack cocaine usage, you have increased violence and theft.

"To add insult to injury, most municipalities have added additional penalties if a Black person is arrested with crack cocaine near a housing project or school.

"Now this is stupid! First of all, Blacks who use crack cocaine live predominately in the projects. They don't use it on the ritzy downtown street corners.

"Secondly, violence and theft are part and parcel of living in the slum areas. No studies have been conducted that show that the violence is a direct result of crack cocaine usage as opposed to the general inhumane conditions of living in the projects.

"Thirdly, no one can show that crack cocaine usage is any more of a danger to our society than marijuana usage. The difference, of course, is that when Whites were using marijuana in the 60's, they did not get put in jail for 10 or 15 years. No, they were children of wealthy parents. It was acceptable.

"In reality, alcohol is more dangerous to our society than crack cocaine. When was the last time that you heard someone say that a train wreck, car accident, ship mishap like the Exxon Valdez or any major or minor accident of any kind was caused by crack cocaine.

"Yet, on a daily basis, we hear of people being killed by motorists who are drunk out of their minds on alcohol or marijuana.

"Crack cocaine has become the White man's justification to incarcerate Black men. Judges have replaced the slave master in the role of severing the Black families and insuring that Black men have no promise of a decent life in this country or as head of the family.

"Crack cocaine is enabling Whites to insure that the forecast becomes reality that by the year 2000 all Black men will either be dead or in jail.

"Yes, there are deaths associated with the use of crack cocaine. There are deaths alright. Many of these death are caused by racist White police officers who shoot Black suspects justifying it by saying that they were drug dealers. Yes, what I am saying is that more deaths of innocent young Black boys are caused by police officers than by the Black boys themselves."

The people were clapping their hands and stomping their feet. They believed what Reverend Hampton was saying.

"But that is not why we are here today. Many of us understand what crack is doing to our communities. We have enacted drug programs and other community programs to help us deal with the drug problem.

"I wish the problem stopped here with crack cocaine usage. But it only gets worse. After crack, came guns.

"Any neighborhood in which you go in this country and it is predominately Black, you will find that a murder occurred within the last thirty days. That murder was perpetrated by the use of a hand gun.

"Once again, the system is geared to subtlety killing us. How you say? I'll tell you. By making available cheap handguns for every teenager in this country.

"All a teenager has to do is go down to the local gun shop or better yet, the local pawnshop and he or she can get a gun. Who owns these gun shops or pawnshops? You guessed it, Whites do.

"Now, how do we know that they are behind putting guns in the hands of young Blacks to kill themselves with? Again, pretty simple. Anytime any lawmaker in this country talks about gun control, he is silenced either by money from the NRA or ridiculed as trying to infringe on your constitutional right to own a gun.

"How in the hell can it be an infringement of your rights to own a gun by saying that, like with all other dangerous instrumentalities, the state must regulate their sale and purchase.

"Now you can't go simply drive a car. No. You have to get a driver's license. You can't simply get a driver's license, your previous driving history is taken into account to make sure that you don't have any serious driving infractions or accidents.

"Yet the NRA lobbies constantly through the legislators and they try to convince you that if you have some kind of background check when you buy a handgun it is interfering with your constitutional right to own one.

"Who do you think makes up the NRA membership? Guess what, it is not you and me, it is gun shop owners and pawnshop owners. You see, if you have to have a background check, then the information may come back showing that you are a convicted felon or that you used guns in the past to kill or hurt someone.

"Who would be hurt most by this information? Not the convicted felon, because he knows that if push comes to shove, he can get a Saturday night special. But the gun dealer or pawnshop owner loses money.

"My brothers and sisters, you see how once again Whites are subtlety insuring that we kill and destroy one another.

"But with all these subtle ways, it is not enough. Blacks are not all dying out or killing themselves. No, Blacks are learning to deal with their problems. We are learning how to get off of this runaway train to death and destruction.

"We are beginning to operate our own recovery houses, our own youth centers and our own stop the drugs and violence programs.

"Whites see this. Now they have decided to once again begin to kill us. But this time it is open, blatant and just vicious.

"As you know, there have been several murders of prominent Black leaders. The authorities have not arrested any suspects and the murders continue. Reverend Althea Ranson being the latest victim.

"But I say to all Whites everywhere. Murdering innocent Black leaders will not silence the Civil Rights movement. You can't silence me. I will not be intimidated. Death is something that eventually comes to us all, and I for one don't mind dying in the service of the father."

The crowd went wild. It was pandemonium. The Blacks in the crowd began looking at the few Whites that were scattered about. Sensing that the crowd might get ugly, the Whites, one by one, started heading toward the entrance to the park.

Reverend Hampton finished his speech and as usual went out into the crowds. He began shaking the wave of hands waiting to touch his.

The man in the jeans and pullover shirt worked his way toward Reverend Hampton. When he was about 20 feet away, he reached into his jeans pocket and pulled out a small twenty-two caliber revolver. He pointed it toward the ground and fired three times.

The crowd panicked. People began to run in all directions. It was like a stampede.

Reverend Hampton tried to remain calm. He had been in unruly crowds before. He would just try to work his way to a natural barrier such as a tree or park bench and wait out this situation.

Suddenly somebody bumped into him, knocking him to the ground. Several people tripped over him. He was not hurt. He slowly tried to work his way back to his feet.

Someone grabbed him by the hair. He felt a stinging sensation in his throat. He blacked out.

The people were pouring out of the entrance to Prospect Park onto East Flatbush. They ran right onto the street and into the path of oncoming cars. This continued for the next 30 minutes before the crowd settled down.

There were bodies lying all over the park. People had been trampled to death during the panic.

The police and rescue vehicles were heading toward the scene. It would be some time before order was restored on East Flatbush.

Chapter 11

Reginald looked at himself in the mirror. It was nice to know that if his law practice ever failed, he could pursue a second career in modeling.

He looked absolutely ravishing tonight. He was wearing a $2,000 custom tailored Armani suit. It fit just right. His cuff links were 24 karat gold with black pearl insets. You could see yourself in the shiny alligator shoes he was wearing. His shirt was as white as snow.

You could tell this man had money. His fingernails were manicured. His hair was cut very smooth. G Q Magazine would have been proud to have him on their cover.

Reginald walked down to the Winthrop Street Station of the New York City Subway. The station was old and dilapidated.

He walked down the stairs past five people sitting on the stairway. They looked like trolls. The place was dark and dirty. Reginald paid for the token.

Very few people, certainly not native New Yorkers, would have risked riding the subway after dark this well dressed. They would have fearing getting mugged. But there were some people that even muggers on the New York City subway didn't bother. These people had a certain look about them that said mess with me and you die. Reginald Johnson had that look.

The number 2 train finally came. It made clanky, clank sounds as it approached. The cars had to be at least fifty years old. The passengers stepped onto the train and it took off. It shook and rattled its way along.

The people sat facing each other on long benches. Brothers were walking up and down the isles, asking for money or just harassing the riders.

Seated across from Reginald was an Asian man with all kinds of trinkets. He would display how a toy worked or some other gadget. It did not matter to him that no one seemed to be paying attention to him. He just kept on demonstrating his gadgets.

The train made its stops along the route as it headed toward Manhattan. The closer it got to Manhattan, the less like trolls the riders became. The people that got on the train closer to downtown actually began to look human.

Reginald exited the train at the Wall Street Station. He walked up the stairs and onto Wall Street.

Wall Street was where the New York Stock Exchange was located. The exchange was where fortunes were made and lost everyday. Had this been a Monday instead of a Sunday, you would have seen thousands of money grubbing, suit wearing piranha lining the streets. But this was Sunday afternoon, and the place was deserted.

He walked past the Chase Manhattan Bank and continued for five blocks until he got to Church Street.

He marveled at the splendor of the twin towers to the World Trade Center. This was an international land mark. Most people who were world travelers had at one time or another, come to the World Trade Center.

There was always something important going on at the Trade Center. You could always see some important dignitary or famous socialite when you took a tour of the place.

Windows on the World restaurant was located on the 107th floor in the North Tower. The average meal here for two people cost roughly $150.00.

The unwritten rule at the restaurant was that if you weren't prepared to spend at least $50.00, don't come.

Reginald waited to be seated. As usual, the restaurant was packed. No matter how bad the economy, there were always people with money and people without money, who went out to expensive restaurants.

Reginald was seated at a booth near the window. He looked out at the Manhattan skyline. It was magnificent at night. No city in the world could compare with the New York skyline at night. It was breathtaking.

Seated three tables over was the former mayor of New York, John Haskins and his party. Reginald didn't notice him at first.

Mr. Haskins had recently lost the election in New York. He had made history in doing so. It was the first time that a democrat had lost to a republican in a New York Mayoral race in about 50 years.

The former Mayor Haskins, like so many Black mayors had not fared well during his tenure as mayor. He had tried to please everyone instead of making the tough, necessary decisions it took to run the city.

Inner city crime had almost doubled, which was another legacy of Black mayors.

The city was left in financial chaos. The city payroll could hardly be met, never mind trying to repair the crumbling infrastructure such as roads and bridges.

Taxes had to be increased on an already overburdened city populace. Even with the increase in taxes, city services declined each year.

Increased taxes led to an unfavorable business climate. Many businesses relocated to other parts of the country, taking their high paying jobs with them.

As a result of the increased crime, high taxes, lack of city services, and loss of jobs, New York was no longer considered a desirable place to live.

People, like the businesses, began migrating south. For one of the first times in the history of the city, more people were leaving New York than were coming into the city. Even lifetime, diehard residents left the city.

It was because of this that a republican won the election. People wanted to reverse the trend. They were willing to try anything. They wanted New York restored to its former glory. They wanted it to truly be known once more as the "Big Apple".

John Haskins looked like the job as Mayor had gotten the best of him. Even though he had been Mayor for only four years, he looked twenty years older than when he took office.

Reginald gave a careful glance over in the direction of where Mr. Haskins was seated. He instantly recognized him.

He thought to himself, "Hum, what an unexpected break. The former major of New York is here. It must be fate. As big as New York is, I can't believe that I would just run into him like this."

Agent Stone was also watching the Mayor. He knew that he was disobeying orders by not investigation the White hate groups as ordered. But damn it, he knew he was right. There was something sinister going on here.

Agent Stone had convinced Agent Kelly that it would be better for them to split up. They could cover more ground that way. Besides, who wanted to work with that taskmaster all day long. Who needed to hear that he was the boss and you were the underling.

Agent Stone prided himself on his investigative skills. While Agent Kelly had gotten all the glory for the serial cases solved in the last three years, it was actually Agent Stone who had been instrumental in solving most of them.

Now with that buffoon out of the way, Agent Stone felt that he could go a long way toward solving this case.

He had studied the pattern of the killings. There had been one in Washington D.C., San Francisco, Atlanta, and Chicago.

The people who had been murdered were extremely well known in their particular cities.

Agent Stone had decided that there were two major cities in which Blacks lived and were politically active where there had not been any killings. The cities were Los Angeles and New York.

There had been a killing in San Francisco. So he gambled that whoever was doing the killings had already had a trip to the West Coast. Now it was the East Coast's turn.

It had been a toss up for Agent Stone in deciding who was the most likely target in New York. The Reverend Hampton was certainly a well known, highly publicized civil rights leader. But he was mostly known in the New York area. Whereas, the former Major was known nationally. Agent Stone chose the former mayor.   He began following Mr. Haskins early this morning when he left his home near Central Park.

Agent Stone felt that Mr. Haskins or some other prominent figure in the New York area was in grave danger. Each of the murders had been no longer than two weeks apart. It was time for another murder.

"May I take your order, Sir," the waiter asked Agent Stone in the typically pushy New York fashion.

"I'll have the house special, thank-you."

"That does not include wine.   May I suggest a Chardernay to compliment your meal?"

Agent Stone quickly scanned the menu. How in the world was he going to justify the cost of this meal on his expense account. Or better yet, how was he going to justify being in New York when he had told Agent Kelly that he was heading to North Carolina.

"Yes, I'll trust your choice of the wine."

"Very good Sir."

Agent Stone turned around and spoke to the man seated at the table next to his.

"Wow, this place is expensive isn't it?"

Reginald replied, "Yes it can be. It especially seems that way if it is your first time."

"Hi, my name is Julian Stone. I'm pleased to meet you."

"I"m Reginald Johnson, glad to make your acquaintance. Is this your first time in New York?"

"No, I have been here many times visiting relatives and on vacations."

"Are you on vacation now?"

"As a matter of fact, I am."

"Well I hope you enjoy your stay. As you know, there is a lot to do in the Big Apple."

"But how about you, do you live here or just visiting?"

"I'm just visiting some friends."

Mr. Haskins got up from his table. He headed toward the back of the restaurant where the restrooms were located.

Reginald was about to get up when Julian Stone jumped to his feet and headed toward the restroom area. Reginald stayed at his table and finished his meal.

Agent Stone went into the bathroom. He saw Mr. Haskins through the crack in one of the stalls sitting on the commode. Agent Stone washed his hands. He reached for a towel, dried his hands and left the bathroom.

When Agent Stone returned to his table he noticed that the gentleman had finished his meal and left. Whoever he was he was apparently not hurting for money. On the table was a twenty dollar tip. Agent Stone thought that his waiter better not expect him to leave a twenty. He was going to leave two dollars.

The gentleman in the Armani suit had paid for his meal and circled around the other side of the restaurant and headed toward the restroom. He saw Julian Stone exit the restroom and head back to his table.

The gentleman went into the bathroom. He heard a man flush the commode. Out stepped Mr. Haskins. He went over to the sink to wash his hands.

While he was bending over the sink splashing some water over his face, he saw a man in the mirror come up behind him. Mr. Haskins was about to move out of the way so the man could wash his hands in the sink when the man grabbed him by the collar. A powerful arm wrapped itself around Mr. Haskins' neck.

He recognized the man. Yes, he definitely knew who the man was that had him in a choke hold. Mr. Haskins elbowed the man in the stomach as hard as he could. The man did not break the hold; rather, he tightened the choke hold almost to the point that Mr. Haskins felt he was going to pass out.

Mr. Haskins saw the man reach in his pocket and grab what looked like a straight razor. He immediately panicked. Surely this man was not going to kill him. Why would he? He knew this man to be a highly respected member of society. Why he had even met the man on one or two occasions. He had had conversations with him. If he was not going to kill him, then what? Was he going to rape him. What?

The man behind Mr. Haskins took his free hand and flicked his wrist. The razor opened. He held it up in the air. Mr. Haskins began to struggle violently to no avail. The man was just too strong. Mr. Haskins was frail and weak.

Mr. Haskins eyes popped wide open as he saw the man bring the razor over to his neck. He watched in horror as the man slit his throat. He felt the pain. It was a stinging sensation. He saw himself in the mirror as his eyes began to close. Everything went black.

Agent Stone was really enjoying his meal. It was quite good. The wine was excellent. In fact, this was one of the best meals that he ever had. He was feeling good. The wine was making him feel loose. He began smiling at a lady seated at a table across from his. She had nice legs. Maybe he would walk over and join her.

Agent Stone suddenly realized that Mr. Haskins had not returned to his table yet. It had been at least 10 minutes. Perhaps he had better go back to the bathroom to take a look see.

He walked to the bathroom door. He pushed the door open and went inside. Lying over in the corner was Mr. Haskins.

Agent Stone ran over to him. He grabbed his arm and felt his pulse. Mr. Haskins was dead. His throat had been cut.

There were some markings on the mirror written in blood. No doubt written by Mr. Haskins. A clue perhaps. Agent Stone could not make any sense of what it was. Written on the mirror in blood appeared to be "at jhnoo," which trailed off into a smeared line.

Agent Stone felt a sickening feeling in his stomach. How could he have let Mr. Haskins be killed right under his nose. Had he not been so caught up with the meal. Had he simply went into the stall next to Mr. Haskins and waited until he left the bathroom. Had he not let his guard down.

To make matters worse was, how was he going to explain all of this to Agent Kelly. He had no business in New York. Agent Kelly was going to hit the roof. There would probably be some disciplinary action involved as a result of this.

There was a way out. He would slip out of the bathroom. Let someone else discover the body. There would be no reason for Agent Kelly to ever know that he was here. He would pay for the meal with his own limited funds. If by chance Agent Kelly found out that he had been in New York, he could justify the trip by claiming that he was to checking out a lead from a snitch. All he had to do was pick a hate group based in New York.

Agent Stone was careful not to touch anything else. He certainly did not want his prints to be discovered at the murder scene of Mr. Haskins.

He poked his head out the door to see if anyone was coming. He was in luck, no one was coming. He slipped out of the bathroom and headed back to his table.

"How was your dinner, sir?"

"It was very good waiter. Oh, may I have my check, please?"

"Here it is, sir."

The total bill was $73.34. All in all, not too much considering the restaurant and how good the meal was.

"You can pay me if you wish."

"Sure."

Agent Stone handed the waiter $80.00.

"You can keep the change."

The waiter did not reply. He gave Agent Stone a look of disgust for giving him such a small tip.

"There is a man dead in the bathroom," yelled an elderly looking socialite. "He was just lying there."

The commotion started. People were talking. Some were heading back toward the bathroom to take a look. Others were signaling their waiters to get their checks.

Agent Stone left the restaurant. He went straight to the elevator. The door opened the moment he pressed it.

The ride down the one hundred plus floors in the elevator seemed like an eternity. Once at the bottom, Agent Stone went to the parking garage and retrieved his rental car. He headed back to his hotel. He would catch a flight in the morning.

Reginald took the subway located at the World Trade Center to 34th Street. He left the station and went into Macy's Department Store. This was the largest store in the world. The prices were reasonable considering the quality of merchandise that the store carried. You could spend all day in this store. There was something there for everyone. The only shortcoming that Reginald felt the store had was in the area of men's shoes. Florsheim was just not on par with a store this upscale.

Reginald browsed the store for about 45 minutes. He purchased an expensive scarf and gloves. One could never have too many scarfs and gloves when traveling in cold climates a lot. It was beginning to get really cold in New York.

It did not just seem to get cold in the air, rather everything seemed to carry the chill. The buildings, the concrete, the cars, the people. The whole aura about the place was cold.

Reginald exited Macy's onto 6th Avenue. He walked up to 5th Avenue and turned left and walked to 42nd Street. He stood in front of the New York City Library. He looked at the large, imposing lion statutes atop the stairs leading to the entrance of this city landmark.

The 42nd Street area was known as the theater district. If you wanted to see a play, this was the place to come. If you wanted to see how the truly wealthy lived, then this was the place to come.

Reginald walked down 42nd Street to Broadway. He watched as limos and scores of yellow cabs dropped off and picked up couples who had come to watch a play. Most of the women were wearing fur coats. The men wore expensive suits and wool coats. You could sense the wealth and power of these people.

Reginald walked back to 5th Avenue. He continued walking down 5th Avenue to 50th Street. He headed left on 50th Street. This block contained the well known Rockefeller Center. The Center was visited by most New Yorkers this time of year. In the winter, the central sunken plaza contained an ice-skating rink. As he stood on 50th Street, he could look down on the ice-skating rink. As usual, there were long lines of people waiting to skate. It was exciting to watch people of all ages and skill levels skating together.

Had Reginald come to Rockefeller Center the previous night, he would have witnessed the lighting of the large Christmas tree. The tree now stood proudly in an area up and behind the skating rink. It was a large tree. Scattered throughout the tree were places for members of choirs to stand and sing carols.

Reginald headed back to 5th Avenue. He walked to Trump Tower which was located at 5th Avenue and 57th Street. This was a fairly new office building, one of the many properties of the allegedly financially troubled Donald Trump. It was worth walking into the lobby which was laden with Italian pink marble and taking the escalator to each of the first five floors to browse in the pricy shops and restaurants.

Reginald left Trump Tower and headed back down 5th Avenue to Saint Patricks Cathedral. He went inside. The place was packed this time of year with worshipers and onlookers. Reginald marveled at the high ceilings and just the general craftsmanship.

Reginald left Saint Patricks and headed toward 48th Street. On the way he stopped at one of the many sidewalk vendors for a pretzel and coke. These were the best pretzels in the world. The vendor took one out of the warmer. It was hot. Reginald put mustard on it and bit into it. What flavor!

He flagged down a yellow cab which had to be going at least 50 mph. The cab screeched to a halt, ignoring the barrage of horns behind it.

"Where to Pal," yelled the cabby.

"Delancey Street and hurry."

Delancey Street was no place for the poor nor weak at heart. This area was run by the Jews and the merchandise that they carried was top notch. All you had to have was money and the ability to haggle until you got a satisfactory price.

Reginald came to Delancey Street tonight to buy a nice leather coat. He saw a shop and went in.

"Hello, sir, how might you be today? Can I help you with anything," a man of obvious Jewish decent inquired.

"Well I'm looking for a nice, heavy leather coat, but I noticed that your prices are too high. Maybe I should look elsewhere."

"Nonsense, we have the best prices in town. I'll tell you what, you pick out a coat and we will see what we can do. How much would you like to spend?"

"As little as possible."

Reginald perused the store for about 20 minutes. "How about this leather coat right here? Maybe we can work something out."

The coat was perhaps the nicest and most expensive in the entire shop. Reginald tried it on. It fit his broad shoulders perfectly. It looked good on him.

"Now, sir, I want to work with you, but you have to be realistic. This coat is not cheap."

"I did not say that it was. What price are you asking?"

"The asking price is $7,500.00."

"I can see that you are not serious about selling me something. Perhaps you can direct me to another store. I'm sure that someone will help be get into a coat of comparable quality for around $4,500.00".

"You must be-- I mean, I know that we have something that will fit you bill."

The man, obviously excited about making such a good sale this late in the day, pulled another coat from the rack. Reginald knew it was of lesser quality but did not let on.

"Now, this coat I could let you have for say, $4,000.00."

"I'll tell you what, I'll give you $4,800.00 for the first coat and not a penny more. You have ten seconds to make up your mind before I go to another store."

"$5,000.00 and you have a deal."

"$4,700.00 and you have a deal."

"Okay, I'll take the loss and sell it for that. Mister, you drive a hard bargain."

Reginald did not respond. He took out his gold card and gave it to the salesman. The card cleared, to the man's surprise.

"There you are, sir, thank you and come again."

"I'll see you next trip."

Reginald took a cab back to 34th Street and 5th Avenue. He looked up at the Empire State Building. On his next trip, he would take the tour up to the Observatory. He took the subway back to the Winthrop Street Station in Brooklyn.

He walked back to his friends brownstone. He packed his belongings and went to bed. He had a 6:00 a.m. flight to Los Angeles.

He just lay in bed awake for a while. He thought about the events of the day and the evening. He relished in the thought that he had gotten lucky with former Major Haskins. What he had pulled off in such a crowded place was remarkable. May be it was luck. No, it was not luck.

Successful people become successful by being consistently skillful rather than lucky. Not that luck did not come in handy at times, but one should not put too much faith in it. Luck was both good and bad.

He suddenly had a horrible thought! "What if that Julian Stone was an FBI agent? After all, he was no wealthy socialite. Mr. Stone was completely out of place at the restaurant. He did not know what to order and was concerned with the price. He was dressed in the typical detective, polyester, bland attire.

"Why had he gone to the bathroom right behind Mr. Haskins? It was too much of a coincidence. What about the way he sprang to his feet. He was restless."

Reginald ran the image of Julian Stone through his mind time and time again. He would remember this man. If he saw him again in some other part of the country, his suspicions would be confirmed.

Good lawyers have excellent instincts. Reginald trusted his instincts. His instincts told him that Mr. Stone was trouble.

The best way to handle trouble was to devise a strategy to handle what may come about before it actually happened.

Reginald began to contemplate some theories. What if the FBI had detected some pattern to the killings and could now anticipate who would be next?

That would certainly explain the presence of Mr. Stone at the restaurant. He was there to observe Mr. Haskins. It might have been sheer chance that he left the bathroom when he didn't see anyone else present except Mr. Haskins. Had there been someone else inside, Mr. Stone might have waited either inside the bathroom or somewhere outside of the bathroom within view. If that had happened, he would have seen and perhaps caught the murderer.

But members of the FBI and other federal agencies tended to work in pairs. At least they did in the movies. Mr. Stone was all alone. He looked uneasy. Perhaps he was working on his own. Maybe he was working without authorization. That would explain his behavior and his concern with the prices of the menu.

What if Mr. Stone was working without authorization? It would make him more dangerous than if he had authorization. It meant that he was a risk taker. He followed his instincts rather than orders. He would be a force to be reckoned with.

But it also meant that if something should happen to Mr. Stone, it would not be readily known to his superiors. It might be days, even weeks before word got back to his superiors of what happened.

His superiors would not be privy to any information that Mr. Stone might have uncovered since he would not keep any records of his activities.

Nor would Mr. Stone have given his superiors any current updates of his progress.

When and if the time came, Mr. Stone would be dealt with. For now, Reginald had to be very careful. He had to check to see if he was being followed or monitored in anyway.

Another thought ran through his mind. He was the national spokesperson for the NAACP. It was a certainty that Mr. Stone would recognize him on television. Mr. Stone would recall their chance meeting in New York. This might make Stone key in on him even more. Certainly his suspicions would be raised concerning the death of Mr. Haskins and the spokesperson for the NAACP being present.

Attorney Johnson had learned long ago to never underestimate one's opponent. It was always a mistake. Oftentimes, it was a fatal mistake.

He had to operate on the premise that Mr. Stone would he thinking along the lines that there was a connection between him and the death of Mr. Haskins. This would be even more likely if Mr. Stone saw the spokesperson in another part of the country at about the same time another murder occurred.

Reginald resolved that if he saw Julian Stone again, he would have to eliminate him. It was simply too risky to allow him time to piece anything together.

What was the death of one more man when you were on the way to liberating millions?

Chapter 12

Agent Stone could not sleep. How could he have been so careless? While he was feasting on good food and wine, looking at a beautiful woman, the man whom he was supposed to be protecting was murdered under his very nose.

He began reviewing the events of the evening. Who had he seen at the restaurant. For one thing everyone there was a potential suspect with the exception of the staff.

It was unlikely that a restaurant worker had the motive or the means to carry out the murders that had been occurring all over the United States.

The former Mayor had been out of his sight for roughly ten minutes. During that time, the murderer had gone into the bathroom, killed the mayor and either left the restaurant or returned to his or her table.

Agent Stone spent the next 30 minutes recalling in his mind what had gone on during the ten minutes in question. The only thing of significance was that the man sitting next to him had finished dining and left his table by the time Agent Stone returned from the bathroom after checking on the former Mayor.

Agent Stone kept putting the man's face up on the screen of his mind. The man was very well dressed. His name was Reginald something or other. Reginald Johnson, that was his name.

It would have been nice to go back to the restaurant and question the staff. He had better not though because asking questions about a murder would draw attention to himself and in the process local authorities might learn that Agent Stone worked for the FBI. Word might get back to Agent Kelly. He would follow-up on Reginald Johnson at a later date.

His instincts had been right about a murder happening in New York. Now that meant that the next murder was probably going to occur in Los Angeles because it was the last of the top five major cities where blacks lived in which no murders had occurred. He would take the next available flight to Los Angeles in the morning. Next time he would be more careful because one mistake and someone else would die.

He called several airlines until he was able to confirm a flight to Los Angeles from Kennedy Airport departing at 6:00 o'clock a.m. This flight was perfect because when you added the six hour flying time minus the three-hour time differential, it meant that you arrived in Los Angeles at 9:00 o'clock a.m.

Agent Stone planned to head directly to the campus of the University of California at Los Angeles. There was a rally scheduled at the campus which was to include a speech by Russell Moore, the current President of the Black Student Union.

The sound of the alarm clock caused Agent Stone to sat upright. He barely had enough time to get dressed and get to the airport in order to catch his flight.

On the way to the shower, he flicked on the television. The commentator immediately got his attention. Agent Stone sat on the bed and listened.

The news commentator continued, "This was the second death of a prominent Black leader in less than eight hours. Last night the former Major of New York was found murdered in a bathroom of the famous restaurant, 'Windows on the World'.

"Mayor Haskins' throat had been cut just like the victims in the previous murders. Once again the police reportedly don't have any leads nor suspects. The overwhelming theme here seems to be that if you are a prominent Black leader, you had better hire yourself some bodyguards.

"Earlier on yesterday, Reverend Jessie Hampton was found dead in Prospect Park in Brooklyn. Police had thought that he was merely trampled to death from the ensuing panic that erupted in response to gunshots. However, when his body was examined more closely by medical personnel, it became apparent that he too had been murdered. His throat had also been cut.

"What troubles this reporter is that these murders are occurring in broad daylight or in crowded places. There appears to be no apparent motive other than the victims were Black and prominent. None of the victims have been robbed or assaulted. Why would anyone want to kill these people?"

Agent Stone felt sick to his stomach. He had not been forceful enough with Agent Kelly. He should have been more adamant about his theory of this case. Maybe the lives of these two men could have been spared.

Who was he kidding? There was no way to convince Agent Kelly that placing the blame for these killings on White supremacists groups was way off base. Agent Stone was certain that these killings were the result of one person, possibly two at most.

He turned off the television and hurried into the shower. Twenty minutes later he was dressed and headed to check out of his hotel room. With luck he would make his flight.

It was a long flight from New York to Los Angeles. During the flight, passengers would be treated to breakfast and lunch as well as an in-flight movie.

Breakfast consisted of orange juice, pancakes and syrup, bacon, eggs and fruit. Afterward, Reginald had some coffee and began reading a magazine. He reclined in the large, spacious seat in the first class section of the Boeing 747 aircraft and read for most of the flight.

Agent Stone began to snore just a little. He had stayed up late and gotten up early in order to catch this flight. He just made it to the airport in time and was one of the last passengers to get on the airplane. One Agent Stone got to his seat and sat down, he fell asleep.

As he slept, he was unaware that up in first class was the very man that he had seen in the restaurant where the former Mayor of New York was killed. Had he arrived at the check-in counter just ten minutes earlier, he would have come face to face with Reginald Johnson.

The pilot came on the intercom, "Ladies and gentlemen, we are about 20 minutes from landing at L.A. International Airport. The weather in Los

Angeles is sunny and 78 degrees. We on Delta Airlines hope that you have enjoyed your flight. Thank you for choosing Delta."

Reginald continued to relax in his seat after the plane landed. He never rushed off the plane with the rest of the passengers just to wait in Baggage Claim until the luggage arrived. He waited on the airplane until the stampede was over, then he leisurely exited the plane and went to the rental car area in the terminal.

On this trip he only had his garment bag. This was the only thing that he usually carried, along with his briefcase. The coat and other stuff that he bought in New York he had left at his friend's apartment in Brooklyn. He left a note for his friend to ship them to Atlanta when she returned from her trip.

Reginald proceeded through the terminal to the rental car agency. While he was renting the Lexus GS300, he did not notice the man at the opposite counter with his back to him. This man had an athletic build comparable to his own. The man with his back to Reginald Johnson was none other than Agent Stone. As fate would have it, neither man saw the other, even though they were within five feet of each other.

Reginald left the rental car area of the terminal and walked outside to wait for the shuttle to the rental car lot. The shuttle was there within five minutes just as the rental car agent had said it would be.

Once at his car, he placed the garment bag and his briefcase in the trunk. He drove to Beverly Hills. He had a room reserved at the Regent Beverly Wilshire. This famous hotel faced Rodeo Drive and Hollywood Hills.

Beverly Hills was located on the Westside Section of Los Angeles. This area of Los Angeles encompassed the area from La Brea Avenue westward to the ocean. Rents in this area were the most expensive in L.A., the real estate prices sky-high, the restaurants the most famous and the shops the most chic. The living in this area represented the epitome of the California life-style; fast-paced, carefree and materialistic. There were few places on earth where the living was this good.

Agent Stone checked into the Beverly House Hotel, a small elegantly furnished bed-and-breakfast hotel in Beverly Hills. The prices at this hotel were about as reasonable as could be found in this overpriced area.

He unpacked his belongings and sat down at the small desk in his room. He pulled out a list of local prominent Black leaders who he thought might be potential murder victims. He narrowed the list down to three people. His top pick was Russell Moore, who he had already chosen before he left New York. The other two people were just potentials.

Agent Stone knew it was time to check in with his supervisor, Agent Kelly. It had been four days since he had spoken with his supervisor. One more day of no contact and Agent Kelly would begin to suspect that he was up to something other than following up on the list of hate groups.

Agent Stone called the Eastern Regional Office of the FBI. He gave his security codes and was put through to Agent Kelly's voice mail.

"Hi, this is Agent Kelly. I am out in the field on assignment. You may contact me at 601-529-2473. If you are working on the taskforce investigating the Black murders, please be ready to give me an update on your progress."

Agent Stone dialed the number. It was to a Days Inn Motel in Jackson, Mississippi. The motel operator put the call through to Agent Kelly's room.

"Hello, this is Agent Kelly."

"How are you, sir? This is Agent Stone."

"Where the hell are you, Agent Stone. I have not heard from you for almost four days. I hope you have some good news for me. You better not be running off on your own following up on your hunch about the NAACP."

Agent Stone thought very carefully about his response. He knew he could not tell Agent Kelly the truth. If he did, he would get reprimanded. This would hurt his chances of ever getting a promotion in the FBI or any other federal agency.

"Agent Kelly, now you know that I would not do any such thing as that, especially since you told me not to. After all, if you can't follow orders, you have no business working for the FBI. I have been investigating a group called,

"Sons of Our Forefathers", located here in North Carolina. I think I may pick up the leader of the group tomorrow sometime for questioning."

Agent Stone knew that he had to keep the conversation short because the more he talked, the more lying he would have to do. While Agent Kelly had a lot of shortcomings, a poor memory was not one of them. In fact he almost had a photographic memory. This was the reason that Agent Stone had picked "Sons of Our Forefathers" as the group to report on. Very little was known about them other than they seemed to be heavily financed and armed to the teeth.

"Well, Agent Stone, I'm glad to hear that. Rather than give me a complete run down, call me after you have questioned the leader of the group."

"Will do, Sir. I will call you in a day or two with the information. Talk to you then."

He had done it and he only had to tell a couple of lies in the process. Now he could fully concentrate on his task here in L.A. without the distraction of worrying about his boss.

*   *   *   *   *

The University of California at Los Angeles is located in the Westwood section of the city and is bounded by LeConte Street, Sunset Boulevard, and Hilgard Avenue. It is the home of the very popular UCLA Bruins basketball team.

Russell Moore attended UCLA on an athletic scholarship to play basketball. As luck would have it, he was injured in his freshman year. Unlike a lot of failed athletes, he buckled down and studied rather than wallow in depression about the loss of a potentially profitable sports career.

Russell was very active in campus politics starting in his sophomore year. As a junior, he ran and was elected as President of the Black Student Union. If ever anyone was a reincarnation of someone, Russell was a reincarnation of Martin Luther King.

Just like Dr. King, Russell could write and then give speeches that were brief, on point and inspiring. He was more like Dr. King than any of his offspring. Russell even sounded and looked like Dr. King.

Russell Moore had gotten famous in California for organizing successful marches to protest the conditions in South Central L.A. He had been instrumental in helping to quiet some of the unrest following the Rodney King riots.   Russell preached and practiced non-violence as a means for accomplishing social change. In the tradition of Dr. King, Russell dedicated himself to helping others even though he was from a wealthy family and could have resorted to enjoying the good life.

Many observers of the Civil Rights Movement felt that Russell was going places. At last there was someone who could really make a difference. Someone who was young and sincere, who had not been spoiled by fame and power.

The Black Student Union had organized a rally to protest the perceived lack of results by the government to solve the murders of the slain Black leaders. The rally was scheduled to begin at 8:00 p.m. in the Franklin Murphy Sculpture Garden.

The rally was scheduled days before the murders occurred in New York. As a result of the murders in New York the day before, the speakers at the rally now intended to give more insightful speeches.

The crowd was beginning to file into Franklin Murphy Sculpture Garden. The crowd consisted mostly of young Black male college students. Many of them had their heads shaved. There seemed to be no end to the types of hairstyles that Black men could wear. These styles ranged from the flat-top Arsenio Hall look, to the bald Shaft look with the Jerrhi Curl somewhere in between.

Russell Moore began to work his way through the crowd toward the podium that he and some of his fellow Black Student Union members had set up some two hours earlier. Russell was unaware that two men were following him through the crowd. The man closest to Russell Moore was wearing loose fitting jeans, large sweat shirt and a head scarf. The other man was wearing a black jogging suit.

Suddenly a man in the crowd yelled, "They are rioting in New York; they are burning the city! Someone has killed the Black Mayor up there!"

Another man cried out, "We ain't got no more time for talking. They gonna kill us all. Let's burn the whole damn country. The hell with this here rally, let's go burn L.A.!"

The crowd began to head toward the entrance to the park. There were too many people trying to go through the small entrance. People began to topple some of the sculptures and breaking the ones that would break. The crowd had turned into a mob.

The man wearing the scarf ran up the Russell Moore. He grabbed Russell by the head. With one quick motion, he drew a razor and sliced Russell's throat. The other man in the black jogging suit yelled out, "No, don't, stop!"

The man with the scarf began to run into the crowd. The one in the jogging suit gave chase. They pushed and shoved people as they worked their way to the park entrance. Once out of the park they ran across the North Campus and onto Sunset Boulevard.

The man with the scarf was a world class runner. He quickly settled into his pace of about a five minute mile. Still the man in the black jogging suit was gaining. The two men were running faster than some of the cars on the traffic ladened Sunset Boulevard. The man with the scarf on ran as fast as he could. He began to gasp for breath. He quickly realized that he could not outrun whoever it was that was chasing him.

The man in the scarf ran behind Joss's Restaurant. He pulled off the sweatshirt and threw it and the scarf in the dumpster. The man in the black jogging suit ran right past the man who now was wearing jeans and a white polo shirt.

Attorney Johnson entered Joss's Restaurant which specializes in Mandarin cuisine. Many people claim that Joss has the best cooking west of

Downtown Chinatown.   The waitress seated Reginald in a booth near the window.

Seated directly across from Reginald was a very dark woman who looked to be of Caribbean descent.   She was having a drink and apparently having a good time all by herself.   You could tell that she had good taste by the way she was dressed.   Her clothes were expensive and coordinated perfectly with her handbag and shoes.   She had magnificent legs.   She was actually stunning.   She had sex appeal.

Reginald was not one to come on to women.   Ordinarily he found it as distasteful as the women found it to be.   But this woman had that special something.   It was hard to describe, but you knew it when you saw it.   She had presence.   Reginald decided that he would break his usual rule and say something to this woman.   Besides, the best deserved to be in the company of the best.

"How are you doing tonight, ma'am?"

"Oh, I'm doing alright."

"Are you dining alone?"

"Why, can't a woman dine out by herself?   Is there a law against it?"

"No, I suppose not.   Look, I just wanted to meet you so I started a conversation.   Is there a law against that?"

"No, but you brothers always want to meet a woman.   You always want something.   It has gotten to the place that a woman can't go out for an evening by herself and just be left alone."

Reginald could not help but notice her large beautiful eyes and her beautiful curves.   This was the kind of woman that made you feel glad to be born a man.   When she spoke, she had the most pleasing Caribbean accent.   Actually it was a combination of Caribbean and probably New York accents.   The way she looked and her accent turned Reginald on.

"Well look, I can appreciate what you say.   My name is Reginald Johnson and I am pleased to make your acquaintance.   If you would rather be left alone, then it was my pleasure and have a good night."

"Look, I'm sorry, it's just that the brothers get on your nerves. They are always trying to hit on you, telling you that you so fine and all."

"Well, I certainly would not want to break the stereotype, so let me say that you are indeed fine, but in an elegant sort of way."

"My name is Shirley Whitaker. I'm glad to meet you. Why don't you join me at my table?"

"I'll be glad to, Shirley. Tell me, where are you from? I noticed that you have the loveliest accent. I hope you don't take offense to my question."

"Oh, I don't mind. I take pride in my accent. I am proud of where I come from. I am from Costa Rica. I grew up in a town called San Jose'. I lived there until I was twelve years old, then my mother moved us to New York."

"Yeah, I just came from New York not more than a week ago. I was up in Brooklyn. What part of New York did you live in?"

"I still live in Brooklyn. I am out here in California visiting a girlfriend of mine. Well, I was visiting her. You see, she led me to believe that she had this big place in L.A. and invited me here for a week. But when I got here, I discovered that she lived with her mom in a small condo, and there was not even enough room for me bunk in the living room. So I rented a hotel room here in the Westside."

Reginald and Shirley talked for an hour about how L.A. was a better place to live versus New York and vice-versa. They just seemed to hit it off. They planned to meet at Joss's tomorrow for lunch at noon. Reginald bent over and kissed Shirley on the cheek. He left the restaurant at 10:30 p.m.

Chapter 13

Agent Stone was glued to the T.V. set in his hotel room. The newscaster continued to describe the fires and looting that were occurring in New York City. The rioting had begun earlier in the day when word had gotten out about the deaths of the former mayor Haskins and civil rights activist Hampton.

The Blacks in Harlem, the Bronx, and Brooklyn went berserk. They started burning buildings, destroying parked cars and looting stores. There were reports of several White police officers being shot while trying to control the crowds.

The national guard was called out to help control the rioting and looting. The current mayor ordered an eleven o'clock curfew with instructions to arrest anyone caught outside who was not a city law enforcement official.

The curfew made little difference. Tens of thousands of Blacks filled the streets. Fires were engulfing whole blocks of brownstones in Brooklyn. In Harlem many of the stores which had been rebuilt since the fires that accompanied the riots after Martin Luther King's death were now burning.

Blacks were yelling in the streets, "Kill the whites before they kill us! They are trying to wipe us out! We are not going to let that happen. Kill the white devils!"

It was a sad sight to see. Just when New York seemed to be making a comeback as the greatest city in the world, like L.A., it was being destroyed by riots.

Most of the rioting and looting was centered in Brooklyn and Harlem. The Mayor decided to block the major entrances into downtown Manhattan. He instructed the police to block the bridges and shut down the New York City Subway system.

Once the bridges were blocked off, thousands of motorists were stranded on the bridges because they could not go forward or backwards. Many of the motorists fearing for their lives left their cars and headed back across the bridges to their respective burroughs. Blacks set fires to many of the stranded cars which caused a domino effect, igniting hundreds of other cars in the process. The bridges became burning infernos catching scores of people in the flames.

Planes could depart from New York City Airports, but planes were ordered not to land at New York City Airports due to the violence that was ensuing in the New York area.

As the night wore on, even seasoned New Yorkers began to stay inside for fear of their lives. The Blacks were out of control. They were directing their anger at anyone who was not Black.

The news report changed location from New York City to Atlanta, Georgia. In Atlanta, the students from the University Center took to the streets once word got out of what was happening in New York.

The Chief of Police had assured everyone that the city would not see a repeat of the students breaking glass and spaying graffiti in Atlanta that had occurred following the Rodney King riots in Los Angeles. The police chief was correct. This time the students didn't just break a few windows in the Atlanta University area and along Peachtree Street. They set cars on fire, threw bricks at White pedestrians, and looted the stores along Peachtree Street. The students went on a rampage.

Agent Stone had seen enough. He turned the television set off and went into the bathroom. He looked himself in the mirror and pondered over the fact that he had the possible murderer of Black civil rights leaders within his grasp and the murderer had gotten away. No one had ever gotten away from Agent Stone in a foot chase since he had been with the FBI. This was not your typical killer. This person obviously worked out, had played professional sports or both.

* * * * *

The phone buzzed by the bedside. The man in the bed tried for an instant to pretend that he did not hear it. It buzzed again. The man looked at the clock on the wall near the foot of the bed. It was 2:00 o'clock in the morning. He picked up the phone.

"Hello, this is the president"

"Mr. Clinton, this is Bob! We've got trouble, big trouble!"

How many times had Bill Clinton heard that line? Since taking office almost two years ago, hearing someone tell him that phrase had become common place. Mr. Clinton ran all of the current crises through his mind: Bosnian uprising, Haitian presidential overthrow, South African elections, Whitewater scandal, sexual harassment suits, North Korean nuclear armament, domestic terrorism, military accident, or natural disaster. What could it be? It was enough to drive you crazy.

Mr. Clinton replied, "What is it Bob?"

Bob was Mr. Clinton's press secretary. The press secretary was usually notified about a crisis before the president. This way the press secretary could already be formulating a statement for the president to read to the media by the time the crises was widely known.

"Mr. President, there are reports of violence all around the nation in most major cities. The violence is being perpetrated by Blacks in response to the most recent civil rights killings. The Blacks are demanding that something be done about the murders of the civil rights leaders, or the Blacks say they will burn the nation to the ground."

Mr. Clinton looked upset. "How could this all happen so quickly? Why was I not informed of the likelihood of something like this happening? To the best of my knowledge, the last information that I had on this was that there was some sporadic outbreaks of violence in Chicago after a minister was killed there. Bob, has any of the national black organizations tried to contact the White House?"

"Well, Sir, to be honest, the new spokesperson for the NAACP, a prominent lawyer from Atlanta, did request a meeting with you. I denied the request because of the arrogance of the man thinking that he could get a meeting with the President of the United States by simply making a phone call to the White House."

"What was the person's name," blurted out Mr. Clinton.

"His name was Reginald Johnson. He is the newly appointed spokesperson for the NAACP. Would you like me to set up a meeting between the two of you, sir?"

"Yes, as soon as possible. In fact, I would like for you to call the office of the NAACP no later than 8:00 o'clock this morning."

Mr. Clinton was completely awake and alert. In his position one had to recover quickly from the shock of anything and begin to formulate strategies to minimize the political fallout. If you were lucky along the way, you might even find a solution that might correct the problem.

The president continued, "Just how bad is the violence and is it likely to get worse?"

"To tell you the truth, Mr. President, we are not sure. The last time that we had this kind of violence by Blacks was during the time shortly after the death of Martin Luther King. We have already seen the level of violence escalate to a degree much greater than the Rodney King riots in Los Angeles. To put it bluntly, sir, you are going to have to intervene. If the violence continues to escalate, you may have to issue a national curfew."

"Are you telling me that we may have to have national Martial Law?'

"That is exactly what I am telling you, Sir. The Blacks in this country have gone crazy. My advice to you is that you must show a strong show of force or they will think that they are in control. I don't have to remind you that the Blacks feel that violence gets things done. When they destroyed South Central L.A., the cops in the Rodney King beating were retried and then convicted."

"Well you may be right, but let me have a talk with the NAACP spokesperson first. There still may be a way to quiet things down. I don't want to react too prematurely."

* * * * * *

All things considered, it was still fairly quiet in the Beverly Hills section of Los Angeles. Most of the violence was limited to the South Central area. Many of the buildings that had been sparred during the Rodney King riots were destroyed this time around. From the look of things, it would take at least four years of constant construction to repair the damage.

Shirley Whitaker arrived at Joss's restaurant thirty minutes early. She wondered if the perfectly groomed, smooth talking gentlemen would show up. There had been some serious rioting during the night and a few people had decided not to venture out today. Her heart beat a little faster each and every time that she thought about the gentleman. She knew that if she got to know him just a little bit better, she would wind up making love to him. She would have to make sure that she did not look too anxious. At least she would try to make him work for it a little.

The skirt she wore today was very short. It was solid white, which was in sharp contrast to her jet black Vaselined legs. Her legs were one of her best attributes. If this gentleman had a penis that worked at all, when he saw her, he would have to have her.

Reginald Johnson drove the short drive from his hotel to Joss's restaurant. He had spent the morning talking to the White House Press

Secretary. A meeting with the President of the United States was set for day after tomorrow. At the meeting the President and Attorney Johnson were to devise strategies to help calm the Black populace.

Reginald found a parking space directly in front of Joss's Restaurant. This was unusual considering that normally, you were lucky if you found a space ten blocks away. But today was different with the riots and all.

Reginald saw Shirley sitting at a table out on the patio of the restaurant. She looked very sexy. He knew that he would have this woman, most likely today. He would have to concentrate to make sure that he did not appear to horny. This was going to be hard considering the raw sex appeal that she exuded today. He wanted to go straight to her table and start rubbing on her legs right now.

When Shirley saw him, she spoke up. "Hi, I was not sure you were coming with the riots and all."

Reginald replied, "Actually, hell's horses could not have kept me away. As it happens, I was busy answering a request from the White House regarding a meeting with the President of the United States on day after tomorrow.

Shirley tried not to act too impressed. But deep down, she was thrilled. This guy had the smarts to go along with his great buns. If something was going to happen between them, it had to be today. Otherwise, Reginald was going to be too busy to think about her.

"So, how are you doing, Shirley?"

"How should I be doing? What do you want me to say?"

"Say that you looked forward to meeting me today."

Shirley noticed that Reginald was checking her out from top to bottom. He looked at her cleavage, and then his eyes lowered to look at her jet black thighs. Since he was checking her out, she decided that she may as well check him out. He was a hunk of a man. He was polished. Everything was in its place. His clothing was expensive, right down to the shoes. Even his fingernails were manicured. But it was not his nails that she was interested in at the moment. What she was interested in was also apparently interested in her.

The bulge in his trousers was starting to take on enormous proportions. Her juices began to flow.

"So tell me, Shirley Whitaker, how is it that a beautiful woman like you is unescorted?"

"Oh, its not so hard to understand. The brothers are usually full of it. Rather than have to endure some trash talking brother, I would rather be by myself."

"What do you mean trash talking brothers?"

"Well, it is not just the trash talking; the brothers are not about nothing."

"Now, Shirley, not all of the brothers are bad. Some of them are down right successful or at least up and coming."

"Not from where I sit. From what I have experienced, most of the brothers want to get something from you. They want to live with you, drive your car and eat your food. They don't want to work. If they do work, it is usually a menial job, and they have no drive to better themselves either by getting more education or on-the-job training. The brothers spend all day chasing women, and when they get lucky enough to catch one, they use her up. If they can't control her, then they become abusers. When the sisters put them out, they become stalkers. Sometimes they even kill the woman and then themselves."

"Maybe you just had some bad experiences."

"Well, we all have, but the brothers are just full of it. You see, we spoiled them in the eighties. We women read all these magazines which told us that we all did not have to hook up with Wall Street types, that there were a lot of good, hard working blue collar men just waiting to be given a chance. Well, we gave them a chance and it nearly got most of us killed.

"What the magazines failed to tell you was that women must have men that are their equals, both financially and educationally. If they are not your financial equal, then over time you will not respect them because you cannot look up to them. They are always needing to borrow money from you, or they can't buy you even the smallest of gifts on a holiday. The two of you can't go on shopping sprees or take vacations. The brother can't even buy you a drink when you go out on a date. Over time, all he wants to do is to sit at home, and in this way he is not embarrassed because he always has to say 'maybe we can do this or that some other time.

"If the brother is not your educational equal, then women find themselves not able to talk to the brother about anything except sex or sports. This might be okay for a very short time. After all, the blue collar brothers always have great bodies and know how to make love, but it ends there. After the lovemaking, they are simply boring. They can't discuss world events or current issues. Most of them can barely read. What they spend their time doing mostly is watching sports with their buddies. When it is time to go out to a social occasion that includes co-workers from your job, the women are always embarrassed to take the blue collar brothers because they are out of place. These brothers can't socialize because they have no conversation to speak of. They wind up sitting in a corner just waiting for the event to be over. In time, Black women go to these occasions by themselves. The blue collar brothers are simply boring!"

Reginald noticed that Shirley was laid back in her chair. Her legs were gaped open, revealing her white bikini panties. He tried to act nonchalant. Meanwhile his loins were aching. No, not aching, they were throbbing. He had to make his move soon or he was going to explode.

"Look, I'll tell you what, lets drop this conversation about the brothers. I'll be the first to concede that the sisters work harder. They will get a job, no matter how menial, and they will support their family off of the income."

As Reginald was talking, he placed his right hand on Shirley's thigh. The touch was electric. He slowly slid his hand up her skirt and began to massage the family jewels. He slid his hand under her panties and touched the warm, wet folds of her womanhood. He slipped a finger inside of her. She began to sigh.

"Lets go to your hotel room."

"Why can't we go to yours, Reginald?"

"Well, if you get there and change your mind, it would be safer, I mean less awkward at your place."

"I don't want to feel safe, and I promise you, it will not be awkward."

They rushed off to Shirley's hotel. Twenty minutes later, they were at the door to her room. Shirley opened the door and they went inside. Reginald pushed her on the bed. He pulled her skirt up and pulled her panties off. He buried his head between her legs and began to taste her womanhood.

Shirley spun around, took his organ and began to reciprocate. It was not long before they both brought each other to mutual orgasm. Afterward, they both fell asleep for about an hour. When they woke up they talked for about thirty minutes and then made love again. Shirley told Reginald that in all her years a man had never penetrated her so deeply. She screamed as wave after wave of orgasms came.

Reginald spent the night. They made love once more in the middle of the night, then they cuddled up and slept until 7:30 a.m.

"Wake up, my darling. It is morning."

Shirley let out a moan, then said, "What did you do to me? Were you trying to kill me and I mean it literally?"

"I enjoyed it very much. I would like to see you again, Shirley Whitaker."

"You can count on it buster."

"Listen, I have to go to Washington D.C. tomorrow. Why don't you come with me if you are free. I will pay for all of your expenses, including hotel accommodations and food."

"Why not? It sounds like fun. Besides, who could turn down a trip to the White House? But before we pack and all, do you think you could try to kill me again?"

"No trouble at all, it will be my pleasure."

Reginald and Shirley spent the day, laughing and talking and making love. They just seemed to hit it off. They were like long lost friends, who after several years, had run into each other again. It was like magic.

Chapter 14

Bill Clinton was elected to the White House in 1992. He was the first Democrat to occupy the White House since Jimmy Carter won the Presidency in 1976.

Like all Democrats who run for political office, President Clinton won on the strength of the Black vote. There were as usual many promises made.

But like most Democratic candidates, once they were in office, they either forgot or didn't care about the Black vote that put them there. This concept was not a new one. Throughout the history of this country, Blacks have always looked to the government to do something for them.

Why is it that Blacks looked to the government as a savior? Possibly because it was the federal government in the time of President Lincoln who freed the slaves through the Emancipation Proclamation. It was also the federal government that attempted to pass and enforce school desegregation and the civil rights legislation of the 1950's and 60's. Who but the federal government was responsible for affirmative action programs, under which many Blacks for the first time got a taste of what it was like to be middle class.

Somewhere along the way it became gospel that the only way for Blacks to achieve anything in this country was by governmental intervention.

What Blacks were refusing to admit, however, was that the feelings in this country were changing. People, specifically White people, no longer believed that Blacks were owed something. Many Whites believed that Blacks didn't deserve the help that they got. The term "affirmative action" became synonymous with the word "quotas". In effect, affirmative action was no longer accepted nor practiced.

Economics also began to play a major role. As international competition from Japan, Korea, and Germany intensified, American workers found themselves in a job crunch. This job crunch has led to the firing of a lot of the Blacks who were hired in jobs under affirmative action in order to make way for unemployed Whites.

After twelve years of Republican rule, Blacks perceived that the clock was turned back and they were turned out. As a result, they rallied behind whatever Democrat was running for office in 1992. They just knew that their troubles would finally be over.

Bill Clinton was elected, alright, but aside from a few high profile appointments, Blacks found themselves worse off under Mr. Clinton than during the Reagan/Bush era. Not only had Mr. Clinton neglected the Black issues, he had so many personal problems of his own that it was very unlikely that he would ever have the time or the political pull to do anything for Blacks.

Attorney Johnson and Shirley Whitaker were picked up at the airport by limousine and taken directly to the White House. They were accompanied by three secret servicemen who searched him and her and all of their belongings. These same three secret servicemen had done a thorough background check on Attorney Johnson the day before. They did not uncover anything in his background that caused concern. The search on Shirley Whitaker had been initiated early this morning and it came back satisfactory.

When the limousine reached the White House, Attorney Johnson and Shirley Whitaker were quickly ushered into the oval office. President Clinton was standing at the window looking out.

The President turned and said, "Hello, Attorney Johnson. Hello to you, too, Ms. Whitaker. Attorney Johnson, I am pleased that you came. We have a situation on our hands that I hope you can shed some insight on. As you, of all people, are aware, there has been some murders of prominent Black leaders all around the country. In retaliation, Black protesters are rioting, looting, and burning within most of the major cities of this nation. What suggestions do you have regarding the matter, Attorney Johnson?"

Reginald noticed the lavish decor of the oval office. He was glad to be here indeed. His sole motive here was to cause even more confusion and chaos around the country with the aid of the President of the United States himself. Reginald had decided in advance that the crux of his suggestions would be a national 10:00 p.m. curfew. He knew that there would be no practical way to enforce the curfew, and it would lead to even more animosity between the system and Blacks.

Reginald spoke up, "Mr. President, I am pleased that you are considering using the advice that I am going to give you. I too believe that these riots are out of control, and if something is not done soon, we will have a national catastrophe on our hands. The advice that I have for you, Mr. President, is simple and to the point.

"The first thing that I feel that you should do is to address the nation. I would suggest that you take a positive but firm stand. Let the Black population know that you are behind them one hundred percent, which is demonstrated by your commitment to use all of the available resources to solve the murders.

"The second thing that I would stress is doing whatever is necessary to restore order. The best, most efficient way that I know of, is by ordering a national curfew. I don't know if the President has the legal authority or not to do so, but I am sure that if you request it, the local authorities will comply. Some cities already have curfews in place.

"The third and final strategy that I think is appropriate is for you to schedule a televised conference with the major Black leadership to discuss ways in which the quality of life for Blacks in this country can be improved."

Shirley listened intently to what Reginald was saying. She was so impressed at the ease in which he was conversing with the President of the United States, the most powerful man on the planet. Reginald had his undivided attention. The power the Reginald exuded turned Shirley on. She could hardly wait until their next sexual encounter.

The President scratched his forehead. He said, "That sounds like solid advice to me, Attorney Johnson. The only thing that I would add is that you appear on national television with me as a show of support for what I will be doing."

"Sounds like an excellent idea to me, Mr. President. I would be glad to stand at your side. When do you suppose you will be addressing the nation?"

"I have had my aides inform all of the major television networks that I will be addressing the nation at 9:00 p.m., Eastern Standard Time, tonight."

"Well, Mr. President, I guess the sooner the better. Something has to be done about these riots. Otherwise, there won't be anything of this country left to protect."

"You and Ms. Whitaker are welcome to stay here at the White House until tonight's press conference. In the meantime, I will get my speech writers to incorporate your ideas into my speech."

Reginald was very pleased with himself. He had accomplished exactly what he set out to do. It had been embarrassingly easy. Well, at least to him, considering the fact that most Whites, no matter what their level, never suspect Blacks of having anything except honorable intentions. For the most part that is true. Blacks usually are trying to infiltrate or become a part of a White institution and, as such, form extreme loyalty to those organizations.

Blacks are more loyal to White organizations than they are to their own organizations. They are proud to serve and feel that they have arrived, once allowed to be a part of the organization. Blacks are the only people on earth that will sell out their own in the name of loyalty, duty, and honor to an organization made up of non-Blacks.

Reginald and Shirley were given a room in the White House. The moment they closed the door, they stripped off their clothes and jumped into bed. They made passionate love for the next hour and fell asleep.

When they awakened, they began to talk. Reginald asked Shirley, "So what do you think of the male population now?"

"My, aren't we a chauvinist. Just because I enjoy sex with you, does not mean that you can chance the way I feel about anything, especially the Black male population."

"So you are telling me that you don't want to be with a man?"

"Look, being with a man and living with one are two entirely different things. I let you lay me and I enjoyed it, but not enough to live with you or have anything long term. Besides, I have two children and it is best not to have a man around them."

"And why is that, Shirley?"

"My children don't get along with men that I bring around them. Just because I am having fun is not enough to overcome the guilt feelings that come from knowing that my children are not enjoying themselves. This is to say nothing of the fact that my mother never had a man around us once our father died."

"Look, sweetie, you are making the same mistakes that hundreds of thousands of women make. They sacrifice themselves and their own happiness for their kids. While parents, single parents or whatever, definitely have a responsibility to care and provide for their children, that does not mean that single parents, most of whom are women, can't have companionship. You see the two are not mutually exclusive.

"The fact of the matter is, that children are selfish. They don't won't their mothers to have any fun. They think mothers are is just there to serve them, to wash their clothes, do the dishes, prepare meals, clean the house, and give them an allowance. In return, these kids give nothing. They mess up the house, get into trouble, and just generally are time consuming.

"It is only when these same children reach around thirty years old that they realize how unfair they have been to their mother. They realize that they now are the ages that their mothers were when they were making the sacrifices. They see that their mothers were in their prime. Of course, by the time these kids realize this, most mothers are about ready to croak from a broken heart. Many of them do die. The children are always the first to shed rivers of tears, but the end result is the same. So I'll tell you, you better start enjoying yourself. Your children are not going to like any man you select. But if you just tell them that it is your choice, they will adjust."

Shirley knew that the words Reginald spoke were true. Still, she knew in her heart that she would continue to sacrifice herself for her children. That is what mothers do.

"Oh be quiet, Reginald, and maybe I'll let you lay me again."

"Sounds like a winner to me."

After another pounding session, Reginald and Shirley showered, dressed, and headed off to the press room. They were accompanied by one secret service agent. The press room was filled to capacity with representatives from all the major networks. The President and three other men, probably advisors, were standing in a corner going over notes. Shirley was ushered to a seat in back of the podium. Reginald was seated in one of three chairs on the podium.

One of the technicians yelled out, "Five minutes to air time. Gentlemen, please take your seats. All others, please clear the floor!"

The President came up onto the podium and sat in the center chair. On the right side of him sat his press secretary. Reginald was seated on the left. The President was dressed impeccably. He looked like he stepped right out of Hollywood. The only person in the whole room that was dressed better was Attorney Johnson.

The technician yelled, "Quiet! Four, three, two, one, we are on the air! Go, Mr. President!"

"Good evening, ladies and gentlemen. As you know, there is a situation currently going on in this country that must be addressed. Right now there is rioting and looting occurring in most major cities in response to the slayings of several prominent Black civil rights leaders. I, along with the cooperation of other people, most notably, Reginald Johnson, national Spokesperson for the NAACP, have come up with a plan which we hope will solve this problem.

"Let me begin by saying that the first priority is the safety of the citizens of this country. That safety can only be maintained by restoring law and order to our communities. Only with law and order restored, can we then begin to address the root cause of the disturbances which we already know are the deaths of these prominent Black leaders. We simply cannot allow the rioting, looting, and in some cases, deaths to continue. Otherwise, we will have chaos

"Starting tonight, I am ordering all national, state, and local authorities to enforce a national 10:00 p.m. curfew. The only people that are out in the streets after that time should be law enforcement officials and persons going to and from work. Those workers should get letters on company letterhead from their employers stating that this is the case. Anyone else caught outside will be subject to immediate arrest."

The people in the press room began to mumble amongst themselves. They wondered how the President was going to really enforce this. What if the states or certain cities would not comply? Was there any case law or court rulings on this subject? What if it later turned out to be unconstitutional? Would that open the government up to lawsuits if someone is arrested or hurt as a result of this curfew?

Reginald Johnson smiled. He knew that there was no way the brothers were going to comply with any curfew. Not now, not ever. The outcomes to this curfew were going to be bloody at best. Reginald felt warm inside knowing that his mission with the President had been accomplished.

Mr. Clinton continued. "I want the Black population of this country to know that this office is committed to arresting and prosecuting the perpetrators of these murders. As of right now, I am directing the FBI to place every available resource to try and solve these murders. I am going to request daily reports on the status of their investigations. I will update you, the general public, on my weekly radio address. This office will not let up until these murderers are found."

There were several minutes of hand clapping. The room quieted down again.

"Like with any great catastrophe, someone has to take the blame. I am putting the members of my staff on notice that it is our fault that something like this could happen in our great nation in the 90's. I believed that this happened because of a lack of communication between this administration and the Black leadership of this nation. This will not happen again. I am setting up a meeting with the Black leadership of this nation to take place on January 4th of the new year. At that meeting we will discuss the general concerns of the Black population of this nation to include education, crime, and economic development. I am asking Attorney Reginald Johnson, national spokesperson for the NAACP, to coordinate this meeting for me. At this time I will field a few questions."

This was icing on the cake for Reginald. He would make sure that he did everything in his power to incite his members by the time of the meeting. When the President met with them, the Black leaders would make such ridiculous demands on the government that no administration could achieve them. This would also give Reginald that little something extra that would go a long way to lifting his credibility as a Black leader.

Reginald turned around on the podium and motioned Shirley to head toward the door. But as he stood up, he suddenly found about ten microphones in his face.

"Mr. Johnson, I'm Tim Matson from the Daily News Network. Do you agree with what the President proposes?"

"Of course I agree with it. You may recall that the President pointed out that the strategies that he outlined were formulated with the help of several people, including myself."

"JoAnn Harding, with The Post. Can you tell us who you think is responsible for these killings?"

"I have said from the very beginning that I believe it to be one of the violent White supremacists groups. It was weeks ago that I predicted that there would be more deaths unless these groups were investigated. The powers that be have not done their job, and so the killings continue. I am somewhat hopeful, though, because of the commitment shown here this evening by the President."

Reginald and Shirley left the press room after twenty more minutes of grueling questions by reporters. Most of the questions centered on the upcoming meeting with the President and the Black leaders.

Reginald and Shirley returned to their room and packed their bags. They were escorted back to the limousine which took them to the airport. They caught a flight to Newark, New Jersey. Shirley had talked Reginald into coming to Brooklyn to visit her family. She intended to introduce him to her children as well as her mother, sisters, and brother. She would not tell Reginald that he had touched a nerve in her during the conversation about companionship. Of course, the great sex also had a lot to do with it.

When they landed at the Newark Airport and retrieved their luggage, Reginald made a call to the NAACP office in Atlanta, Georgia. He spoke to the Executive Director. During the conversation, they decided to set up a meeting to discuss what the President had said. The meeting was to be held on December 21st. This would give them enough time to formulate some strategies of their own and revise them if need be. At the meeting there would be some discussion of what was to take place at the NAACP meeting in January in Atlanta. The Executive Director congratulated Attorney Johnson on a job well done. The conversation ended.

Reginald and Shirley proceeded to the rental car area of the Newark Airport. They did not notice the man a few paces behind them. He had been following them since they left the White House. His name was Charlie and he was an FBI agent. He was loyal to Agent Stone. The agent had been given instructions by Agent Stone to follow Attorney Johnson 24 hours a day. Agent Stone had recognized Attorney Johnson on television during the President's Address to the Nation. Stone's instincts told him that Reginald Johnson was somehow connected to the murders. Attorney Johnson also possessed the athletic build that was capable of the feats that the suspect in L.A. had performed.

Agent Stone would take the next available flight to Atlanta, Georgia. Somehow he felt that all of this was going to boil down to that town.

Chapter 15

Lenox Mall in the Buckhead area of Atlanta, Georgia was just about deserted. If a count was made of the patrons currently in the mall, it would number less than 100. During this time period, the second week in December, there should have been tens of thousands of patrons. There should have been standing room only. There should have been Christmas carolers at various strategic points filling the ears of passerbys with sounds of Noel.

This was true in most of the major malls around the country. People, especially White people, were afraid to venture out. They were afraid that if they did go out, they might not make it back. People were being killed all over the nation. The incidents of random violence were escalating.

The curfew was actually working in most major cities. The problem was that the curfew did not start until 10:00 p.m. Most of the violence that was occurring was during the daylight hours. By 10:00 p.m., people, including the looters, were tired and went home to get some sleep. It was not practical to have a daytime curfew unless the country shut down entirely. Besides, people would not accept it.

With the malls being empty, stores were losing billions of dollars at a time when they would have reaped this much in profits. Some mall stores, those with small profit margins, would have to close.

Many of the hard working, middle to lower class Blacks, were staying home. They, like White people, were afraid to venture out. The effect of these Blacks staying home was felt almost immediately. These were the people that make up the bread and butter consumers of the country.

The businesses that were hit hardest were convenience stores, hair product shops, cleaners, video stores, liquor stores, and check cashing establishments. These businesses were always located in the heart of Black neighborhoods, but owned by whites, Koreans, and Arabs. If you really thought about it, most Whites and other non-Blacks always got rich off of consumer product businesses, most of which were patronized by Blacks.

Now, with the rioting and looting, these stores were being burned down to the ground or vandalized to the point that they could not do business. It did not matter that much to the owners, because most had insurance. Once these riots were over, the owners would collect the insurance monies, rebuild the stores and reap more profits than ever off of these same Blacks that burned the stores down.

There was a sadder side to all of this. Not only were the adults staying inside, but the children were staying inside as well. Many of the children wondered if Santa Claus would be too afraid to venture to their house through the riotous streets. Many children believed that he too might just cower by the fire and stay in his cabin up at the North Pole. Even if he were to come out, his sleigh would be vandalized the moment he went down a chimney, and they still would not get any toys.

There was a somber mood all over the country. People were beginning to wonder, how could the country have gone from the usual day-to-day hustle and bustle to rioting, looting, and killing in just the space of a few months? Most White people and more than a small number of Blacks felt that these rioting, murderous Blacks were the gremlins that stole Christmas.

The gremlins were everywhere. These Black gremlins came out in the streets each day about noon. They threw rocks at everything that moved. They roamed in gangs, looting and injuring people, mostly White people. There were daily encounters with the Army National Guard.

The National Guard was both praised and criticized at the same time. They were praised by Whites and middle class Blacks for the job they were doing to make the streets safer. This was important to those who had to work. At least with the National Guard out in the streets, they could make it to and from work in one piece.

The criticism leveled at the Guard was that they were becoming increasingly brutal. There were reports of the Guard shooting young Black males on site if they were in a group of more than three. The critics contended that the command structure of the Guard was White, and they did not value the lives of young Black males. They did not bother to ascertain if these Black males were actually committing or about to commit a crime. It was merely open season on these males, under the guise of making the streets safer.

Still, no one could argue that where there was a strong concentration of the Guard, there was less rioting, looting and injuries. The number of incidents where roving Black gangs had cornered walking White pedestrians and killed or molested them, had markedly decreased because of the National Guard. Even in the face of this, the complaints about their methods were growing.

Not all of the random killings that were occurring were the result of Black gangs. Nor were all of those being killed White. There were many instances, particularly in the South in small rural towns, that Blacks were being murdered. It was like in the 40's and 50's when a Black could be killed, and there was little or no investigation into the death. While Blacks in the large inner cities roamed the streets with reckless abandon, the Blacks in these small rural towns rarely ventured outside unless it was absolutely necessary.

Many Whites overlooked the killings of Blacks in these small towns because they viewed the situation in the light of, "it is either us or them." The Whites, they felt, had a right to defend themselves from the hedonistic Blacks. Had Whites not been so naive in the first place, with all of that affirmative action, integration, and emancipation of Blacks, Whites would not be dealing with all the crime and destruction they were facing today.

There were still areas of the country, such as the mid-west, that were essentially unaffected by the goings on in major cities. In the small mid-western towns, there were either no Blacks, or if there were Blacks, they were a negligible percentage of the population. As such, they did not cause any trouble.

*   *   *   *   *

The man in the chair began to cry. He could not stand any more pain. He hoped that by crying, perhaps his oppressor would stop hitting him so hard and so often. He did not know the answers to the questions that the man who was hitting him kept asking.

"Please, Mister, I don't know the answer. If you want me to, I will make something up. Just don't hit me again, please!"

The man responded by slapping him across the face with such force that the two front teeth of the man strapped in the chair came loose.

"Look, Jimmy, I know you know something about these murders. If you don't tell me what I want to know, I'm going to beat you to death. Do you hear me?"

A young man standing in the corner spoke up, "Sir, why don't we use the truth serum on him? Once he is under the influence of the truth serum, he is sure to tell us what we want to know."

The man doing the beating yelled, "Look, asshole, if I had wanted to use serum, I would have administered it myself by now! This punk's name was given to me be several snitches as belonging to 'Whitewash America'. These snitches informed me that if anyone knew who was doing the killings, this man, Jimmy Sharpe, knows. If you interrupt me again, I'll put your ass in the chair and question you."

Jimmy Sharpe did indeed belong to the White supremacist group, 'Whitewash America'. He and some of the group's members had done quite a number of things, but murdering Blacks was not among them.

Like the members of a lot of hate groups, they got together to merely let off steam; to vent their frustrations upon people with similar beliefs and frustrations. Sure, they had done some pranks on occasion. These pranks ranged from burning crosses in front yards of Niggers to actually fire bombing a residence or two. But with the way law enforcement was cracking down on such things, it was just too risky to engage in that kind of behavior.

Agent Kelly's eyes were black. They were perfectly round and had an empty look to them as though he had no soul. He looked at Jimmy Sharpe. The rage and anger inside of him grew to the point that he felt that he was going to explode.

"Look, you son-of-a-bitch, if you don't tell me what I want to know, and tell me right now, I'm going to beat you to death!"

"Mister, I belong to a hate group, but I don't know anything about any murders. I hate Niggers, but I haven't ever killed any of them. Now please, mister, let me go, let me go. I don't know nothing."

Agent Kelly walked over to Mr. Sharpe. He balled up both fists and started hitting Mr. Sharpe in the face. First a right, then a left. He did this over and over again. Mr. Sharpe began to bleed from the nose profusely. His jaw broke from the pounding. As a result, his mouth fell open. After a few more rights and lefts, his teeth went flying to the floor.

Agent Kelly took a step back. He gathered all the energy that he could in his right arm. He swung as hard as he possibly could at the face of Jimmy Sharpe. The blow landed directly to the nose, shattering it. The blow was so hard that it caused bone fragments to pierce Mr. Sharpe's brain. Death was instantaneous.

The young agent in the corner reached for his revolver. In a split second he thought about killing Agent Kelly. Just as quickly, he regained his composure and removed his hand from his revolver. One day, he was going to kill Agent Kelly. After all, he deserved to die.

Agent Kelly turned to the young agent. He looked at him for about ten seconds before he spoke.

"Look son, I was like you when I started with the agency. I was young, idealistic and by the book. Don't worry, your idealistic nature won't last too long. For you see, if you went strictly by the book, you would never get anything done. Our laws and all those pesky defense lawyers protect these scumbags so well that you would never get anything out of them. My methods get results. Sure, sometimes people get hurt, but in the end, more people are saved than injured."

"Sir, if I may speak freely, I will never be like you. I will quit the agency before I let that happen."

"Son, you are already like me, otherwise, you would have shot me just now when you had the chance, but you didn't. You just have not had the opportunity to use the tactics that I use, but you will when the stakes are high enough."

The phone in the room rang.

"This is the hotel operator. Is everything alright in your room? I have reports of loud noises coming from your room as though a struggle of some sort is going on."

"No, everything is fine. Perhaps it is another room. My room is as quite a funeral parlor. In fact, I was sleeping when you called."

"Okay, sorry to bother you sir."

Agent Kelly hung up the phone, then turned and barked out some orders for the young agent

"Look, we have to clean up this mess. I want you to stay here in this room until it gets dark. Then take this body out and down the stairwell and throw it in the dumpster. Make sure that you go down to the maids room and get some cleaning supplies and clean that blood off of the carpet. Wipe everything down good. Can you handle that?

"Yes sir, I can."

"When you have finished, check out of the room and drive back to the bureau headquarters to join me."

"Got you sir."

Agent Kelly never got rid of the bodies himself. He always let the underlings do it. That way if they were caught trying to get rid of a body, they would take the heat for the death. He would simply deny having had any part in the killing.

Agent Kelly knew he had to return to headquarters in order to stay on top of things. Especially Agent Stone. He knew that Stone was up to something. He always was. Stone had always made the mistake of underestimating him. Didn't he know that you don't get to be the senior man without being able to out maneuver fools like Stone.

Agent Kelly had put a tail on Agent Stone the moment they split up. He had known about the incident in New York, the mess in Los Angeles and now he was equally aware of the fact that Stone was headed to Atlanta to meet with Agent Charlie Smith.

Agent Smith was completely loyal to Agent Stone except when it came to Agent Kelly. It was Agent Smith who had told Agent Kelly about the instructions that Agent Stone had given him. Agent Smith had told Kelly about Attorney Reginald Johnson and how Agent Stone suspected that he was somehow connected to the killings.

Agent Kelly was not mad at Agent Stone for disobeying his orders. Because of Agent Stone's luck in solving some past cases, Agent Kelly had gotten quite a bit of notoriety. His plan was to let Stone continue these wild goose chases. He might get lucky again.

Chapter 16

The radio talk show host was the most famous in the country. He had worked hard to get where he was. He was always the underdog. He was not very educated, nor did he have any looks. He did not even have a pleasant voice. Yet, he had achieved the pinnacle of success in his chosen field. That success netted him roughly 30 million dollars per year.

His talk show was broadcast all around the nation in the time slot of 12:00 o'clock p.m. until 3:00 o'clock p.m., Monday through Friday. On December 19th, his show began as usual.

"Hi, you ladies and gentlemen out there, this is the Rush Limbaugh program broadcasting to you live from the EIB, Excellence in Broadcasting network. This is day 719 for the middle class, day 920 for the rich and the dead.

"Today, ditto heads, we are going to spend the show talking about the current crisis in this country. You know, all the rioting, looting, and general lawlessness brought on by the Clinton Administration.

"I told you that this was going to happen. The democrats simply do not have the courage nor the ethics to demand law and order in this country. These liberals are so caught up on letting everyone have their way and now this is the result.

"Ladies and gentlemen, these current riots and killings are not the result of a few black leaders being murdered as the liberal, whining democrats would have you believe. Rather, the current situation is the result of years of allowing Blacks and other minorities in this country to march and protest and even riot every time things don't go their way. And, you know when these minorities feel that things aren't going their way? You guessed it, when someone tells them that they have to work and earn a living. When they are told that they have to take responsibility for their actions.

"Okay, there are some of you out there moaning, but, Rush, their leaders are being killed. They are simply responding in the only way that they know how.

"Horse hockey! These Blacks look for any excuse to rape and pillage our no, their communities, any chance they get. That's right. They are so stupid that they burn and destroy their own neighborhoods, the places where they have to live. How stupid can you be? Well, I'm mad at you, so I'm going to burn down my own house to get back at you.

"Look, I admit that a few alleged Black leaders, if there are such people any more, and I have my doubts, being killed. But so what? People are killed everyday. When the President of the United States is assassinated, you don't see Whites going on the rampage and burning everything in sight. No, they let the system do its job and investigate what happened. Ultimately, there is an arrest and prosecution of the perpetrator.

"But no, let a Black person get killed, and Blacks start destroying the country. They do this because they allege, Oh, my God, Whites are responsible. They are killing Black people. Let me burn down some building to get their attention. And you know what, the liberal democrats fall into the trap every time. They allow these subhumans to cause billions of dollars in property damage that you and I have to pay for in the form of increased taxes, and then these sickening liberals slap them on the hand and give them a few more handouts, and the cycle continues for another five years or so.

"Ladies and gentlemen, this is ridiculous. When are we going to say, enough, "we won't stand for it anymore." You know, the national guard has been taking a lot of criticism for the tactics that they are using to restore law and order in our communities. Of course, most of the criticism is coming from the lawbreakers themselves or from their relatives. You've heard it, "my son is out there killing innocent people and the guard shot him, it's so terrible." The rest of the criticism is, of course, coming from the liberal pinko democrats. They say, 'Oh, you're too rough on these murdering, thieving young Blacks. They come from broken homes. They need some understanding.' Yeah, tell that to the victims that they killed.

"I think that the guard has the right idea. If you are out their looting, destroying property, you ought to be shot on sight. It does not matter whether you are Black or White. If you break the law, then you ought to pay for it. In this case, you are looting and killing innocent bystanders, so you ought to pay with your life.

"Now I'm going to take some calls in a minute, but before I do, lets talk about the killings of these so-called Black leaders for a moment. Blacks and liberal democrats would have you believe that the killings must be done by evil White supremacists. Every time something goes wrong regarding the Black race, it must be caused by the White evil empire.

"Now, let's think about this for a moment. Let's suppose that we Whites are evil, cold-blooded, Black haters. I ask you, why in the world would we want to kill off Black leaders? That does not make any sense. These alleged leaders are useless. They have not done anything for the Black race in recent years. It makes far more sense for us evil Whites to protect these Black leaders. They are bumbling idiots.

"Now, who would have the greatest motive to kill these losers? Whose interests would be best served by getting rid of these dummies? I'll tell you who, it would be Blacks themselves. 'But Rush you say, Blacks would never kill their own leaders? After all, these leaders put pressure on the system to get Blacks welfare and food stamps.'

"Well, I'll tell you what, food stamps won't buy you Mercedes Benzes. Welfare checks won't buy you decent housing. Maybe Blacks are tired of living in slums and watching each other being killed off by drug dealers and the like. It could be that Blacks are fed up with the current leaders and have decided to get rid of all those with the current philosophy and get new ones who aren't afraid to stand up for personal responsibility and hard work.

"Fellow ditto heads, I know that this sounds far fetched. But most of the things that Rush puts forth sound far fetched at first until they become true later on. Of course, by then ,some liberal democrat tries to step in and take the credit.

"So, there you have it, now I'm opening up the call lines."

A young redneck calls in from Tennessee.

"Hi, Rush, Mega-dittos."

"How are you, caller? What is on your mind?"

"Well, Rush, I would like to congratulate whoever is doing the killings. I would like to see them branch out and start killing all Blacks while they are at it."

Rush Limbaugh cut the caller off.

"Look, you people out there, this show does not promote violence toward anybody, not even liberal democrats. I want to make it clear that this talk show host does not in anyway condone the killings that are going on. If any callers want to call in to condone them, then don't call this show."

A middle-aged housewife from Kansas is the next caller.

"Mega-dittos Rush. I'd like to say that I agree with you. Every time something happens to Blacks, they want to blame Whites for it. I'm sick and tired of Whites always being held responsible for all the bad things that happen to Blacks and never getting any credit when something good happens. We White people are not responsible for what happens to Blacks. Sure, our great grandfathers may have enslaved them, but that was way back then. I did not enslave no Blacks, and I am sick and tired of being blamed just because I'm White."

"You hit the nail on the head, darling. No Whites currently living have enslaved Black people. Think about this for a minute. What we have here is a deep seated problem. Every time Blacks have to be self-sufficient, they immediately scream racism, slavery, White supremacy. It's is a kind of defense mechanism which keeps Blacks from facing the hard core reality that maybe they are lazy. Of course, they are never willing to admit that they don't have an education or usable skill, and that's perhaps why they can't find a job or open a business. But no, blame Whites; it's easier. It's their fault that I can't compete in life. It's their fault that I'm too lazy to get up and go to work each day. It's White peoples' fault that I sell drugs and shoot innocent bystanders on the street rather than earn an honest living; like, you guessed it, White people."

*   *   *   *   *   *

Reginald reached over and turned off the radio. The cabin was now whisper quiet in the Mercedes S 600.

Shirley spoke up, "I must be out of my mind to let you talk me into spending another week away from my children."

"No, my dear, you're not out of your mind, just horny as all get up."

"You wish. I just enjoy your company. I'll admit, the sex ain't bad either."

The toll plaza on Georgia 400 was coming up fast.

"Say, aren't you going to slow down. According to that sign back their you have to pay a toll."

"I purchased fast pay. It reads a meter in your car dash and debits accordingly."

When Reginald crossed over I-285, he began to pick up speed. As he did so, he noticed the white Ford Taurus behind him did the same. It had been following them since they left Hartsfield Airport. It had sped past the Mercedes to pay the toll, but had slowed to allow the Mercedes to overtake it once through the toll plaza. It had to be driven by the man who had followed them while they were in New York. The man had to work for the FBI. He wore the same bland clothing and had the same crewcut hairstyle. He probably had instructions from Agent Stone.

It was 20 more miles to Reginald's house. He intended to lose the agent before then. The chances were that the rented Taurus did not have a radio in it. Still, the agent would have the tag number of Reginald's Mercedes ran. When he did, he would only find out that the car was registered to his lawpractice. The address would be for the office's downtown location.

Reginald eased his foot down on the accelerator. The response was instantaneous. The Mercedes quickly picked up speed. Reginald looked down at the speedometer. He was going 120 mph, then 130, 140. When he hit 150 mph, he eased back a bit.

"Reginald, why are we going so fast?"

"What do you mean going so fast?"

"Well, the other cars seemed like they are stopped. We must be going at least 100 ."

Reginald smiled. It was hard to gauge your speed in the big Mercedes. Shirley certainly would have been panic stricken if she knew they were cruising at 150 miles per hour.

Reginald checked his rear-view mirror. The Taurus was completely out of sight. Reginald would maintain this pace for another two miles or so, then exit. It was a miracle that no Georgia State Patrol had spotted him yet. This was especially true considering the fact that it was only 10:00 o'clock p.m. on a Sunday night.

Reginald knew for certain that Agent Stone suspected that he had something to do with the murders now. Perhaps Stone had made a report to someone other than himself. He certainly had informed the agent that was following him. It was a safe bet that the agent had told someone else, and so forth. Reginald would have to keep in mind that wherever he went from now on, he was going to be followed. He had to be very careful. He was just too close to completing his plans to let some idiot like an FBI agent interfere. At this point, everyone, including his own mother, was expendable if they got in his way.

When Shirley saw Reginald's mansion, she was impressed. She had never seen anything like this. She had spent most of her adult life in Brooklyn, New York. Where she lived, all the homes were attached and the only yard you had was a patio. One look at Reginald's house and New York living just didn't seem to stack up anymore. In fact, compared to this, where Shirley lived looked like a slum.

Once in the house, Reginald and Shirley unpacked and had cold cuts for dinner. They looked at some adult movies and made love. They fell asleep about 2:00 o'clock a.m.

Reginald woke up at 5:00 o'clock a.m. He eased out of bed so as not to wake Shirley. He looked in the top of the hall closet and retrieved a pair of powerful binoculars. He looked out of the window in the guest bedroom, which faced the gate to his driveway.

The Ford Taurus was there, parked about 50 feet down the street from the gate. This was exactly what Reginald had expected. Agent Stone had done his home work. He knew where Reginald lived and probably where he worked. Stone himself was probably on the way to Atlanta, if he were not already here.

None of this was as bad as it seemed. The good thing about this was that Reginald knew who was following him and had already spotted his trackers. The time frame in which to complete his plan was nearly at an end. When the NAACP meeting was over in January, the killings would stop. There were no witnesses to any of the murders, and even though he may be a suspect, there would be no way for anyone to prove it.

Reginald did his normal exercise routine for Monday, which was upper body. After he finished showering and getting dressed, he fixed breakfast.

"Shirley, wake up."

"Is it morning yet? I'm still sleepy. Let me go back to sleep."

"No, my darling, it's time to get up. I have fixed breakfast and everything."

"Oh, you're so sweet. Not only are you a great lay, but you're sensitive, too. If a girl is not careful, she could fall in love with you."

"Sorry, I'm not the fall-in-love type of guy."

"I know. Me neither. Just kidding."

"Look, after you eat breakfast, you can do whatever you want for the rest of the day. I have to go into town and take care of some business. The keys to the Range Rover and the Mercedes C280 are under the sun visors in each vehicle. Feel free to take either one that you want, if you would like to go for a drive to the mall or something. Northpoint Mall is not very far away, and it has some very nice stuff. Here is $300 spending change if you need it."

"Oh, no, you are not going to leave me up here in the boonies. I'll be dressed in thirty minutes and we can go to your office together. I want to see what you do on a daily basis. I'm not some floozie who makes love all night and sleeps all day.

Reginald and Shirley arrived at his office at 7:30 a.m. Reginald immediately reviewed all of his messages and began making phone calls. Shirley looked around the office at first, then she sat down and began reading a copy of the <u>Daily Report</u>.

Reginald's secretary gave Shirley the evil eye. The secretary knew that something must have been going on. Attorney Johnson never brought women to the office to let them just hang around. This one must have some good stuff to rate such treatment. The secretary had wanted to give Attorney Johnson her stuff for months, but he was just not interested. She had worn tight dresses, ass-high skirts, see through blouses, and glove-fitting pants. None of the get-ups worked. Oh well, this was life.

Reginald called Shirley into his office, "Shirley, I have to walk down the street to a business meeting. Please wait here until I get back. When I return, we can look at some of the sights downtown."

"You just keep trying to dump me, aren't' you?"

"No, I just don't want you to get bored."

"Look, Reginald, I won't get bored. I never told you what I did, because you didn't ask me. Well, let me tell you, I am a law school graduate. I am waiting to take the bar in February. Like I said, I'm not just a great lay, but I have brains to go along with this nice ass."

"I see. I'm impressed. But I still want you to wait for me until I get back. I will only be gone for an hour. My secretary will keep you company."

"Alright, I'll wait for you."

Reginald headed out of his office and walked down Peachtree Street to the Five Points MARTA Station. He walked into the station and purchased a ticket. He went through the turnstile and waited for the train headed toward the Westend Station. He noticed that the same man that had followed him in New York was also waiting for the train on the lower end of the platform.

The train blew its horn as it approached. Once it stopped, people exited, then more people entered the train. In about fifteen seconds there was the usual warning beep. The doors started to close. All at once Reginald rushed to the doors and held them open just long enough for him to squeeze out. The train took off. The FBI agent was still on Board.

Reginald exited the MARTA Station and walked back up to Edgewood Avenue and then down to Butler Street. He made a left on Butler Street and walked to the YMCA.

Every Monday the YMCA had a speaker. This week's speaker was Marcus Luther Bing, III. Mr. Bing was an okay speaker. He had been brought up in the shadow of his father's accomplishments. Like most kids who were raised in such circumstances, he could not measure up. It was not his fault, of course. People such as Marcus Luther Bing, Jr. only came along about once a century. Offspring of such people should find their own niches, and at all costs, never try to imitate their famous parent.

Mr. Bing stepped up to the podium. The usual suck-ups began to clap. The clapping lasted for about two minutes.

Mr. Bing began, "Let me say that I'm happy to be here today. There is no finer cause than to try to do something that will enrich our young people. Too many of our young people today are lost in the muck and mire of crime, drug addition, and illicit sex. I'm going to do my part to change this. That is why I am here today.

"We must convince our young people that the struggle continues. We must not let them forget from whence they came. Let me repeat that, less we remember, less we forget. What happened to so many of our young people today is that they think that the battle is over and the victory is won. Nothing could be further from the truth. We, as Black people, have never been under attack as much as we are now. Most, if not all, of the gains that people such as my father made have now been eroded. If the current trends continue, you won't even have the right to walk down the streets in this country once again.

"Young people, you better wake up. Just because you are driving a fancy car to school and wearing nice clothing, that does not mean that everything is fine. Once you have to look for a job, there is not going to be one forthcoming. What that means is that you will live far better as a teenager than you will as an adult.

"How, in the first place, do you think that your parents were able to get that good paying job which allows them to buy you that expensive car? I'll tell you how, they got it through the affirmative action programs of the late 70's and early 80's. Without those programs, you would still be walking or catching public transportation instead of driving twenty plus thousand dollar automobiles."

Attorney Johnson was sitting near the back of the room. He could hardly contain himself, listening to Mr. Bing speak. He was sick to death of this same old rhetoric. Of course, you could not tell this from his facial expression. Looking at him, you would think that he was filled with nothing but enthusiasm. Attorney Johnson would stay until the end of the speech, no matter how aggravated he was from listening to it.

Outside of the YMCA building across the street was a parked black Ford Taurus. Agent Julian Stone sat inside. He was watching the front of the building, waiting for Attorney Johnson to come out.   Agent Stone had anticipated Attorney Johnson trying to give anyone following him the slip. To cut down on the risk of that happening, he had placed two agents, along with himself, on Attorney Johnson. Each of them had the best walkie-talkies that the agency had in its inventory.

When one of the agents lost Attorney Johnson on the MARTA train, he simply relayed this to Agent Stone, who was waiting outside of the station and followed Attorney Johnson to the YMCA. Agent Stone instructed the other two agents to join him here.

At last, Marcus Luther Bing, III was finished. Good thing, too, because in five more minutes, Reginald felt he would have exploded. Mr. Bing went around the room shaking hands. He was congratulated on a job well done by the program organizers.

Reginald noticed just how bad Mr. Bing looked in a suit. He reminded Reginald of a stuffed turkey, just waiting to be slaughtered. Reginald slipped out of the side door to the YMCA. He descended the flight of stairs to the street level. Parked between the YMCA building and the adjacent building was Mr. Bing's black Mercedes. Reginald walked up to the car to see if he could be seen from the street by passersby. When he looked back at the street, he saw the black Ford Taurus.

Reginald recognized the man in the Taurus immediately. It was Agent Stone. At last they meet again. But this time, Reginald was going to be the aggressor. He would call the shots.

Reginald headed back up the stairs and into the building. As he pulled the door open that led into the building, Mr. Bing was coming out.

"Hello, Marcus, how are you?"

"I'm fine, Attorney Johnson. I did not know that you were here."

"You know that I'm always going to be present when something of substance is happening that helps to educate our youth about what is going on in the world today.

"Listen, Marcus, which way are you headed?"

"Well, to tell you the truth, I was going over to Ebenezer for a minute."

"I don't suppose that I could impose on you to give me a ride somewhere along the way?"

"Oh sure, I don't mind. My car is right downstairs. Let's go."

Attorney Johnson got in the Mercedes and slumped down in the seat just a little bit. The Mercedes backed up onto the street and headed toward Auburn Avenue.

Agent Stone was watching the front door to the YMCA intently. He was looking to see if Attorney Johnson was coming out. About 30 more people came out of the front door and still Attorney Johnson was not one of them. Agent Stone was so caught up in watching the front door that he did not pay close attention to the occupant of the black Mercedes that backed out on the street. He had no reason to, since Attorney Johnson had walked to the YMCA from the Five Points MARTA station.

The agent that had been left behind to observe Attorney Johnson's office and the one that had taken the MARTA ride arrived at the black Ford Taurus almost simultaneously. They were given instructions to watch the other entrances to the YMCA for another ten minutes, then to go inside to see if they saw Attorney Johnson. If they did not see him, they were to meet back at his office on Peachtree street and wait for him.

Marcus Bing leaned over to his passenger, "Where to, boss?"

"Actually, I'm going to Ebenezer Baptist Church."

"Wow, that is not what you said when you asked for a lift."

"That's true, but I'm going there to see someone."

"If you don't mind my asking, who is it?"

"Actually, the person that I am going to see has no idea that I was coming, nor does he know why I want to see him."

"Sounds weird to me, but life can be a little weird sometimes."

The black Mercedes pulled into the parking lot of Ebenezer Baptist Church. As usual, the parking lot was deserted this time of day. There were the usual winos and homeless people going up and down the street.

Attorney Johnson reached into his coat pocket. He pulled out the straight razor that he had used on so many occasions. Marcus Bing reached for his door handle. As he did so, he felt a hand grab him by the shoulder. He turned to see what Attorney Johnson wanted. He saw the razor, but not in time. His throat was cut. Marcus Bing slumped back into his seat.

Attorney Johnson got out of the passenger's side. He took his handkerchief and wiped the door handles. He had been careful not to touch anything else. He looked closely to see if he had dropped anything in the car. He did not see anything, not even a hair follicle. He closed the door and locked it. He glanced around the parking lot. There was no one of substance to be seen. Any of the drunks in the area would merely have seen another uppity brother wearing a suit getting out of a Mercedes.

Reginald walked back up Auburn Avenue to Peachtree Street. He went into his office building. One of the FBI agents was seated in the lobby reading a newspaper. Once he saw Attorney Johnson, he radioed his boss, Agent Stone.

"Sir, he is back from wherever it was that he went after leaving the YMCA."

"Fine. Make a note of the time that he arrived. Keep him under surveillance. We can't afford to lose him again."

Chapter 17

Agent Stone was furious. He threw the newspaper against the wall. He knew Attorney Johnson had something to do with the murder of Marcus Bing, III. It was because of his own blunder that this murder took place. He should have arrested Attorney Johnson on suspicion alone. But no, those stupid constitutional protections about probable cause and all that.

No, damn it, he had had it. Attorney Johnson's march of death and destruction was at an end. He was going to arrest the son-of-a-bitch right now. He knew that he would not be able to hold him, but, got damn it, he couldn't do any more killing, at least while in custody.

He went over to the wall and picked up the newspaper. The headlines described how Marcus Bing, III had been found in the parking lot of Ebenezer Baptist Church in broad daylight. There were no witnesses, but police were classifying the murder as another link in the chain of killings of prominent Black Civil Rights leaders.

The streets of Atlanta were deserted today. The current mayor had ordered city workers to stay at home in light of the impending violence that was sure to come following the death of one of Atlanta's own freedom symbols.

Oddly enough, there were few incidents of violence. It was as though people were just at their wits' end. No Black leader was sacred. Whoever was doing the killings had no respect for anyone that was Black. Marcus Bing, III had been killed at the very place where his father had risen to fame and fortune. What was worse, he had been killed in a parking lot in plain view, and yet no one saw it.

Blacks were becoming more afraid rather than angry. They feared that somehow all Blacks, not just the prominent ones, could become targets of this murderous plot. The government was not doing anything about these murders.

After all, the government and white people were one and the same. Whatever feelings of 'I'm an American and I'm safe in this country', were fading away.

The violence that was occurring in the country seemed moot in light of the fact that the killings were continuing. The death of Marcus Bing, III seemed somehow more real than the others. Many Blacks were becoming down right depressed. Blacks were beginning to fully understand just how helpless they are in this country. They only were as free as whites let them be.

Reginald continued his workout. He was in contest condition and he knew it. Every muscle in his body was ripped to shreds. His body fat content was less than six percent. He would be glad when his plan was finished, and he could really concentrate on entering a body building contest.

Reginald and Shirley had spent yesterday afternoon dining at some of Atlanta's finest restaurants. They went dancing in the evening, despite the news that there was going to be trouble following the death of Marcus Luther Bing, III.

When they returned to Reginald's house, there were three messages on his answering machine. They were from the Executive Director of the NAACP. Reginald contacted the Director. They set up a meeting for day after tomorrow afternoon at 7:00 o'clock p.m. at the Hyatt Hotel.

Reginald had to figure out what to do about Agent Stone. He knew that Stone would be hot on his trail. The fool might even try to arrest him on suspicion alone. He could not allow that to happen. He had to go on the offense, take Stone out of action before he called in more of the robots who call themselves agents.

The plan was simple, get in his car and have Stone follow him. When the time and place was right, he would confront Stone. But first things first. He finished exercising, cleaned up and got dressed.

"Shirley, I have breakfast ready for you my love."

"Why do you have to get up so early? Why can't you get up at a decent hour like the rest of the world?"

"Because, my darling, I don't want to be like the rest of the world. To be first, you have to do things first. Starting your day before everyone else is just one of a series of things that put you on top."

"I suppose you are going to tell me that you have an errand to run, and you want me to stay here in this mausoleum until you get back."

"No, no, madam. Today I am yours to do with as you want. I am going to take you shopping."

"Well you know what they say, the way to a girl's heart is through a shopping cart."

Reginald and Shirley spent most of the day shopping at Northpoint Mall. With the exception of large cities such as New York and San Francisco, most of the best shopping was in the malls. The inner cities were left with the five-and-dime stores which catered to low income poverty stricken minorities.

Reginald bought Shirley a beautiful tennis bracelet which cost five thousand dollars. She was grateful and would thank him all night long.

After shopping for four hours, Reginald and Shirley ate dinner at an expensive Chinese restaurant. They laughed and joked and got drunk off of the house wine.

Once back at his house, they made passionate love and fell asleep. At least Shirley fell asleep. Reginald got out of bed and took a shower. He dressed and left Shirley a note informing her that he would be back by ten p.m.

The big black Mercedes S 600 pulled out of the driveway and headed for the freeway. It cruised effortlessly at seventy-five mile per hour. The white Ford Taurus was right behind. The Mercedes stayed on Georgia 400 until it merged with I-85. It continued through the downtown on I-75/85.

Once past the stadium, the Mercedes exited onto the University Avenue off ramp. At the light it turned left and then a quick right at the next light. It proceeded one mile and turned into the large Atlanta Housing Project known as 'Carver Homes'. It stopped at about the twentieth apartment building.

It was getting dark. The windows to the big Mercedes were slightly tinted. Just enough so that you could not see inside from the outside. Reginald pulled off his shirt and tie. Underneath he was wearing a black jogging shirt. He then pulled off his pants to reveal a matching sweatpants bottom. He put on his running shoes and socks. He got out of the car.

There was a young black male eyeing the car. Reginald walked over to him.

"Like the car huh?"

"Yeah man it sure is nice. Why you down here in a ride like this?"

"Come here, young man."

When the young man was within reach, Reginald grabbed him by the collar and threw him against the Mercedes.

"Listen you little punk. You see this car? It does not have a scratch on it. I'm going to give you a $100 bill to watch it. When I get back, it better be in the same condition or I'm going to break your little neck. Got it?"

"Yes sir, you're hurting me, mister!"

Reginald released the young man. He reached in his pocket and pulled out a crisp one hundred dollar bill. The tore it in half. He handed the young man one of the halves.

"You get the other half when I return."

"Don't worry, mister, for a $100, even the police can't get this car. Your car is safe with me."

Agent Stone and the two FBI agents were watching what was going on down the street.

One of the agents spoke up, "Sir, what do you think is going on? Why would a man of Attorney Johnson's stature be hanging around a dump like this?"

Agent Stone responded, "That's a very good question, but I intend to find out."

Reginald walked between two apartment buildings. Agent Stone and the two agents got out. Agent Stone instructed the two agents to split up. They would maintain contact through their radios if need be. They were to meet back at the car in fifteen minutes at all costs.

Carver Homes, like most housing projects, was a war zone at night. If you did not live in this jungle, you had no business being there. There were brothers everywhere. Danger was around every corner. Tonight there was a quietness in the air. It was cold and damp. It was also now pitch black due in large part to the broken lamps which were supposed to provide some light.

No one could be expected to live under these conditions and turn out normal. These places bred crime. Politicians visited them only during the last week before an election and never visited them again until the next election. These hell holes were here to stay unless the land was needed for a stadium and something of that magnitude.

Reginald turned the corner. Under the stairs of the building were two black males molesting a young black girl who seemed no more than sixteen years old. One of the men was having intercourse with her from behind. The other was kissing her in the mouth and fondling her breasts. They ignored Reginald completely.

Reginald turned another corner. Coming down the alley was one of the agents. They had split up no doubt. That was exactly what Reginald had expected.

The agent walked slowly down the alley. He could sense that something was wrong. He knew that they should not have let Attorney Johnson lead them into this trap. Yet they had a job to do and most of the time it was dangerous.

Reginald hid under the stairwell. The agent did not see him in the shadows since he was wearing all black. As the agent walked past, Reginald pounced upon him, knocking him to the ground. The agent was stunned. He was just barely conscious. It was good that he was because he felt just a pin prick as his throat was cut. He died instantly. Reginald removed his wallet and his radio. He undressed him down to his underwear. He then started cutting the agent in the face again and again until he was not recognizable.

Reginald took the agents clothing in a bundle and walked down the alley. He threw the clothing in the nearest dumpster. He headed further into the complex. He heard a scuffle. He hurried around the corner to see what it was.

A black man wearing a suit was lying on the ground. He was bleeding profusely from the mouth. An apparent robbery victim, he was moaning, asking for help.

Reginald walked over to the agent on the ground. He stood over him, lifted his head back and cut his throat. Reginald took out the radio that he had taken from the first agent. He keyed the radio.

"Stone, where are you?"

"Who is this unauthorized user on the radio?"

"You know who it is, asshole. Meet me by my car, now."

"What happened to the agent whose radio you are now using?"

"Let's just say that he is out of commission for now. Get your ass to my car, Stone."

Agent Stone was once again mad at himself. He had let Attorney Johnson outfox him. No telling what had happened to his agents, and if he did not get out of here now, no telling what was going to happen to him. He knew he should have informed the rest of the department about what was going on. He should have had it out with Agent Kelly. If he had, none of this would be happening now.

Reginald keyed the radio again, "Stone, get in your car and follow me. I am going to a place where we can talk. I don't want any trouble. I know we can work this out."

"Well, I don't know if that is possible, but I am willing to hear you out."

Agent Stone knew something had happened to his two agents. He would not attempt to contact them on the radio because he knew that Attorney Johnson would overhear the attempts. Instead, he would try and activate the small pagers hidden inside of their belt buckles. Each agent was now equipped with one of these little devices. You dialed an 800 number and put in the respective agent's code. The page let the agents know that they were to abort their current mission and return to the last base of operations.

Agent Stone reached into his glove compartment and retrieved a small cellular phone. He dialed the 800 number and entered the pager codes for both agents. The mechanical voice on the other end of the line confirmed that the pages had been sent. This was no consolation to Agent Stone because in his heart he felt that both of these agents were dead.

Reginald headed north on I-75/85. He passed through the downtown and continued until he reached Georgia 400. From Georgia 400 he exited at Lenox Road. He took this road to Lenox Mall. He parked on the second level of the parking deck. It was deserted except for an occasional car here and there. Agent Stone parked a couple of spaces away.

Reginald picked up his car phone and dialed Shirley.

"Hi, sweetie. I won't be much longer. What are you up to in the mausoleum as you call it?"

"Oh, I'm just relaxing, reading a book while soaking in the hot tub. I'll tell you, what a life you have, Attorney Johnson. So what are you doing?"

"Me, I'm just getting rid of some nuisances that have been bothering me."

"Sounds like fun, hope you enjoy it."

"Okay, see you in about an hour."

Reginald got out of his car and walked over to the Ford Taurus. As he was approaching, Agent Stone got out.

"Well, Attorney Johnson, we meet face to face again. Somehow I just knew our paths would cross again after that New York incident. That was you in New York that killed that city's former mayor, wasn't it?"

The two men starred each other down for about a minute. Each could see that the other was a formidable adversary. Neither one of them was sure that he could take the other in a fair fight.

"I see that you place being an interrogator above being polite. Making accusations that are not founded on fact seems reckless and unprofessional, Agent Stone."

Reginald was watching Agent Stone intently. He had to figure a way to get Stone close enough to him so that he could punch him in the face. Not many men could stand a punch from Attorney Johnson.

"Where I come from, Agent Stone, when you meet someone for the first time, you usually shake hands with them. It is called courtesy."

Agent Stone did not trust Attorney Johnson. Each and every time that he underestimated Attorney Johnson, someone got killed. This time that someone could be him. Agent Stone took consolation in the fact that he had his revolver tucked into his pants in the small of his back. He would not hesitate to shoot Attorney Johnson if provoked for any reason. First, he would hear him out, then he would place him under arrest.

Agent Stone walked over to where Attorney Johnson was standing. When he was within arms length he held out his hand. Attorney Johnson did what appeared to be the same. The two men shook hands. Both of them used a vice-like grip and held the handshake for about ten seconds.

Reginald shifted most of his weight to his back foot. When he released the handshake, he drew his hand back as though he were going to lower it to his side. Instead with cat-like quickness, he threw a punch with his right hand at Agent Stone. By the time Agent Stone thought about ducking, it was too late. The punch landed squarely on the chin.

The punch staggered Agent Stone, but not enough to lose his footing. Reginald quickly followed up with a barrage of lefts and rights. Still Agent Stone did not fall. He had taken some very hard shots during his football days. Shots that would have put the average man into unconsciousness for a week, Stone was able to absorb. Aggravated, Reginald kicked Stone in the groan. Stone doubled over. As he did so, Reginald delivered a karate chop to the back of the neck. Stone lapsed into unconsciousness.

Reginald placed Stone, who was as heavy as his name implied, into the trunk of his Mercedes. He closed the door to the Taurus and locked it. Then he went to the trunk of the Taurus and opened it. He took the key out of the lock and put it in the trunk, closing the lid with the key inside. There was construction going on at Lenox. Anyone seeing the Taurus would think it belonged to a construction worker or something.

Reginald drove back to his home with Stone in the trunk. Upon his arrival, he pulled into the garage. Shirley came into the garage by the time Reginald got out of the car. She ran over to Reginald and gave him a hug.

"I have been waiting for you. I've got something for you. It is warm and moist. Do you want it?"

"Absolutely."

"Well I have to serve it up in your room. So why don't I go up there and prepare it."

"Sounds like a winner to me. I'll be right up. I have to get some garbage out of my trunk that I threw in there earlier. I'll be right up."

Reginald opened the trunk. There was Agent Stone still out cold. Reginald lifted him out of the trunk. He gave him another karate chop to the neck just in case Stone was faking it. He carried Stone in through the kitchen and down into the basement. He placed him in a chair and tied his hands and legs to the chair. Agent Stone was then gagged securely. Then up the stairs and into the bedroom Reginald went.

Shirley was lying on the bed. All she had on was a white tee shirt. The shirt did not cover her buttocks which were sticking in the air like two mounds. Reginald headed into the bathroom and took a quick shower. He ran out of the shower and jumped on top of her for the next hour.

Reginald fell asleep almost instantly after the lovemaking session. He had had a full day tangling with Stone and his boys. He needed rest. Tomorrow he had the NAACP meeting. He wanted to be fresh and alert. He also had to figure out what to do with Shirley. He had a lot to do before the NAACP meeting in January. She was beginning to get in the way. Not that he did not enjoy being with her every second. It was just that she might see or hear something. As cold-blooded as Reginald was these days, he wasn't sure that he could bring himself to hurting her. He would convince her tomorrow that it was time for her to return to her family in New York.

Agent Stone opened his eyes. It was pitch black. His head hurt something terrible. It felt has though someone had tried to twist it off. Then he remembered who that someone was. It was Attorney Johnson. At least he had not decided to kill him or he would have awakened in Hell instead of where he was now. But where was he? Wherever he was he had to escape. He had to warn the remaining members of the NAACP of the danger that they were facing. Someone had to stop this madman.

Chapter 18

Shirley opened her eyes. As usual, she expected to find Reginald up and dressed. This morning she did not smell the coffee pot or anything in the kitchen. She rolled over to find Reginald sleeping right next to her. She looked at her watch. It was ten minutes to five. She shook Reginald.

"What is it, my little chile pepper?"

"Nothing. I just woke up before you and wanted the pleasure of waking you up for a change."

"So how does it feel?"

"Wonderful, just wonderful."

"Listen, Mi Amore, I have to meet with the NAACP this afternoon at the Hyatt Hotel Downtown. I don't want you to get bored waiting for me here all the time, nor do I want you bored sitting at a function waiting for me either."

"Who said that I was bored?"

"Look, we have had fun. It has been wonderful to me. But I am starting to feel guilty knowing that I'm the reason that you are away from your children."

"That's just like men. They get what they want, then they are ready to dump you. I thought that you were different."

"I care for you very much. More than I have for anyone in a long time. But I know that you have responsibilities. Why don't you let me fly you to New

York today, check on your kids and fly back anytime you want. That way I will feel much better and so will you."

Shirley thought about what Reginald said for a minute. Deep down she knew that he was right.

"Alright, I'll fly to New York today. I guess I do miss my children a little. I'm coming back to Atlanta in about three or four days. But I'll call you first to let you know that I'm coming."

"Hum, I like the sound of that."

"You are such a pervert. Come here you little pervert and let me show you what the word means."

Reginald went through his usual morning routines. He and Shirley watched the news. The situation in the country was getting worse. The violence that was occurring was reaching epidemic proportions. Unless someone did something soon, there was going to be all out war between Blacks and Whites.

Reginald took Shirley to the Airport. He gave her some spending money and purchased a ticket which would allow her to fly back to Atlanta whenever she chose.

Agent Stone woke up. He did not know what day it was or how long he had been asleep. It was daylight now and he could see the room in which he was in. Wherever it was, the place was beautiful and clean. The ceiling was high and floor was hardwood. This had to be Attorney Johnson's house. This looked like the sort of place that he would live.

The ropes that held Agent Stone were very tight around his wrists and ankles. As a result, the circulation was somewhat cut off. He was beginning to get numb all over. He did not want to die, but he also did not what to lose a limb due to poor circulation either.

There was the sound of breaking glass upstairs. Footsteps could be heard on the main level of the house. Someone was inside. Whoever it was, they were now heading down the stairwell. It certainly was not Attorney Johnson. He would have no reason to break into his own house, or would he.

No, he would not, unless he was going to claim that Agent Stone was a burglar or something and he had to kill him.

The door sprang open to the basement. There stood old leather face himself. Agent Stone's heart beat faster.

"Well, well, if it isn't Agent Stone. The same Stone that I told not to act on the NAACP theory. Now I wonder what Agent Stone is doing here all tied up in the basement of a nationally famous Black lawyer? Thought you could fool old Agent Kelly, did you?"

Agent Kelly went over to where Stone was tied up. He ungagged him but left the rest of the bindings in place.

"How did you find me, Sir?"

"Do you think that I got to be where I am by letting some little punk like you outfox me? I have had one of my loyal agents following you and those other two fools all along. If you are going to use other agents to try to do something behind my back, you better make damn sure that they are loyal to you. One of the agents working with you kept my agent informed all along. I knew your every move.

"Once you let yourself be captured last night, my agent called me, and I thought I better come running. By the way, my agent tells me that your two agents did not come out of that housing project with you."

"That is true, Sir. I fear that they might be dead. It is all my fault. I should have not underestimated Attorney Johnson. If I hadn't, those two agents would not be dead now. Sir I would appreciate it if you would untie me."

"Oh, now you need my help, Agent Stone. Now you see that perhaps there is something to be said for teamwork. I'll untie you alright, but not before you tell me all that you know about this Attorney Johnson and his involvement with the murders."

"Agent Kelly, my circulation is cut off. I am beginning to get very numb. I would appreciate it if you would untie me. I will tell you what you want to know."

"You're right, asshole, you are going to tell me. You are going to tell me right now. Otherwise, I'm going to leave your ass to rot right here.

"Better yet, Agent Stone, I think that I have an opportunity here. How often am I going to have you in such a compromising position? Now is a perfect time for me to interrogate you. The last guy that I interrogated decided to black out on me in a permanent sort of way, if you know what I mean. I realized too late that I should have used truth serum on him. That is what I'm going to do with you. That way I'll get the whole story instead of a piece here and there."

"I would remind you, Agent Kelly, that we work for the same side. What you are doing is unethical."

"You should talk, asshole. You disobeyed my direct orders, and in the process, you got two agents killed. Don't tell me that we work for the same side. If we were at war, I would kill you where you sit without a moment's hesitation."

Agent Kelly went upstairs and motioned to his agent outside. When the agent got within hearing distance, he told him to bring the truth serum.

Attorney Johnson passed through the toll plaza on Georgia 400. He was heading back to his house in order to prepare for tonight's meeting with the NAACP and to give Agent Stone some food. He would spend some time interrogating Stone to see what he had told other members of the FBI. He knew that he could not convince Agent Stone to join him in his quest to liberate Blacks. He would have to kill Stone because he was the only man who knew that Attorney Johnson was involved in the murders.

He liked Stone well enough. It was just too much of a risk to let him live. If Stone somehow escaped, all of the planning and carrying out the tasks would be all for nothing. Stone had to die.

The needle hurt badly going into Agent Stone's arm. But it should have hurt much worse. Stone knew that his lack of circulation was getting critical. He had to somehow, someway appease Agent Kelly so that he would loosen his bindings.

Almost instantly, Stone saw that the room began to spin. He felt as though he were having an out-of-body experience. His spirit was flying all around the room, looking down at his body which was bound to the chair. It was like being drunk with absolutely no inhibitions. Stone actually wanted to begin to tell his life story. Like most FBI agents, he had not had enough training in how to resist the effects of truth serum.

Agent Kelly watched from a corner of the room. He saw Agent Stone's head begin to bob and weave. It was time to start asking questions.

"So, Stone, how do you feel about me?"

"With all due respect, Sir, I think you are the biggest asshole in the animal kingdom. If it were not for me, you couldn't determine why it stinks when you go to the bathroom."

"Is there anything that you know about me that you intend to ever use against me?"

"Yes, I know that you killed that suspect that you were interrogating in Boston last year. I videotaped the whole thing unbeknownst to you. If you ever tried to discipline me or hurt my chances for promotion, I intend to give it to your superiors."

"Where is the tape now?"

"I keep it locked away in a safe deposit box at the Central Bank in Washington, D.C."

"Did you make any copies of the tape?"

"No, I only have that one copy."

"Are there any special passwords or codes that you need in order to get into the safe deposit box?"

"All you need is my social security number which is 459-23-9873 and my special password which is 'covert'."

"It takes a dumb shit like you, Stone, to come up with a password like that."

"Reginald turned on his turn signal to enter his driveway when he suddenly spotted a man coming down his driveway dressed in government dull attire. He turned off his signal and continued down the street. He parked around the corner and got out of his car. He took off his jacket and threw it over his shoulder. He started walking back towards his house. He picked up the newspaper out of the driveway of one of his neighbors and put it under his arm.

The agent in the Taurus saw the man coming down the street with his coat over his shoulder and newspaper in hand. As far as he was concerned, just another rich jerk out for a stroll. The Agent leaned back in his seat and propped his head on the headrest.

Attorney Johnson picked up his pace as he headed for the Taurus. He reached into his pocket with his free hand pulled out the razor. He walked right up to the man in the Taurus. The agent had shut his eyes. He was tired. He intended to take a five minute nap and then go back to the house to see what was happening. He didn't see or hear the man that approached him. He never opened his eyes again.

"So, Stone, I want you to tell me all you know about these murders and then tell me what you think needs to be done to solve them. No, wait a minute. I intend to have some fun with you, Nigger. I'm going to teach you a lesson you won't forget. You see, it is uppity Niggers like you who don't know their place in this life and it is up to White people like me to show you what it is.

"Now listen very carefully, Stone. You can't resist me. You are under my power. You must do anything that I say. Do you understand?"

"Yes, I understand. I have to do as you say."

"I want you to give me a blowjob. I want it to be the best damn blowjob in the world, got it?"

The effects of the truth serum were just too strong. Once an individual was injected with it, he or she became helpless. Not only did they have to tell the truth, but they were completely open to suggestions as long the level of serum was high enough in their bloodstream. The effect was short lived though. It usually lasted for about twenty minutes.

Agent Kelly walked upstairs and looked around until he came to the master bedroom. He searched through the closets and drawers until he found a video camera and tape. He did not know if the tape had been used. He didn't care, he would simply tape over it. He went back down the stairs and into the basement. He set the camera up in a chair and made sure that it was focused on Agent Stone's head.

He pulled his pants and boxer shorts down to his knees. He held his penis in his hand as he walked over to Agent Stone. He placed his penis in Stone's mouth. Stone began to suck on the head of the penis ever so gently until he had the whole thing in his mouth.

The video camera was recording the whole thing. All you could see was Agent Stone sucking on a man's penis. You could only see the midsection of the man.

"That's it, Stone, faster, faster, deeper, take it deeper. Now I want to see the look on your face when you try and threaten me with your tape and I show you this."

Agent Kelly was really getting into the blowjob. He did not hear the low sound of footsteps behind him. An arm grabbed him from behind. He was startled. He saw the razor coming for his throat just as he was starting to ejaculate. Agent Kelly experienced pain, pleasure and fear all at the same time. His body fell to the floor.

Attorney Johnson saw the needle and vial on a chair. He looked at Agent Stone's right arm and saw a blood spot. He must have been injected with some drug that made him acquiesce to what was occurring in this room.

Reginald could not decide what to do with Stone. May be he should just cut his throat while he was in this semi-conscious state. Stone would not know the difference. It would be like a mercy killing. No, Stone was a man. He deserved to die like a man.

"Agent Stone, can you hear me?"

"Yes, I hear you."

"Do you have to tell the truth?'

"Yes, I have to tell the truth."

"Have you told anyone in the FBI about me?"

"Only the two agents that were with me here in Atlanta."

"Do you know if they told anyone else?"

"I don't think so. We were supposed to decide today what to do about that."

"Who was that man just in the room with you?"

"He was Agent Kelly, my boss."

"How did he get here?"

"He had one agent following me all along."

"Do you know if your boss told anyone in the FBI about me."

"I don't think so. He told me that he wanted to hear what I had to say before he called in the troops."

"Do you have to do what I say?"

"Yes, while I am under the effects of this serum."

"What about when the serum wears off?"

"When it does, I will only remember what happened up to the moment I was injected with it."

"Alright, Stone, go to sleep. Sleep deeper than you ever slept before. I want you to sleep a solid eight hours. Nothing will wake you up. Now sleep."

Agent Stone's head fell forward. He began to snore. Attorney Johnson had found out what he wanted to know most. He could breathe easier. He would get rid of all of the bodies once night came and he returned from the NAACP meeting.

Reginald went outside and walked to the Ford Taurus. He pushed the dead agent over onto the passenger side and got in. He drove the car into his garage and closed the doors. He then walked back up the street and retrieved his Mercedes.

Once back in the house, he headed to the master bedroom to take another shower and change clothing. He relaxed for ten minutes and then spent the next three hours preparing his strategy for the meeting.

His strategy was very simple. He would subtly manipulate the members in attendance to agree with him to have the president of the United States come to the national NAACP meeting on January 16th instead of them meeting with the President on January 4th of next year. That way, Reginald could control the outcome a lot better than it being somewhere in Washington, the President's home turf.

The second thing that he would do is the suggest that the NAACP organize a march from Atlanta to Washington D.C. on the 17th of January, the day after the national meeting. This way, the members would be distracted with the logistics of planning a dumb march instead of seeing any kind of pattern to the killings.

The Executive Director struck the gavel. As he did so, all conversations stopped in the conference room. People took their seats.

"Gentlemen, I call this meeting to order. There are a lot of no shows tonight. I imagine the reason is that some of the members are afraid. I want to take this opportunity to say right now that no one will be looked down upon for not coming to the meeting. People, no not people, we the members of this organization are being killed. That is the simple reality. I have never seen such intimidation of Blacks since I started working in this organization some thirty years ago.

"As all of you are aware, our very dear friend, Marcus Bing, III, was killed two days ago. This death struck at the very heart of the Civil Rights Movement. I fear that if we don't take some kind of significant, effective response, we will all be picked off like flies."

A man interrupted from the rear of the room, "Mr. Director, I'm scared. All we are doing tonight is talking. Meanwhile, the members of this organization are being murdered. This is my last meeting. It just ain't worth it to die for some organization, and you don't even know why you are being killed!"

The room erupted into many small conversations. The net effect was a loud mumbling sound. The Director struck the gavel and again the room quieted down.

"Gentlemen, are we cowards who run and hide anytime that we are threatened? Or are we men sworn to ensure that Black people will achieve racial equality in this country no matter what the cost or how long it takes?"

A young man jumped to his feet, "The hell with giving your life for these ideals. I have a wife and kids to think about. These murders are different from the killings of the 60's. At least then you were out marching somewhere. Now people are just being killed anywhere and anytime for no apparent reason. I say we should may be lay low for a while, not have any meetings until the authorities get whoever it is that is killing us."

Many of the members in attendance began to clap. Most of them felt the same way and were glad that someone had the guts to vocalize what needed to be said.

The Executive Director waved his hands in the air and then began speaking.

"If we give into these terrorist, whomever they may be, we are doing a disservice to all of the Civil Rights leaders who went before us. These people gave their lives so that you and I could walk openly and proudly along the highways and byways of this country. Now when the going gets tough, you are going to turn tail and hide. They did not hide when they were being hosed down with fire hoses and bitten by police dogs. When their friends were being hanged, they still did not quit. We have an obligation to continue this legacy or we will never be free."

Attorney Johnson had been totally still during this whole exchange. He felt that the time was right for him to make his move. He stood up.

"May I say a few words? The opinions of all of you in this room are right. Just as the young man said, we can't allow ourselves to be killed for no apparent reason. At the same time, we can't give up the fight for Civil Rights that is so vital to us all. I for one do not intend to die.

"But what can we do to solve this dilemma? I propose that we put more pressure on the President of the United States, who in turn can and will exert the kind of pressure needed on the law enforcement agencies of this country. How can we use the President to do this? For one thing, I say let's not have a meeting with him on the 4th of January. If we do, it will just be another affair in Washington and as soon as it is over, all will be forgotten. Now as you know, the President asked me to help coordinate that meeting. Let's have the President come to us."

There were murmurs in the room. The suggestion caught the members by surprise.

"That's right, let's have the President come to us. Not on January 4th, but on January 16th, the day of our national meeting. This way, our meeting will be taken very seriously by everyone. All of the press in the nation will be in attendance, and we can demand all kinds of things. People will be very receptive to us.

"The next thing that I suggest to you is for us to follow up on the suggestion that was given to us some months ago. Let's have a march. Let's march from Atlanta to Washington D.C. Let's do it the day after our national meeting. Most of our members and supporters will be in Atlanta anyway and we will have the necessary momentum to pull it off. If we are successful, I believe the pressure on the law enforcement in this country to stop the killings will rise to the level that they will do something, anything to save face."

The room was quiet. The members pondered this. It seemed like a good idea. Marches had been used effectively many times in the past. When nothing else worked, marches always did.

The room erupted into clapping. Everyone stood up. This was just the shot in the arm that the organization needed. The Executive Director then took over the floor. He praised Attorney Johnson for coming up with such brilliant suggestions. He spent a few moments congratulating Attorney Johnson on the way he performed on the nationally televised news conference in Washington the previous week.

Reginald took it all in stride. He acted as humble as he could. He was excited at the prospect that he might actually pull this whole thing off. The national NAACP meeting was just three weeks away. It seemed like an eternity.

The meeting lasted for another hour. During that hour, the members agreed to meet on January 2nd in order to finalize the agenda for the national meeting. It was also agreed upon to let Attorney Johnson take whatever steps necessary to convince the President to come to the national meeting. There was a committee set up to begin to organize and prepare for the march.

Chapter 19

The members of the NAACP began to leave the hotel. Most of them felt good about what had transpired. The Executive Director had rented a room at the hotel. This was his usual practice. He would make notes on what had happened at that particular meeting and what may need to be brought up at the next meeting.

There was a knock on the door. The Executive Director got up from the desk in his room and walked over to the door. He looked through the peep hole and recognized the man standing at the door. He opened the door.

"Come in, Attorney Johnson. I did not expect you, but I'm glad that you are here."

"I'm not so sure that you will be once you realize why I'm here."

"What on earth do you mean?"

"Have a seat, Sir. I think that it would be better if you were sitting down when you hear what I have to say."

The Executive Director walked over to the chair by the window and took a seat.

"What is it, Attorney Johnson?"

"Sir, I hate to inform you that I am here to kill you."

"What? Is this some kind of joke, Attorney Johnson? It is not like you to make such absurd statements."

"I wish it were a joke, Sir, but I assure you that I have come here to kill you."

The Executive Director did not know what to think or to do. In his highly skilled political demeanor, he acted as though it was perfectly logical for Attorney Johnson to do what he said.

"So why must you kill me, Attorney Johnson?"

"I'll tell you in a moment. But first there is something else that I must make sure you are informed about. What I am talking about are the killings of the various Black leaders around the country. I know who is responsible for doing the killings."

"But how would you know that when the best law enforcement officials in this country don't have a clue as to who is responsible?"

"I know because I did all of the killings myself."

The Executive Director looked at Attorney Johnson in disbelief. This was not possible. He could not have been so wrong about an individual. There was no way that this man, the man whom he had held in such high esteem in recent months, have committed all of these killings. One would have to be madman to do such a thing.

"Why in the world would you, a successful Black man, go around murdering innocent Civil Rights leaders? Why, this very moment you are working with the organization dedicated to the betterment of Blacks."

Reginald looked at the Executive Director with a cold-blooded stare. There was no compassion in his eyes. If a stare could kill, the Executive Director would have died right then and there.

"The current crop of Civil Rights leaders are not innocent. They are guilty. Guilty of what you ask? Well I'm going to tell you. The reason that Blacks in this country are in such a poor state of affairs is because they have listened to the Black leadership of this country for the last thirty years."

The Executive Director listened to Attorney Johnson intently. He was compelled to listen just as the man in 'Rhyme of the Ancient Mariner'. Reginald continued.

"You see, the basic premise of the Civil Rights movement in the 1990's is wrong. The Civil Rights movement originated as a means to assist Black people in this country to achieve basic human rights. Those rights were already there into the Constitution to begin with, they just were not applied to Black people. Of course, that makes sense considering that when the Constitution was written, many of the framers had slaves.

"Now, what rights are we talking about? We are talking about the right to vote, own property, eat in public places, and so on. In other words, to have the same basic rights and protections from the government that Whites do.

"The mistake made was the notion that the only way to achieve these rights was through integration. That way, if we where allowed in the same places, to work side by side, and interact with our oppressors, then everything would be fine. Nothing could be further from the truth. There is no such thing as integration. You can't integrate two races. All you can do is establish a state of mutual co-existence.

"To have true integration, you must have total acceptance, total empathy, and total respect from the dominant race toward the inferior race. What you idiotic Civil Rights leaders failed to realize, is that no movement, Civil Rights or otherwise, can accomplish that. Whites are Whites. They have displayed a consistent pattern of behavior for the last 1,000 years. They have raped, pillaged, conquered, destroyed, and just generally taken the best land and amenities from every non-White person they have come into contact with. Not once have they ever faltered from this pattern.

"But no, you idiotic Civil Rights leaders think that because they let you eat at the same restaurant, hire a token Black here, and there, and occasionally donate some money to one of our Black colleges, they are going to accept you and treat you fairly. Well, it ain't so. What has happened in this country is that the more Black leaders have pushed integration, the worse the condition of Blacks has become in this country. Because of integration, we have inner city slums as Whites move further out of the cities trying to get away from Blacks. We have high unemployment rates among Blacks because Whites are not going to hire you. The only reason that Whites hired the few token blacks anyway was to comply with the mandates that came from a few White liberals in the 70's. Well, those liberals are no longer in power and they have gotten older, more conservative and thus, more White."

"Now, I'm not saying that the Civil Rights movement did not accomplish anything. In fact, Black people have been granted those basic human rights as a result of the movement. But that is all that a Civil Rights movement can do.   Once the basic rights have been obtained, then the movement is dead."

The Executive Director came out of his trance. He got angry and decided that he would not hold his tongue any longer. He spoke up.

"Attorney Johnson, you are wrong. The Civil Rights movement is needed now more than ever. The instances of racism in this country are on the rise. Whatever gains that were made have been eroded. We must re-double our efforts. Otherwise, Black people in this country will never have the decency and dignity that they deserve. Young people such as you always think that the older folks don't know what they are doing, even though you are enjoying the fruits of our labors everyday. If it were not for the Civil Rights movement, you would not be living in a million dollar house, driving a Mercedes, and working in a lavishly appointed office as a lawyer in the heart of Downtown Atlanta. Now, at a time when racism is on the rise and the movement needs you, you turn your back and say the movement is dead. I should be killing you."

The two men stared each other down for a moment. Reginald actually felt sorry for the Executive Director. Here was a man who believed in a cause strongly enough to give his life in vain for it. It was sad indeed.

Reginald responded, "When the Civil Rights movement was conceived, it was absolutely necessary. At that time, Blacks did not have the basic human rights. Blacks could not ride in the front of the bus. Hell, they could not even go into most places through the front door. No other movement could have accomplished so much for Blacks as the Civil Rights movement did back then. Most likely, the only way that those rights could have come about was through integration, public and governmental integration that is.

"But the fight today, in the 90's is not for basic human rights, rather it is the condition of the individual that is at stake. The Civil Rights movement cannot improve the individual. That is something that each and everyone of us must do for ourselves. Black leaders must now teach that we must become strong individually so that collectively we are a race that can determine our own destiny.

"Merely integrating with someone is not going to strengthen you financially, mentally, emotionally and spiritually. Those things must come from within. Just because I let you live next to me does not mean that by osmosis you are going to become just like me.

"Now, lets talk about racism for a moment. Racism has been around since the dawn of time. It will always be around as long as you have different races. What the heck is racism? Well, it is a combination of feelings of superiority, competition, and dislike of oneself projected onto other races. Sure, there are things that cut down on people acting out racial hatred. Probably the thing that does it most is getting to know each other. Integration comes into place somewhat here. But the competitive component of racism is not going to allow feelings of racism to go away because each race wants to believe that it is superior to the other. One way to prove superiority is to be economically superior. Whites are money driven. Anything or anybody that takes money from them and redistributes it elsewhere is not going to be voluntarily tolerated for long."

The Executive Director did not share Attorney Johnson's beliefs. He, like most of the older Black leadership, had spent a lifetime trying to ensure that Blacks could integrate with Whites. That was the only strategy that they knew. They felt that if you could appeal to the consciousness of Whites, make them feel guilty about what they were doing, then they would be compelled to treat Blacks fairly.

"So, what are you suggesting that Black leaders in this country do, Attorney Johnson, to help our citizens?"

"The first thing that I suggest that Blacks as a whole do in this country is to stop listening to the current Black leaders. Of course, I am making sure that happens.

"The second thing that I suggest is that Blacks stop spending so much time trying to integrate with Whites and start integrating with themselves. How in hell can Blacks expect Whites to accept them when they have not accepted themselves. Blacks must learn to get along with each other, to trust each other and start working for the common good of each other. We must utilize our own goods and services. We must depend on each other"

"It is time for Blacks to understand that Whites are not responsible for them. It is time for Blacks to understand that self worth comes from you, the individual, not someone that conquered and enslaved you. Whites have never accepted and treated any other race as equals before. Why do Blacks think that they are going to start now?"

The Executive Director, furious, spoke up, "But Whites do owe us something. It was them that brought us here in the slave ships. They took us from our homeland. They kept us from being educated. They raped our women and killed our men. They put us in the slums, which is another name for public housing.

"At first, Blacks did not know how bad off they were. That was because we were not allowed to get an education, nor allowed to see how life was meant to be lived. But thanks to those of us who had the courage, the vision, the strength of our Lord and Savior, we were able to make a difference.

"Attorney Johnson, you bet Whites owe us something. They owe us for all of the years that they enslaved us, took our dignity, kept us from being competitive and had us thinking that we were inferior. Of course, we seemed inferior because they kept us from learning to read and write and learn useful skills in order to build and to have something.

"Now, damn fools like you, Attorney Johnson, come along and have gotten complacent. It's because of idiots like you that Whites once again are treating us like we're less than human because there aren't people who are not afraid to stand up and call them down on the carpet for what they are doing. Whites have to be told what they are doing wrong. We have to tell them. The louder and the more often that we tell them, the more they will listen and take action on our behalf. Attorney Johnson, you have set the movement back twenty years because you have silenced those voices who were the most willing to speak out for injustice."

The Executive Director continued. As he did so, Reginald set down. He would give this man and those he represented the decency and respect to have his say. Reginald knew that if this conversation was taking place twenty years ago, what the Executive Director was saying would have more merit.

"Justice, Attorney Johnson, is not something that just happens. Justice is something that has to be fought and died for. It is not obtained any other way. Even Jesus himself had to die in order for mankind to receive justice. Here was a man that was superior in every way. He was more educated, he controlled the wealth of the world and could have taken whatever he so chose from his enemies. But he knew that to have long lasting peace and harmony, mankind must listen to his inner voice. That inner voice speaks of forgiveness, trust, love, and peace. Until Blacks and Whites have that in this country, there can be no equality. That is where the Civil Rights leaders come in. We are the inner voices of whites."

The Executive Director lowered his voice, "Attorney Johnson, the Civil Rights Movement has and can accomplish more than all the racial competitiveness that you want Blacks to have. What you are forgetting is that Whites out number us ten or more to one. It is only by the grace of God that they allow us to live in this country in some kind of decent state at all. Were it not for Civil Rights leaders prodding their consciousness, they might just all well kill us all off. Whites control everything in this country. You go around trying to compete with them, pissing them off, and you are going to have a backlash, the likes of which you have never seen. What are you going to do then, Attorney Johnson?"

Reginald spoke up. "That is exactly the kind of thinking that Whites want us to have. They want us to believe that we are not in control of our own destiny, that we can only have and do what they allow us to do. That is simply not true. How do we know that it is not true?

"All we have to do is look at other minorities. Take the Japanese for example. These people don't look White. Like us, there in no way for them to pass as White. You can spot them a mile away. Yet, they are not dependent on Whites. They actually think and behave as though they are superior to Whites. They out perform, out think, out purchase and out produce Whites in every way. They are out numbered by more than ten to one, yet it does not seem to matter.

"How do they do it while we wallow in poverty? I'll tell you how. They trust each other. They demand the absolute best from each other. They take advantage of the educational system in this country. They study while our students are playing cards. They attend classes while our students are in the activities lounge trying to be seen. Other races such as the Japanese, the Koreans, the Chinese, Jews, you name it, are driven by competition while we are driven by blame and excuses.

"We can't make anymore excuses. It is true that we were enslaved, but so were many other races. We are not the only ones that were oppressed. Look at the Jews, look at what is going on in Russia. The reality is that everywhere in the world, Blacks are in last place. Why is this so? It is because we don't demand the standards of ourselves as other races do. Now, we have those standards when it comes to sports. We must now have those standards when it comes to finances, services, childrearing, and morals. But we can only have this if we each take a look at our individual selves. If we, the individuals, are strong, then the race is going to be strong. Black leaders must start preaching this now."

The Executive Director got up and turned his back to Attorney Johnson. He spoke as though he were talking to himself.

"What you are talking about is elitetism. Only the best survive. If you are not the most fit, then you die. We are not animals, we are people. We have only been given the opportunity to compete in the last thirty years. We don't have the history that the Jews, the Japanese, and all these other peoples that you named. Those people have been free most of their history with the exception of ten or twelve years or so. We Blacks, on the other hand, have been enslaved for generations and only experienced some semblance of freedom since the late 60's, early 70's.

"What you want, Attorney Johnson, can't be achieved in a day, a month, or a decade. A century is more likely the time it will take for us to become competitive. Thanks to your insane actions, it may take even longer.

"No movement is perfect, but this is the only one that we have. It is the only one that has worked consistently for us. It you destroy it, what will we have? I'll tell you. We'll have nothing, nothing, and no one to speak out for us. We'll be completely at the mercy of Whites with no one to jog their consciousness."

Attorney Johnson stood up. He was going to turn his back to the Executive Director, but thought the better of it. This Director might be old, but he was no fool. He not going to willingly let his life be taken. Of that much, Reginald was certain.

"You are wrong, Mr. Director. With the current crop of Civil Rights leaders out of the way, people will look to new solutions. They will no longer be shamed or brow beaten into acquiescence by a group of leaders that have not really made a meaningful difference in a decade by leaders that spend most of their time bickering and backstabbing each other. You're familiar with the old 'crabs in a crab bucket' syndrome.

"I believe that there are many people out there that feel the same way that I do. They have kept quiet because the things that I am talking to you about are not fashionable. I intend to provide a way for them to be able to come out, to work towards the same goals that I have. There will be nobody to shame them. Rather, they will be encouraged to let young Black males know that we will not tolerate their behavior anymore. They won't be afraid to demand that Blacks get up off of their asses and accomplish something. They won't be bound by the premise that all Blacks are equal, and the reason that we all don't perform well is because of a broken home or some other asinine reason that masks individual laziness.

"All men are created equal. What you do with it after that is left entirely up to the individual. We have left it up to Whites. The reason that we have left it up to them is because there had not been anyone to tell us that we did not have to. But now there will be. That someone will be me. I will make more of a difference in five years than you buffoons would have made in a hundred. Blacks are the smartest people on earth. It is time that we proved it.

"I intend to become the new movement in this country. I am going to use the NAACP as my forum. It is a good organization in theory. I will run it the way it should be run."

The Executive Director looked at Reginald with disgust. He knew that this fool actually believed what he was saying and might possibly be able to carry out these plans. He had to be stopped. The only person that could do it was an old man who could not match him in physical strength nor persuasion. He would find a way.

"You certainly are not going to prove it by murdering people. By doing so, you have already proven that you are inferior. You can't allow people of a different viewpoint than yours to exist. You can't kill someone every time they don't share your view. When you take an objective look at your actions, they seem to be the actions of an insane man. I believe you to be that."

Reginald started to slowly ease toward the Executive Director. He knew that the old man was up to something. He would not take any chances. The Executive Director tried to grab the pitcher of water on the table near the window. If he could just hit Attorney Johnson with it. He got the pitcher, held it up and brought it down with all of the force that he could muster. The pitcher landed squarely on the head of Attorney Johnson. The pitcher broke into pieces when it came into contact with his head. Unfortunately for the Executive Director, the pitcher was made of thin glass. It did not do any real damage other than wet Attorney Johnson's expensive suit.

Reginald shook off the blow. He grabbed the Executive Director by the collar and pulled him closer.

"Before you kill me, Attorney Johnson, consider this. We were segregated in this country for hundreds of years. Segregation did not work for us then and it won't work now. What you are doing will lead to nothing more than the return of segregation. We can never be equal under segregation. The reason is because Whites control the government. If we move in the direction of segregation, then we won't have any say so in what they do as a government because they will only worry about Whites when they make a decision. With integration however, we will be intertwined not only physically but mentally with Whites. If they hurt us, they hurt themselves. It can be no other way, Attorney Johnson."

"Your time has passed old man. You may look upon me as a murderer. I see myself as a liberator. Only history, most likely the White man's history, will tell. As far as segregation goes, no other race has tried to integrate, only Blacks. As long as our society is based on the democratic process, anybody, any race can survive at the highest level as long as they earn the right. I'm sorry, old man, this is the way it has to be. The time has come for us to control our own destiny."

Reginald pulled the trusty razor from his pocket. This razor had served him so well. That service was almost at an end. He sliced the Executive Director's throat in one quick motion. The old man's eyes did not close. They just stared at Attorney Johnson as he removed his coat and threw it over his shoulder. He walked out into the hall and pulled the door. He was careful to grab the doorknob with his coat sleeve.

Reginald had to get back to his house. There was still work to be done. Work that must be done tonight. He had not thought about Agent Stone all evening. The man had to be fed and those ropes had to be loosened. What was he going to do with Stone anyway?

Reginald was melancholy on the drive back to his house. He had listened to the Executive Director intently. For the first time since he had began this plan he felt uncertainty. Not that what he proposed was not totally correct.

Rather, that the fastest, surest way to accomplish it was, in fact, to rid the nation of the current leaders. If only there had been another way.

Reginald pulled the Mercedes S 600 into the driveway. He walked around to the main entrance to his house and unlocked the front door. He walked in the foyer and headed for the stairs that lead to his basement. He descended the stairs quickly.

Seated in his chair was Agent Stone. He was still fast asleep. Reginald untied the ropes that held him to the chair. He picked him up and threw him across his shoulder. He carried Stone up to the guest bedroom and placed him on the bed. Reginald went downstairs and looked into an old trunk that contained all kinds of paraphernalia. In it he saw the pair of handcuffs that had been given to him by a police officer years ago when he did criminal work. He returned upstairs and cuffed Stone to the iron bedpost.

"Still sleeping like a baby, huh, Stone? Go ahead, it is better that you don't awake. When you do, I will most likely have to kill you. I'm going to deal with you, though, either way, in the morning."

Reginald went into the kitchen and looked under the sink. He pulled out four large, heavy duty garbage bags. He went into the basement. He pulled one bag over the head of the dead body of Agent Kelly. He took another bag and placed Agent Kelly's feet in it. Where the two bags overlapped, he tied them together. He went over to where one of the chairs in the room was and picked up the video camera. He reached inside the camera and took out the video cassette. He smashed it with his foot. After putting the fragments into a trash can in the corner, he picked up the corpse and carried it up to the garage placing it by the Taurus. He went through the same ritual with the Agent in the car. Both bodies were placed in the trunk of the Taurus.

Reginald drove to a large construction sight about five miles from his home. He placed the bags containing the bodies of the agents in one of several huge dumpsters containing debris. This completed his task for today.

Agent Stone's head lifted off of the pillow. He felt completely rested as though he had caught up on a year's worth of sleep. His joints no longer ached. In fact, the only pain that he was experiencing was in his stomach. He was both hungry and thirsty.

He yelled out, "Is anyone here? I'm hungry and I need something to drink.   Attorney Johnson, do you hear me?   I know that you are here somewhere."

He looked at the wall clock. It read 5:30 a.m. Agent Stone had yelled to an empty house. Reginald had gotten up at 4:45 a.m. He had put on a jogging suit and went downstairs into the garage. He drove the Taurus to the MARTA Station where you could leave your car and take a bus Downtown. The Station was located nine miles from his home. He left the Taurus in the parking lot and began the long jog back to his house.

Reginald arrived back at his house by 6:30 a.m. He went into the kitchen. He prepared a large glass of orange juice, two slices of toast, and some fruit. He took it into the guest bedroom where Stone was.

"Well, good morning, Agent Stone. You look fit as a fiddle this morning. How was your nap?"

Agent Stone looked at Attorney Johnson with a cool and collected stare. He knew that if Attorney Johnson had wanted to kill him, he would be dead already. He had to play along with this man and somehow escape. First, he would establish some kind of rapport in order to find out what he was up to. Especially why he was murdering these Black leaders.   "I'm fine, Attorney Johnson, just a tad bit thirsty and hungry. I hope that you brought that food for me."

"Please call me Reginald. And, yes, this is for you."

"How long have I been out?"

"About two days and nights."

"What is going on here, Reginald? Why are you doing all of this?"

"All in good time, Stone, all in good time. But now I have to get dressed. I have to go into town. You can use your strength to pull the bed over to those double doors. Open them and pull the bed inside the bathroom. I cuffed you to the edge of the bed. That way you can sit on the commode, use it and then pull the bed back into the center of the room and so forth. I'll be back this evening. We can talk then. Meanwhile, I suggest that you relax and watch some TV."

"Reginald, I need to know what happened to the two agents that were with me. Did you kill them? Tell me."

"Yes, I killed them. Look we'll talk when I get back this afternoon. I will answer all of your questions then, I promise. Try and relax."

Reginald left the room and went to his own room to get dressed.

Chapter 20

Attorney Johnson parked his Mercedes at the MARTA Station. A bus was already there. He watched people getting on. Through the windows of the bus you could see people standing in the aisles. This was not unusual for the bus to be this crowded since this was the time that most people were heading off to work.

Reginald waited until the bus departed the station. Then he took his briefcase out of the trunk of his Mercedes and locked his car. He walked over to the Taurus, got in and drove off.

As he was heading down Georgia 400, Reginald began to think about what he had left to do. He had to contact the White House and convince the President that he should come to Atlanta to attend the NAACP meeting rather than hold a Black Summit. He would persuade the President that this would do more toward healing the rift between Blacks and Whites in the country. It would show just how much he supported the Black causes in this country. Reginald would wait to contact the President until news of the death of the Executive Director made the headlines.

The next thing that he had to do was to call the remaining power brokers in the NAACP and set up a meeting to discuss what they were going to do at the National Meeting of the NAACP now that the Executive Director was dead. It was time for him to make his move as interim leader of the organization. It should not be too difficult since most of the people in the organization were afraid that they might get killed if they were too visible.

The final thing that he had to do was to write the opening speech for the national meeting that was usually given by the Executive Director. This speech usually set the tone for the organization for the rest of the year. He would write a speech that would change the direction of the organization. He would not share the contents of the speech with anyone in the organization. This too would be easy since most of the members would be too concerned with organizing that stupid march to realize what he was going to say once he took the podium at the meeting.

Reginald began to feel warm inside. It was not often that you got to steer the course of history. Not many men got to share in this glory. Sure, no one would know that he was responsible, but he was not doing this for the glory, he was doing it to save his race.

Reginald exited off of I-85 onto the airport exit. He found the Alamo Rental Car return entrance and dropped off the Ford Taurus at the rapid return. He took the shuttle bus to the airport and caught the MARTA train back to Five Points. He walked leisurely up Peachtree Street to his office building.

Agent Stone dumped the mattress and box spring to the floor. He dragged the bed frame to the bathroom where he relieved himself. His energy level was beginning to return. He wondered how he was going to free himself from this bed frame. It was solid brass. Not the cheap stuff that you could bend, but the solid, expensive, last forever type. He dragged the frame over to the TV and turned it on.

The scene was all to familiar. A newscaster was showing the picture of another dead prominent Civil Rights leader. Again, there were no clues as to who did it or why. But this time Agent Stone was sure that he knew who did it. It was Attorney Johnson. Agent Stone resolved that when Attorney Johnson returned home tonight, he would pressure him into revealing why he was committing the murders and how many more people he intended to kill.

Attorney Johnson walked into his office. As usual, his secretary was dressed in one of her get-ups. She had on a skirt up to her thighs and was wearing sheer stockings.

"Good morning, Attorney Johnson", she said in her seductive voice. "How are you doing this morning?"

"I'm fine thank you. Listen, I want you to get Chavis Martin at the NAACP on the telephone right away."

"Very well, Sir."

Reginald walked into his office. On his desk was the morning paper. While his secretary's attire left something to be desired, her efficiency didn't. Every morning that he was scheduled to be there, she always had the morning paper, a cup of coffee and his itinerary on his desk when he got there.

Reginald looked at the headlines which read, "HOW MANY MORE BLACKS MUST DIE?"

His secretary interrupted his train of thought on the intercom, "Sir, I have Mr. Martin on the phone."

"Thanks, I got it."

"Mr. Martin, how are you?"

"If you want to know the truth, Attorney Johnson, I'm scared to death. I heard about the death of Mr. Weeks this morning. He was apparently killed right after the meeting yesterday. That is just too close for comfort. I wonder who will be next? We are being picked off like flies. From what I can see, there will be no end to the killings until we are all dead."

Attorney Johnson replied, "Look Chavis, you and I both know that Harrison would want us to continue, no matter what. I'm scared too, scared to death. Right now, I'm the most visible with all this business with the President and all. I fear for my life all the time. I'm afraid to go anywhere at night or during the day if a place is deserted. I'm constantly looking over my shoulder. So I know what you mean."

"But, Attorney Johnson, they are going to kill us all. There can be no doubt now that they are after members of the NAACP or anyone that is prominent and remotely associated with the organization. Whoever is responsible for these deaths has killed at will. Either the people in power don't know who is doing the killings or don't care. We have to protect ourselves. I say that we have to lay low for awhile. Even disband if we have to. Otherwise we are all going to be killed. If that happens, there won't be anyone to further the cause anyway."

Reginald had not foreseen the possibility that members of the NAACP might become so frightened that they actually would be too scared to have the national meeting in January. If that happened, all of his plans would have been for nothing. Without the NAACP, he would have no forum in which to operate. He felt his heart pounding in his chest.

"Listen to me, Chavis, we have a job to do. If we don't display the courage that our predecessors did, all of their efforts will have been for nothing. I don't want to die either. But I'm willing to risk my life to make sure that others of my race can live full, productive, free lives in this country. Now, you are heading the committee that is organizing the march on January 17th. I suggest that you focus on that. How is it going anyway?"

"Actually, I had scheduled a meeting for day after tomorrow to set it in motion. Now I'm not sure if people are going to come to it."

"You just get on the phone and make sure that they do. Tell them that I said the President himself is going to be there to participate in the march. Believe me, when they hear that, they will participate. This can be the biggest march on Washington in history."

"I'm glad that I talked to you, Attorney Johnson. I'm ready to do what needs to be done."

"By the way, Chavis, I'm contacting most of the leadership of the NAACP myself today. I asking for an emergency meeting day after tomorrow to discuss the possibility of me acting as interim Director until the meeting in January. What do you think about that possibility?"

"I think that it is a great idea, Attorney Johnson. Who else is more capable to provide leadership for the organization during this time of crisis?"

"Perhaps we could have the two meetings together. We would get more people in attendance that way. Alright, Chavis, let's get on to our respective tasks. We have a lot of work to do. Goodbye."

Reginald immediately dialed the White House. He had been given a special number to dial and then a code to enter which would allow him to get to the President in a hurry.

"Hello, this is Attorney Johnson calling to speak to the President about the Civil Rights Murders and the upcoming Black Summit."

The voice on the other end of the line acknowledged him and told him to wait for a moment.

The President was in a meeting with his advisors. Among the topics of discussion was the Civil Rights Murders. The President had been informed about the death of the Executive Director of the NAACP and the increase in violence that followed. The President had taken out his frustration on his advisors who in turn began calling all of the major law enforcement agencies in the country. The President had received word that the FBI agents who were heading the investigation had disappeared a couple of days ago. He was not happy with the news. The President had demanded a meeting with the Director of the FBI who in response to that demand was in attendance at this meeting.

The President addressed his remarks to the current Director of the FBI, C. J. Dixon.

"Look, C.J., what in the hell is going on with these murders? I mean, it looks like whoever is doing them is killing at will. You can't possibly expect me to believe that the finest law enforcement agency in the world does not have any suspects nor viable leads into these killings. The country is falling apart. Something has got to be done."

Director Dixon was the youngest Director in the history of the FBI. But he had become know as the most shrewd Director yet. He had a reputation for not being pushed around and he was not about to allow that to happen now.

"Mr. President, you are correct in your assessment. As of right now, the best Agent that we have in the Bureau who has solved most of our major cases of this type is missing. So are several other agents who were working with him. I will tell you, Mr. President, this case baffles me and my staff. We have shaken down most of the White hate groups in this country. Nothing has fallen out. Many of them seemed to be as baffled as we are. It is inconceivable that any organization could pull off this many murders without some kind of leak to somebody. Yet, there are no viable suspects at this time. In other words, we don't have a clue, Mr. President. Have I answered your questions?"

The President looked startled. He had expected Director Dixon to beat around the bush. At least he could have squirmed in his chair a little. Instead, he had boldly sit up in his chair and told the truth. The truth was not something the President was used to hearing.

"Well, I want something done, Director Dixon. I want something done now. People are dying all over this country because we can't find out who is murdering our Black leaders. I am asking you to place every available man you have on this. Shake down whoever you have to. I don't care how you do it, but you put a stop to these killings."

"We will do all that we can, Mr. President. I give you my word. May I be excused now, sir?"

"Of course."

Director Dixon left the room. Outside waiting for him was Supervisor Thompson, who jumped to his feet the moment he saw the Director.

"How did it go, sir? Did he tear into you?"

"No, Supervisor Thompson, he did not tear into me, but I'm going to tear into you and your whole staff if you don't come up with some viable suspects this week. Damn it, we have had more Black leaders killed in the last few months than we had murdered during the whole Civil Rights era thus far. If you don't come up with some suspects in the next two weeks, you are fired. Do you hear me?"

"Yes, sir, loud and clear!"

Inside the room where the President was, someone motioned for him to pick up the green telephone on the table next to where he was seated.

"Hello, this is the President. How can I serve you?"

"Mr. President, this is Attorney Johnson."

"How are you, Attorney Johnson. Did you call to tell me something about the Black Summit that we are having on January 4th?"

"Actually, Mr. President, I'm calling to request that you call off the Summit."

"Call off the Summit! Why would I do that? I thought that's what the Black Leadership in this country wanted."

"They do want to meet with you, Mr. President, but in Atlanta at the National NAACP meeting. As you know, the Executive Director was murdered on yesterday. Everyone is running a little bit scared. The membership has decided to conduct a march from Atlanta to Washington on January 17th to protest the killings. We felt that if you came to the meeting and then participated in the march the next day, it would go a much longer way in showing your support for Blacks than a Summit would."

The President asked Attorney Johnson if he would hold on for a moment. Then he turned to his advisors and informed them of what Attorney Johnson had suggested. They all nodded in agreement.

"Attorney Johnson, you can count on me being there. To assure you of this, when I give my next weekly radio address, I will state that very fact."

"Thank you very much, Mr. President. I will be contacting you again with some more specifics."

The President hung up the phone. He burst into laughter. He roared back into his chair.

"Gentlemen, do you realize that I have been given a way out of this mess. Instead of having to deal with the stigma of being the President and not being able to do anything about these murders of Black leaders, I will now go down in history as the President who marched side by side with Black people in their darkest hour. It's perfect, don't you think?"

Attorney Johnson breathed a sigh of relief. He had what he wanted and he knew it. He was going to be able to deliver the opening speech at the National NAACP meeting in January. Everyone would be there including the President of the United States. People would be there from all over the country and the world to participate in the historic march to Washington. But this time the march would signify a whole new meaning. Blacks would not be marching in the hope that they could get some of the basic human rights that every human being deserves, rather the march would signify Blacks demanding their place in history, in this country, in the world.

Reginald turned on his personal computer. He had to write his speech. This speech had to be the speech to end all speeches. It had to be right up there with Martin Luther King's, I Have A Dream. The speech had to touch on all areas of the Black experience. It had to point out the problems, yet offer solutions at the same time. It had to be the kind of speech that stuck with you. The kind that people quoted at dinner parties, on university campuses, in meetings, in churches and in bars.

Reginald informed his secretary that he did not want to be disturbed for the next three hours unless it was an emergency. He could, of course, be interrupted if the President or someone from Washington called. He would also take calls from members of the NAACP. He told her to take his member contact list of the NAACP and call them to let them know that there was an emergency meeting day after tomorrow back at the Atlanta Hilton. He doubted if they would feel comfortable at the Hyatt in light of what happened to the Executive Director there.

For the next four hours Attorney Johnson drafted a rough outline of his speech. It just seemed to flow out of him as though it had been inside of him all of his life. This speech was going to do what no other speech had done in modern times. It was going to jar the Black consciousness. It was going to change the way Blacks looked at themselves and Whites. The more of the speech that Reginald wrote, the more he felt that his plan had been worthwhile. All the months of preparation, all the killing and all the traveling now seemed justified. It would all boil down to a twenty-minute speech.

Reginald left his office and headed for the MARTA Station. He took the train to Lenox Mall and then took the MARTA Bus back to his Alpharetta Station. On the way to his house from the station, he picked up some wine and cheese to celebrate his apparent victory.

He walked into the upstairs guest bedroom. Agent Stone was seated on the bed which was missing the mattress. You could tell that he had dragged the frame all over the room from the scratch marks on the floor. Stone perked up when he saw Attorney Johnson.

"Did you have a long day, Attorney Johnson? Kill anyone today? Or were you able to get through the day without bumping anyone off? How does it feel to be a serial killer?

Reginald walked right up to Stone and looked him in the eye.

"Look, Stone, I'm in no mood for useless chatter. I have to figure out what to do with you."

Reginald opened the wine and cheese. He walked to the kitchen and got two wine glasses, two china saucers and a knife. When he returned to the room, he saw Agent Stone had dragged the bed over to where the wine bottle was. He was about to pick it up.

"Going to drink it all by yourself, Stone? Don't even think about trying to use that bottle on me. It would mean that I would have to kill you sooner rather than later."

Agent Stone dragged the bed back to a neutral corner and sat down.

"Alright, Attorney Johnson, what is this all about? Why kill all of those people?"

Reginald prepared two glasses of wine and cut some cheese for the both of them. He handed the glass and cheese to Stone. Reginald grabbed a chair and sat down.

"Stone, what I am about to tell you is something that you could never understand. You are the only living person that will know the truth for now. How long you are going to live, I don't know. I have not decided your fate yet."

"Why tell me if you are going to kill me anyway?"

"You are the one that asked the question, Stone. Do you want to know what is going on or not?"

"Of course I do."

"I am killing the Civil Rights leaders in order to take over the NAACP and use it as my forum to change the condition of Black people in this country."

Agent Stone began to laugh. Soon he became hysterical. He could not stop laughing.

"You sound like a madman. In fact, if that is why you killed all those people, you are a madman!"

Attorney Johnson got up out of his chair and walked over to Agent Stone. He slapped him hard across the face. Stone stopped laughing.

"I am far from being a madman, Stone. I am going to address the nation on national television less than two weeks from now. I am giving the opening speech at the NAACP meeting. On the following day, I, along with the President of the United States will kick off a march from Atlanta to Washington D.C. If you look at television in the next few days, you will see that the march is already in the planning stages. You see, I am going to change history, Stone."

Agent Stone was silent. If what Attorney Johnson had said was true, all the killings made sense. No one on earth could have foreseen the plot in all of this. No Black person would be suspected of such sinister actions. But Stone knew he was a lawman. He had a job to do. That job was to bring Attorney Johnson to justice.

"There is no way to convince you to join me in all of this, Agent Stone, because you have been conditioned by the White man to believe in what you are doing. You believe all that nonsense about serving God and country. But the God you serve and the country both belong to the White man. Thanks to me, Stone, the Black man in this country will no longer live as a second class citizen. He will no longer live in the shadow of a race that never will accept him."

"Nothing you can say, Attorney Johnson, can justify the cold-blooded murders that you have committed. If I live and breathe, I will bring you to justice. You will have to answer for these crimes. I am going to put you behind bars where you belong."

"To join all the other Black men that are behind bars? I think not. Stone, I don't want to kill you. I think that you are brilliant in the fact that you narrowed the suspects down to me. I respect intelligence. But I don't respect misplaced intelligence. I don't respect Black intelligence used to better White kind. I believe that you are a man of your word. I believe that if you give your word, you will stick by it. I am the same kind of man. Once I give my word, I stand by it. Now I will give you my word that I will not be responsible for anymore killings of Civil Rights leaders if you don't try to bring me to justice until after the march to Washington. Do we have a deal?"

Agent Stone though about what had been said. He knew that if he did not agree, Attorney Johnson would most likely kill him. Attorney Johnson was not a man to make mistakes and he certainly was not going to chance anything coming between him and his destiny now. Attorney Johnson was also right when he said Stone was a man of his word. He prided himself for such.

"Attorney Johnson, I give you my word that I will not attempt to do anything to stop you before the march on Washington provided that you don't kill anymore Civil Rights leaders. But when the march to Washington is over, you and I are going to settle this thing, once and for all, man to man."

"I believe you, Agent Stone. But there is one more thing. I am going to request that you stay my house guest until the march. You may accompany me wherever I go in order to make sure that I am complying with our agreement. This will also allow you to be a witness for whomever as to the events that transpired up to the march. House guest also means that you don't have any contact with the FBI or other law enforcement agencies."

"Alright, Attorney Johnson, I'll agree to all of your terms. But just remember, I'm going to bring you down."

Reginald went into his bedroom and opened his wall safe. He took out the key to the handcuffs. He came back in the room and uncuffed Agent Stone. The two men stared at each other like two lions out in the wild. Each one not sure if the other was stronger.

"Stone, make yourself at home. I have some work to do. There are some towels in the hall closet, and from the look of you, you can wear my clothes. Feel free to do so."

Reginald went into his study and began working on his speech. He thought of all the great orators of all time. Men of greatness such as Martin Luther King, Jr., Ghandi, Hitler, Churchill, John F. Kennedy, Jesus Christ himself, all flashed through his mind. All of these men had changed history with the power of words, with the power of speeches. Reginald envisioned his own speech as being remembered as one of the great ones. He worked until 2:00 o'clock in the morning. The speech as taking shape.

*   *   *   *   *   *

"Give me a spot, please?"

"Of course, Agent Stone. Not bad for an out-of-shape FBI agent. Not many men can bench press 315 pounds for six repetitions."

"Let's see you do it, Attorney Johnson."

Reginald walked over and placed another forty-five pound plate on each side of the bar. The total amount of weight now was 405 pounds. Reginald assumed the bench press position on the bench. He lifted the weight into the air and pressed it for seven repetitions. Agent Stone could not believe what he saw. He wondered how could a paper-pushing lawyer be in such fantastic shape?

The two men got dressed and ate breakfast. After the meal, Agent Stone asked Reginald if he could borrow a tape recorder to record the events that were transpiring. Reginald agreed.

Reginald asked Agent Stone if he would like to do some sight-seeing today. Stone agreed that he would. Reginald handed him the keys to the Range Rover and told Stone to look around Atlanta until 5:00 o'clock. Then Stone was to come and join him at the Atlanta Hilton at the NAACP meeting.

Reginald smiled as Agent Stone left. He knew that Stone could be trusted because like most Blacks, he was honorable. He was downright trustworthy. Blacks would never conquer the business world because they just did not possess the ability to do whatever it takes to win. Instead, Blacks will play by the rules while everyone else lies, cheats, and steals to win and make money. Blacks tend to believe anyone who smiled and extended their hand.

Agent Stone stopped at the nearest telephone. He called into the FBI office in Washington and asked to speak to Supervisor Thompson.

"Hello, this is Supervisor Thompson. How can I help you?"

"Sir, this is Agent Stone."

"Agent Stone, where in the hell are you, and why haven't you and Kelly and a couple of the other agents working on these Black murders called in for days?"

"Sir, I believe that Agent Kelly and the other agents are dead. I have a good idea who did it, but I'm not sure. I am currently in Atlanta, Georgia. I believe that if I'm right, I can bring the murderer to justice within fourteen or fifteen days."

"Agent Stone, I have the Director here in my office. He wants to speak with you."

"Stone, this is C.J. I want to know exactly what you have right now."

Agent Stone thought about the promise that he had made with Attorney Johnson. He intended to keep his promise. Not because he was a man of his word, but he wanted to bring this man to justice himself. If Director Dixon got involved, it was quite possible that he would not be involved in the arrest. Stone decided not to disclose who it was.

"Sir, I need a couple of days to make sure. I know how important this case is. The very survival of the country may depend on it. But please give me the time that I need. A few more days will not make a difference."

The Director was not a man to lose his cool or be rattled easily.

"Agent Stone, I'm giving you a direct order to disclose all you know about this case right now. If you don't , I'm placing you as of now on administrative leave pending your dismissal from the FBI on the grounds of disobeying direct orders."

"Sir, I must have more time. Don't do this to me. You must trust my judgment."

The Director spoke in even tones, "Agent Stone, I am officially notifying you that I am placing you on administrative leave as of right now. As of this moment, you have no authority to act in any capacity on behalf of the FBI. Please do us all a favor and report back to headquarters right now."

"Sir, with all due respect, I can't. I am going to solve this case, then you can do with me whatever you will. I'll call you back in about fourteen days. Good-bye."

Director Dixon hung up the phone. He turned to Supervisor Thompson and gave him some orders.

"Thompson, I want an 'all points bulletin' put out on Julian Stone. I want him picked up and brought back here ASAP. Use whatever means necessary to accomplish this. Do I make myself clear?"

"Yes, sir, very clear."

Agent Stone headed back to the housing project where he and the other two agents had encountered Attorney Johnson. He wanted to see if he could find out anything about their whereabouts. He owed it to their families to find out what had happened.

Chapter 21

Reginald sat at the head of the large conference table along side one of the officers of the NAACP. As Reginald looked across the room, he was not surprised to see who actually made up the organization. He was the darkest person in the room. Everyone else was light, very light complected. This was typical of Black organizations. Even in the 90's, light skin was valued more than dark skin in the Black race. It was bad enough that Whites were more likely to hire a light skinned Black, but it was worse that Blacks themselves valued the light skin more. Reginald thought about just how little had changed in terms of how Blacks viewed themselves since slavery time.

Reginald leaned over to the man seated next to him and asked if he could open up the meeting. The man gave a nod. This was fine because Reginald knew that now was the time to exert himself. He intended to take as much power as the members would let him get away with. Reginald stood up. He was pleased with how many members had turned out. Maybe they felt safety in numbers.

"Good evening, fellow members. I'm so glad that so many of you turned out this evening. As you know, another tragedy, perhaps the greatest to date, has befallen this organization. Two days ago, the Executive Director was found murdered in his hotel suite. But I stand here today to tell you that his death shall not be in vain. This organization has endured turmoil and death before and it shall continue to shine as a beacon for those who are oppressed and downtroddened. Let me make my remarks very brief.

"I am going to act as interim Executive Director of this organization until the national meeting, which is scheduled to be held approximately two weeks from today. I believe that this is what Mr. Weeks would have wanted. If there are any objections, please voice them now."

Reginald paused. He looked each member in the eye. No one voiced any descent. They were looking for someone to take the lead. They were afraid. Reginald could not have felt better. He had what he wanted, Executive Director of the NAACP.

Reginald continued, "On yesterday, I had a conversation with the President of the United States. He agreed to attend our national meeting and then participate in our march on Washington."

The members applauded. Reginald had instant credibility. No one would challenge his leadership now.

"What we need to do now is to hammer out the specifics of the march. So, I will turn over the meeting at this time to Chavis Martin. He will give you an outline of the things that need to be accomplished to make this one of the greatest marches in history."

Reginald sat down. Seated over in the corner of the room was Agent Stone. He was impressed at how good Attorney Johnson was at manipulating people, himself included. Stone was looking forward to see what Attorney Johnson had to say at the national meeting. If history was indeed to be made, Stone wanted to be a part of it.

Chavis Martin spent the next hour outlining all the things that had to be done regarding the march on Washington. He assigned people the various tasks of contacting the media, inviting celebrities, getting permit approvals along the march path and so forth. The march committee was to meet each Monday, Wednesday, and Friday until the national meeting to keep on top of things. Mr. Martin was to give Reginald daily reports.

When the meeting adjourned, Reginald told Stone to ride back with him. They would pick up the Range Rover tomorrow. When they left the hotel, Reginald drove Stone through Atlanta's major housing projects.

"Stone, I want you to look at these places. Here it is in the 90's and look how Black's live. Look at all the young kids you see running in the streets in these places. These kids are already lost. If the tide is not turned back, our race is going to die. The percentages of Blacks that live in these housing projects and get involved with drugs and so forth, far outweigh the mediocre one or two percent of Blacks that are successful."

"Attorney Johnson, what you are doing is not right. We all know that there is a problem, but killing each other is not the answer. There is two much Black on Black crime now and you have just added to it."

"No, Stone, the few people that I killed were necessary so that millions could be saved. If I thought that my death would save millions, I would gladly give my life."

"Attorney Johnson, only God can change what is happening to Blacks in this country or anywhere else. You are not God, yet you are trying to act like him. I gave you my word that I was going to let you play out this little scenario provided that you didn't kill anyone else. I will stick to my promise. Once the march begins, I intend to take you into custody. Do you understand that?"

"Yes, Stone, it's a deal."

During the next week, the arrangement between Attorney Johnson and Agent Stone worked pretty well. They got up in the mornings and exercised. They ate breakfast together and then headed off to Attorney Johnson's office. Sometimes Stone stayed with Attorney Johnson all day. Other times he went sightseeing around the city. He tried not to spend too much time out in the open because he knew that the Director probably had people looking for him. He did not want to get picked up now. He wanted to see this thing to the end.

*   *   *   *   *   *

Shirley Whitaker hurried to the airport shuttle. She did not want to miss her plane. She wanted to surprise Reginald. She would arrive in Atlanta by 3:45 a.m., rent a car and get to his place by 5:00 o'clock a.m. This would be just about the time that Reginald woke up to begin his exercise routine.

On the plane Shirley kept reliving the times she had with Attorney Johnson. She had had such a good time. Sure, she liked being independent, but it was more fun to have male companionship. She craved to be around him.

Reginald opened his eyes and looked at the clock. It was 3:30 a.m. He got out of bed and put on his slippers. He walked to the kitchen and got a glass of orange juice. He went back to his bedroom and turned on the laptop computer that set on his desk. He retrieved his speech and began working on it. He was almost finished with it. All he had left was a couple of revisions and it would be perfect.

About five minutes to 5:00 o'clock a.m., Reginald heard a car drive into his driveway. He looked out of his bedroom window. Getting out of the car was none other than Shirley Whitaker. Her timing could not have been worse. Reginald wondered how he was going to explain the presence of Agent Stone. He would figure it out somehow. He put on his bathrobe and went to the front door.

He opened the door just as Shirley was about to climb up the steps.

"Good morning, Ms. Whitaker, I guess you were trying to surprise me. You succeeded."

"How are you, you hunk?"

Shirley dropped her bags and gave Reginald a big hug.

"Let's go back to bed. I've missed you. We have some catching up to do."

"Yes we do, but before we go back inside, I have something that I have to tell you. I have a house guest. His name is Agent Stone. He works with the FBI and is here to protect me. The FBI felt that it was necessary because of my close working relationship with the President of the United States regarding the Black Summit meeting and all."

"Wow, aren't you afraid?"

"Well, you do what you have to do in life. Some times things carry risks. Either you take the risk and do what needs to be done, or you cower under and wimp out."

Reginald and Shirley entered the house and walked up stairs. Reginald knocked on Agent Stone's door.

"What is it, Attorney Johnson," Agent Stone said from behind the door.

"I have a house guest that I want you to meet."

Agent Stone opened the door. He had on one of Reginald's bathrobes.

Reginald said, "Agent Stone, I would like you to meet Shirley Whitaker. She is the woman I am currently seeing. I told her that you worked for the FBI and were here to protect me because of my working with the President and being in the spotlight."

Stone understood what Attorney Johnson was doing. He acted as though what was being said was the truth.

"I am pleased to make your acquaintance, Ms. Whitaker. What Attorney Johnson told you is absolutely correct. I am here to protect him."

Reginald cut him off, "Well, Stone, we will see you later."

He and Shirley went to his room and jumped in bed. They made love for about half an hour and Reginald went downstairs to exercise with Stone.

"I appreciate your playing along with me, Stone. I don't want her to know what is going on here. Promise me that you won't do anything that could help her discover the truth."

"I give you my word that she won't find out anything from me. Now, what is on the agenda for today?"

"Well, I'm going Downtown to my office to meet with Chavis Martin to discuss how the plans for the march are going. Then I'm going to contact the President or his staff to give him an update and ask what extra preparations we should make for him. For the remainder of the day, I am going to take Ms. Whitaker out to a nice restaurant and try to convince her to go back to New York."

Shirley took a shower. She was hungry after her workout with Reginald and decided to go to the kitchen to get something to eat. She almost forgot that Agent Stone was there. She decided that she better put something on. Reginald had put most of her belongings in one of the extra bedrooms upstairs. In one of her bags was a nice housecoat. She would go get it. On the way to the bedroom she saw the door to the hall bathroom open. Sitting on the sink counter was a small tape recorder. She wondered why it was there. After a few moments of wrestling with her conscience, she decided to listen to a minute or two of it. She turned it on. The voice of Agent Stone began speaking.

"I know for a fact that Attorney Johnson is responsible for the murders of the Civil Rights leaders. He has told me so. He is a madman who thinks that he can change to course of history by killing off the current Black leadership and himself become the voice for Black people. This man is a cold-blooded murderer who is responsible for the deaths of at least ten innocent people. He should get the death penalty when brought to trial"

Shirley heard footsteps. She pulled the door to the bathroom and stepped into the shower and hid behind the shower curtain. She was trembling. Her heart beat about 200 times a minute. If Reginald found out that she had discovered the tape and listened to it, he might kill her. How could she love a murderer?

Agent Stone pushed the bathroom door open. Shirley's heart stopped. She could not see who it was through the shower curtain. Agent Stone pulled off his workout clothes. He was naked. He stepped over to the bathtub and turned on the water. As he did so, Shirley peeked from behind the curtain only to see his naked buns bending over to adjust the water.

"Damn it, I forgot to get some clean towels."

Agent Stone put the workout shorts back on and walked out of the bathroom. Shirley quickly stepped out of the shower and went into the hall. Agent Stone did not see her sneaking up the hall behind him. When he walked into his room to get the towels that he had laid out earlier, she scurried past his door. She went downstairs. Reginald was in the kitchen preparing breakfast.

Shirley did not know what to do. She could not let on that she knew that Reginald was a murderer. One thing was for certain, she would not let him touch her again.

"Hi, baby, are you fixing me breakfast?"

"You know that I am. You need your strength, if you know what I mean."

"I know what you mean. I can't sleep, so I'm going upstairs and start getting dressed. First I have to go to the spare bedroom and get a skirt I want to wear."

Shirley walked over to where Reginald was and kissed him on the cheek. She almost fell as she felt her knees buckling from sheer fright. She left the kitchen and went upstairs. She hurried down the hall and went into the bathroom where Agent Stone was.

"What the hell are you doing in here," yelled Stone.

"Lower your voice or he might hear you."

"What do you want," Stone said in a lower voice.

"I listened to your tape recorder. I know what is going on here. You're trying to say that Reginald is a murderer. Say it is not true."

"I'm afraid that it is true. You had better get out of here. If he were to find out that you knew his secret, I believe that he would not hesitate to kill you."

"But you know and you're still alive."

"That is because I had information about what the FBI knew of the murders. I also think he had to tell someone. It is a trademark of murderers. If they keep it entirely to themselves, I think that they would explode. Now get out of here."

Reginald turned off the intercom. He had hired a contractor months after he bought the house to install secret microphones in all of the guest bedrooms. He had had few occasions to use the system. Shirley had acted weird in the kitchen. Not overtly so, but to a man like Attorney Johnson, he could tell the difference. He knew she was scared of something and wanted to be upstairs by herself for a moment. He now knew why. She had to be eliminated. It pained his heart. He hadn't felt this strongly about a woman in years. But this had to be done. Any man worth his salt would never let pussy stand in the way of his destiny. Pussy could be replaced, your destiny could not.

"Breakfast is ready, you two," Reginald yelled up the stairs. "Come and get it while it is hot."

Shirley listened to him from the hall as she got to the top of the staircase. Her knees were shaking so badly you could hear them. She was in terror. It sent chills down her spine knowing that the man she had given herself completely to was a cold-blooded murderer. She had to pull herself together, otherwise, Reginald would suspect her. He might kill her sure enough if he found out that she knew his secrets.

"I'm coming, sweetheart. Let me wash my hands."

Shirley went into the master bedroom and washed her hands. She splashed some water on her face. Her nerves steadied a little. At last she felt that she could go into the kitchen and masquerade as though nothing was up.

Breakfast was uneventful. The three of them finished their meals and got dressed. Reginald took Agent Stone back to the Hilton to get the Range Rover. He and Shirley went to his office. Agent Stone was to join them in about an hour. He wanted to do some more sightseeing. Shirley had suggested that she might accompany him while Reginald did some work, but Reginald said that he wanted her with him. He knew that he had better keep her by his side lest she run off to the police or something.

Reginald's phone rang almost non stop. Chavis Martin gave him updates on the march. Newspeople were calling asking about the march and the President's involvement and to comment on the news that the Ku Klux Klan intended a rally of their own. The more aggressive newspeople came directly to his office. The place was becoming a zoo.

Shirley sat in a chair in Reginald's office. She was taking all of the excitement in. If she had not played the tape recorder in Stone's bathroom, she would be enjoying herself right now. The raw appeal that Reginald exuded was hypnotic. She had to remind herself that he was a killer. She could not give into her passions again. She had to do something.

The idea suddenly popped into her head. She would have a wild fucking session with Reginald tonight. Once he fell asleep, she would run away. Agent Stone was there as a back-up in case something went wrong. The only thing was that she was not sure if she could stand for him to touch her. Somehow she would force herself to go through with it.

*   *   *   *   *   *

People from all over the country began arriving in Atlanta. Some of them were there for the National NAACP meeting. Others were there to participate in the march the day following the meeting. Still others were there for the thrill of it. They hoped to get a view of the President of the United States. They just wanted to be a part of it. It was also something to do. The killings seemed to have stopped at least for the moment. For Blacks, something positive was happening for the first time in six months. There was hope after all.

Reginald and Shirley had lunch at their favorite Chinese restaurant in Alpharetta. They drank five glasses of wine each. By the time they returned to his house, they were pleasantly drunk. They headed straight for the master bedroom. They tore off each other's clothes like they were animals.

Shirley tried to remain in control of herself. She tried to remind herself that she was lying in bed with a murderer. She was just too horny to care. There was always tomorrow to deal with this situation. Right now all she wanted to do is make love to this man. To make love as though it was the last time in her life.

Reginald pulled Shirley closer to him and penetrated her. It was pure ecstasy. He made love to her as though it was the last time in his life that he would have the opportunity to do so. Reginald was stroking her rhythmically. Shirley was enjoying it, as was evidenced by waves and waves of orgasms. Reginald slid his arm over to his pants which had been thrown onto the night stand. He pulled his pants onto the bed. He reached into the pocket and pulled out his razor. He began to trust deeper and deeper into her love canal.

"Harder, oh please, give it to me harder! I'm coming!"

She never felt the razor as it cut her throat. She thought the initial gasps for air were because of the mind wrenching orgasms. But she could not catch her breath. She tried to reach for her throat but Reginald held her hands. He kissed her as the last remnants of life left her body.

Reginald began to cry. He squeezed her lifeless body tighter and tighter to his. He held her for five minutes. He got up and turned her onto her side facing her away from the door. He pulled the covers up to her neck. He stepped to the entrance of the room and looked in. It appeared as though she was sleeping from that angle. Her body could stay there for a good two days before it started to smell. That was fine since it was only three days before the NAACP meeting.

Reginald walked back into the room and closed the door. He turned on the television set. He watched the scenes of people coming to Atlanta by the bus loads to participate in the march. It was as though the country had something to rally around again. People were beginning to venture out again. The newscaster reported that shopping malls were full to capacity around the country. White people whose Christmas shopping frenzies had been repressed, were now eagerly flashing their credit cards to make up for lost time.

Agent Stone entered into the front door of the house. He had spent some time driving around the sites where the NAACP meeting was to be held . as well as the site where the march was to begin.

"Hello, people, I'm home. Is anyone here?"

Reginald put on a bathrobe and walked into the hallway.

"We are here, Stone. We're turning in early, if you know what I mean. See you in the morning when we exercise,okay?"

"I gotcha. Have a good night."

Stone wondered how Shirley was doing. Was she sleeping with that monster knowing that he was a cold-blooded murderer? Oh, well, that was something that she had to live with, not him. Stone went to bed.

The next morning at 5:00 o'clock, Reginald knocked on Stone's room door.

"Time to get up, Stone, the weights are just sitting there begging to be picked up."

"Alright, I'll be there in a minute. Go ahead and start."

Reginald walked down to the weight room. He did some stretching exercises and then started his shoulder and arm routine.

Stone got dressed for his workout. He could hear Reginald lifting the weights. He decided to go by Reginald's room and look in on Shirley. He walked downstairs and opened the door to the master bedroom. He saw Shirley lying in the bed with her back to the door. She appeared to be still asleep.

"Shirley, wake up, it's Agent Stone," he said in a very low voice. "How are you doing?"

She did not make a sound. Stone decided that he would risk walking over to her and waking her up. He tipped toed closer to her.

"Come on, Stone, I'm waiting for you. What is taking you so long," Reginald yelled from the weight room. "I'm coming up to get you"

Stone turned in his tracks and left the room. He headed for the weight room.

"I'm coming, Attorney Johnson. Just hold on the your weights."

Stone entered into the weight room. There was Attorney Johnson working his tree trunk sized arms.

"What took you so long, Stone?"

"Nothing, I was just washing my face, that's all."

"Well, Stone, when we finish working out, you and I are going to meet with some of the members of the secret service's advanced scouting team. They want to discuss some of the details about how security will be provided for the President. I told them that the NAACP will give them our full cooperation."

"What about Shirley, what is she going to do?"

"Well to tell you the truth, Stone, she said that she was going to stay in today. She is worn out after last night. There is no life left within her. Know what I mean?"

Stone smiled. He had his answer. Shirley was still sleeping with this monster. He would not think any less of her. After all, this man was charming and had so much appeal and looks that no ordinary woman could resist him.

"Maybe we'll all have dinner tonight. Shirley did say, though, that she might be heading back to New York soon. You know she has children there."

"No, I didn't know. But that makes sense. Attorney Johnson, I would like to drive myself Downtown if you don't mind. After the meeting with the secret service, I would like to go to one of the malls and buy me a new suit for the NAACP meeting. After seeing you, I see that my wardrobe needs upgrading."

Stone had a plan. He would go shopping alright, but after that he would rush back to the house to check on Shirley. He just could not believe that she could sleep with Attorney Johnson knowing what she knew about him. He would suggest to her that she do, in fact, go back to New York. That way nothing would happen to her.

Chapter 22

Candice Reynolds handed the parking attendant her car keys. She opened the door to the back seat of the black Mercedes C280 and got her leather briefcase. She asked the parking attendant for directions to 191 Peachtree Street.

Looking at Candice the way the parking attendant was, all you saw was a well dressed, voluptuous Black woman. She was tall and had great legs. No one would suspect that she was the number one point person for the Secret Service. In fact, she was their best agent.

She had joined the service some ten years ago. She had worked her way through the ranks faster than anyone else. During that time she had made quite a network of powerful, influential people. There were few high level people having anything to do with the national security of this country that she didn't know.

Among her many contacts was the Director of the FBI, C. J. Dixon. She spoke with him on a regular basis. They shared information about their various organizations. This was what kept her ahead of her peers. If anything of substance was happening in the country, she could find it out with a phone call. She could get the most up to date, detailed information from her contacts because she provided the same for them when asked.

During her last conversation with Director Dixon, she learned about what was going on with the investigation by the FBI into the Civil Rights murders. The Director had informed her that some of the key agents that were working on the case had disappeared. The only one that had reported in was an agent named Julian Stone. This agent had told the Director that he thought that he knew who was committing the murders, but could not deliver any suspects until about fourteen days later. The Director had placed the agent on administrative leave when he refused to disclose the name of the suspects and declined to return to headquarters. The agent's last know whereabouts was in Atlanta, Georgia.

Through her other contacts with the Bureau, Candice Reynolds got a photograph of Agent Stone. She intended to look for him after her briefing with the NAACP.

Candice walked into the large foyer of the 191 Peachtree Building. She located the bank of elevators for the floor to Attorney Johnson's office and went up to the 35th floor. She walked into Attorney Johnson's office.

Attorney Johnson's secretary looked up, "Hi, can I help you?"

"Yes, I'm Candice Reynolds. I'm with the Secret Service. I have an appointment with Attorney Johnson."

"Have a seat, I'll get him for you."

The secretary walked into Attorney Johnson's office. He was seated at his desk talking to the strange man that had been coming to the office with him over the last several weeks.

"Sir, a Ms. Candice Reynolds is here to see you."

"Who is she?"

"She says that she is with the Secret Service, but she don't look like no secret service agent to me."

"Alright, tell her I'll be right out."

Agent Stone spoke up, "Your secretary is one fine heifer. How do you get any work done looking at that fine big ass all day long?"

"You seen one big ass, you seen them all. You see, Stone, big asses don't make you rich, but being rich gets you all the big asses you want."

Attorney Johnson stepped into the waiting area. What he saw was a big ass that stood up to greet him. Of course, there was something to be said for a big ass.

"Hi, I'm Attorney Johnson."

"I'm Candice Reynolds. I'm pleased to meet you."

"The pleasure is all mine. We can talk in my office."

They headed down a small inside hallway that lead into a very large office. When they went into the office, Candice almost gasped for air. There standing up to greet her was none other than Agent Stone.

"Ms. Reynolds, this is Mr. Stone, he will be joining us in the meeting."

"Glad to meet you, Mr. Stone. I'm Candice Reynolds."

Agent Stone immediately recognized her from a photograph he had seen in an FBI newsletter on the Secret Service. The question that immediately flashed through his mind was, "did she recognize him?" This woman had connections all over the country. But did she have the kind of connections with the FBI that could have told her about him and the investigation he was conducting? Did she know Director Dixon? Stone was worried. This woman was reportedly the best Secret Service agent in the country. There was probably not much that this woman didn't know. He had to assume that she did know about the investigation and that she recognized him.

"I'm glad to meet you. I must say you don't look like a Secret Service agent."

"How are they supposed to look, Mr. Stone?"

"I don't know, but all the Secret Service agents I have seen up to now have never had better looking legs than mine."

"I have never seen your legs so I can't really comment."

Everyone in the room smiled. Reginald broke up the conversation.

"So how can the NAACP assist the Secret Service in providing security for the President?"

"Well, the first thing that I need from you is a list of the members of the NAACP. Then I need a copy of your agenda for the meeting's activities. I need a copy of the route that the march is to take. I also need the location of the meeting. If you suspect anything unusual about any of the members, that too would be helpful. We plan to place Secret Service agents all throughout the crowd. We also plan to assign an agent to escort each of the remaining prominent Civil Rights leaders left. So I need a list of those who plan to attend, also."

"Sounds like you really know your business, Ms. Reynolds," said Attorney Johnson. "I can give you what you want right now. My secretary has all of that information. I'll tell her to give it to you."

"That will be wonderful. I appreciate it. What will you be doing, Attorney Johnson, at the meeting?"

"I'm going to attempt to deliver the opening speech. I also intend to participate in the march by walking with the President most of the way."

Agent Stone thought to himself that, "all you are going to do, Attorney Johnson, is spend time in a jail cell when I arrest you after you give the opening speech."

Reginald accompanied Ms. Reynolds to his secretary. He told the secretary what she needed.

"When you have what you need, Ms. Reynolds, you can come back to my office and I'll see you out."

"Thanks, will do."

Attorney Johnson headed back to his office. When he did so, Ms. Reynolds asked the secretary if she could use the bathroom. The secretary said yes, but told her that visitors had to use the bathroom down the hall. She handed Ms. Reynolds the key.

Ms. Reynolds walked out of Attorney Johnson's office and headed straight for the elevators. She went to the lobby and found a pay phone. She dialed the FBI headquarters and asked to speak with Director Dixon. She said it was an emergency affecting national security.

"Hello, this is Director Dixon."

"Director Dixon, this is Candice Reynolds. Guess who I found in Atlanta?"

"Who?"

"One of your agents, Julian Stone. Is there anything that you would like me to do with him?"

"Yes, absolutely. Find a way to detain him if you can. I'm taking my private jet straight to Atlanta. I can be there within two hours."

"I'll find a way to detain him for you. But you really owe me one."

"Don't worry, I'll deliver when you need it."

"Sir, what I intend to do is to get Stone to spend some time with me. I will have him in the lobby of 191 Peachtree Street at 2:00 o'clock p.m. Can you be here by then?"

"You bet your sweet ass I will"

The Director and three of his agents, better known as 'goons' around the agency, headed straight for the airport. His private jet was there waiting for him.

Candice went back to Attorney Johnson's office. The secretary had most of the documents that she needed waiting for her.

"I appreciate your getting these lists together for me. Would you buzz Attorney Johnson to let him know that I am finished?"

The secretary got up from her desk and walked back to Attorney Johnson's office. On the way there she thought to herself that here was another floozie that would probably get some action around here while all she did was work her fingers to the bone.

"Sir, Ms. Reynolds wanted to let you know she is waiting for you to walk her out."

"Does she have everything that she needs?"

"Yes, sir. While she went to the bathroom, I compiled all of the lists that she asked for."

"Very good. Tell her to come back to my office, please."

Agent Stone felt a lump in his throat. He wondered if she had gone to the bathroom or ran to make a phone call to inform the FBI of his whereabouts.

Candice Reynolds walked into the office. She was looking so good. One could not help but notice that one more button on her blouse was open, revealing some very enticing cleavage.

"So tell me, where can a girl get a good meal around here?"

Attorney Johnson was about to answer when Stone jumped in,   "I'll be glad to show you, if you will join me for lunch."

"Why, I'd love too. Maybe you could show me around Atlanta a little so that I can get a feel for the place. Perhaps we could go by the site where the NAACP meeting is going to take place."

"I don't see why not. That is going to be at the Georgia Dome. I think that you will get a kick out of it. It is one of the few domes in the country."

Reginald spoke up, "You guys have a good time. I have a lot to do today. I'm meeting with members of the NAACP to discuss the final agenda for the national meeting and to work out the last remaining specifics of the march. I'll see you guys back here around say 2:00, 2:30."

Candice and Agent Stone both gave a nod. They left the office and headed for the parking lot where she had left her car. The parking attendant brought the car around. Unlike when she had brought the car to the lot by herself, now he was indignant. He acted as though she had done something to him because she was being escorted by a man. He no longer flirted with her, but took her money and gave her a cold stare.

Candice did not mind. She was used to Black men behaving in this manner. Anytime they saw a good looking Black woman by herself, they always tried to come on to her as though it was their birth right or something. But the moment they saw her with a man that she really wanted to be with, they got mad, even thought they had only met the woman while parking her car or while doing some other menial task.

"Wow, I did not know that Secret Service agents drove Mercedes Benzes. They must really pay agents well."

"No, it is not that. I rent a Mercedes or some other luxury car every time I go somewhere because those stupid Ford Tauruses are a dead give away. No one would suspect an agent to drive a Mercedes."

"That makes perfect sense."

Stone could not help but notice Candice's cleavage and her beautiful thick thighs, most of which were showing as she drove the car.

"Why don't we go to the Georgia Dome first. I would like to see it before we get something to eat."

"Fine, you're driving."

Chavis Martin and some other members of the NAACP walked into Attorney Johnson's office. Reginald was there to greet them.

"Gentlemen, come on into my office. We have a lot to go over. Mr. Martin, why don't we begin with the latest on the march."

"All is going well, anybody that is anybody is going to be there. The committee and I have arranged for some of the local high school bands to play at the kick off ceremonies. Mrs. King will be there to give the kick off speech, followed by some remarks from the President of the United States. We have contracted with a local company to make t-shirts for everyone that wants one, for a nominal fee. One of the major television networks and Coca-Cola are acting as official sponsors of the march."

"How about the necessary marching permits along the route," Reginald asked.

"As you know, the planned route of the march is from Atlanta to Anderson, South Carolina; to Greenville, South Carolina; to Spartanburg, South Carolina; to Charlotte, North Carolina; to Greensboro, North Carolina; to Durham, North Carolina; to Richmond, Virginia; and on into D.C. All of the cities mentioned have given quick approval on all the necessary permits. They have also been quick to deny approvals to all of the Klan rallies that they scheduled to coincide with the march in these various cities. The justification has been that the President of the United States will be there, and in the interests of national security, the Klan can be kept from assembling."

"Excellent, Chavis, excellent. Now, let's talk about the common sense items such as porta-potties, food, and water along the route, shelter and all of those things."

*   *   *   *   *   *

"Mr. Stone, I appreciate your escorting me to lunch. Sometimes it can be very lonely in my job, you know, going to a city as the advanced scout for the protection of the President. Usually you don't know anybody there and you spend most of the time by yourself. It's nice to have someone, especially a good looking man, to spend some time with."

Stone smiled. He was not fooled for a minute. This lady was up to something. She purposefully wanted him near her. While he knew he had sex appeal, this woman would not fall for it so easily. Perhaps she had told someone that she would keep him occupied until they got there. He would play along. This was going to be a game of cat and mouse, but who was playing which role, he did not know.

"Well, it is my pleasure to escort such a beautiful woman to lunch."

Stone reached under the table and touched her on the thigh. She did not protest. He reached his hand as high as he dared. Still she did not give him a hint that she didn't like it.

"I'm staying with Attorney Johnson for a few days. Perhaps we could drive up to his house and have a few drinks."

"You don't waste any time, do you?"

"You know what they say, you have to strike while the iron is hot. And from where I sit, this is some iron."

"How long would it take to get there from here?"

"Oh, about forty minutes. It's 12:15. We could be there by 1:00 and back by 2:30, if you're thinking what I'm thinking."

Candice had done all sorts of things in the name of God and Country. Sleeping with men was not one of them. She was genuinely attracted to Agent Stone. She wanted to be with him, and she was not going to miss the only chance that she knew she would have. It had been about four months since she had been with anyone, and she was quite horny.

"I am thinking what you're thinking. What are we waiting for? Let's go."

Stone could not believe his ears. Would this woman go to any length to effect his capture? He reached his hand under the table and slipped his finger under her short skirt. She angled her legs so that he could better reach under her panties. She was soaked. Stone figured, "what the hell, might as well fuck her.

At least it will be a good memory no matter what happens." They hurried out of the restaurant.

On the drive up to Alpharetta, Stone placed his hand under Candice's dress. He rubbed her soaked panties for a while, then slid his fingers deep inside of her. More than once she almost ran into the back of a slower car as his fingers worked their magic. At last they arrived at Attorney Johnson's house. They rushed inside and ran up to Stone's room. He threw Candice on the bed and pulled her legs up in the air. He removed her soaked panties and mounted her. She responded like a bucking bronco.

"Fuck me, fuck me," she yelled.

Stone pounded away. He propped her legs up over his shoulders and entered her as deeply as he could. He got in the rhythm of going in as far as he could and then pulling out as far has he could without actually coming all the way out. The sensation drove Candice wild. She screamed in ecstasy. Her screams made Stone come inside of her.

"Oh God you're good," screamed Stone. "Why did you do this?"

"Because I knew that you would be a good fuck the moment that I saw you. Let's get cleaned up. We have to get back."

Stone thought to himself how good this screwing session had been. Ordinarily he would let a beautiful woman like this arrest him anytime. But not today.

They drove back to Atlanta. Candice told Stone that she had forgotten to get some more specifics on the march. She said that they could park the car and walk to the office together. Stone agreed.

Director Dixon had positioned his men. One was seated in the lobby of 191 Peachtree reading a newspaper. The other one was stationed by the teller machine. Dixon himself was inside the Wachovia Bank watching the lobby. They all saw Candice Reynolds and Agent Stone enter the lobby together. Stone was about to walk past the Agent seated reading the newspaper.

Candice said in a very low muffled voice, "Get out of here, Agent Stone, now!"

Stone looked to the left and saw Director Dixon coming out of the bank. The agent reading the newspaper reached for Stone. He missed as Stone dodged him instinctively from all the days of playing football. Candice grabbed Stone by the arm. He punched her in the side, knocking her to the ground. He ran out the door and headed down the block. The agent who had been reading the newspaper ran after him.

Candice yelled, "You idiots, I delivered him to you and you let him get away! What kind of agents are you?"

"Now, Ms. Reynolds, don't take it personally. We will get Stone," Director Dixon said in a very calm voice. "You did your part. I won't forget that. Let's find some place where we can talk. I want you to tell me everything that happened while you were with Stone."

Candice's mind flashed back to the bed in Alpharetta. Stone had really put it to her. It was the best fuck she had had in ten years. She just did not have the heart to betray him so soon after what had occurred between them. She had a feeling that they would run into each other again. She certainly hoped so. If she did see him, she would make love to him again. She needed it. Perhaps she could explain to him why she did what she did. He was an agent. He of all people would understand. No, she had to make him understand that she was not just doing her job when she made love to him. Rather, she was in pure ecstasy and it had nothing to do with her job.

Candice answered Director Dixon. "We did not really talk about anything that was even remotely related to the Civil Rights Murders. But I can tell you that I believe that Stone has somehow become involved in the planning of the upcoming NAACP meeting and the march that will follow. The meeting is scheduled to take place at the Georgia Dome. Station your men there and I believe that eventually you will see Stone show up."

"You did good, Ms. Reynolds, real good. At least we have an idea of where Stone is and what he might be up to. He must believe that the murderer will be present at the NAACP meeting. He probably intends to make his move at that time. We will be there to help him. I'm calling in the troops. I'll see you later. We'll talk again."

The agent that ran out after Stone came back into the lobby of the building. He was sweating perfusely.

"Sir, he got away. I had him in my sights a couple of times, but there was no way to get off a clean shot. Just too many bystanders."

Candice spoke up, "You mean you would have shot and killed him?"

The agent and the Director looked at each other.

"No, Ms. Reynolds, I have given standing orders to all of my agents to do whatever is necessary to apprehend Agent Stone. Those orders do not include killing him. This agent was merely going to shoot him in the leg if that was the only way to stop Stone."

Candice did not believe that for a second. She had heard rumors about how rogue agents in the FBI had been killed by agents in good standing. The justification was always that the agents posed a serious threat to national security. But inter-agency gossip was that the Directors of the FBI simply did not tolerate agents who crossed them. Candice believed that Stone's life was in jeopardy. She prayed that he got in contact with her soon so that she could warn him.

She left the lobby of 191 Peachtree Street and headed back to the parking lot where she had left her rented Mercedes. The parking attendant brought the car around. He began his usual flirtations since she was by herself. Just as she was about to tell him something ugly, she saw Agent Stone run around the corner and head for her car. She got in the car on the driver's side, and he opened the door and got in on the passenger's side. He reached over and grabbed her. He pulled her close to him and kissed her. They drove off. The irate attendant looked on.

Candice took Stone to get the Range Rover. They drove separately to a motel located in Roswell. They spent the night together. After they checked in, she explained to him what had happened and what her role in the whole thing had been. He was pleased to know that their sleeping together had not been because of her job, but because she was genuinely attracted to him. After she finished explaining, they made love again. This time was even more passionate than the first time.

At about 7:00 o'clock p.m, Stone informed Candice that he needed to go on up to Alpharetta and get some of his toiletries and some suits in order to have a change of clothes. He also needed to drop off the Range Rover.

They arrived at the house about a half hour later. Stone opened the garage and put the Rover in it. He closed the garage door and walked back to the front door of the house and let them in. They walked up to his room and packed up one of his suitcases with the stuff he needed.

"Candice, let me look in the master bedroom and see if the lady that is staying with Attorney Johnson is there. I worry about her. Don't give me that look, there is nothing between us."

"Why would you worry? This place seems safe enough. Unless, unless, wait a minute! Attorney Johnson has something to do with the murders. That's it, isn't it? Why else would you be hanging around Attorney Johnson as though you were one of his colleagues?"

"Yes, he does have something to do with the murders. He knows that I know and we have an agreement that I won't move on him until he delivers the opening speech at the national NAACP meeting. Please keep this to yourself. It goes without saying that I'm going to need your help."

"Well, I'll do what I can, but I have to brief the Secret Service people tomorrow. I will be caught up in that all day. The meeting, you know, is day after tomorrow. I suggest that you stay in the hotel room, out of sight, until the time the meeting begins. Believe me when I tell you that the Director and his goons are looking for you, and they will stop at nothing until they find you. The Director told me that he is calling in the troops and that they will be at the NAACP meeting at the dome."

The two of them walked down the staircase and went to Reginald's room. They opened the door. Shirley was there in bed. The covers were pulled up to her neck. She had her back to the door.

"That's funny. Why is she sleeping this time of day? In fact, it does not look like she has moved since this morning. Surely she did not sleep all day. I'm going to wake her."

Stone walked over to the bed and grabbed the lifeless body of Shirley Whitaker by the shoulder and rolled her over.

"My God, she had been murdered," he yelled. "That son-of-a-bitch killed her. He said there would be no more killings. I'm going to wait here and kill him myself. Somebody has to stop him. I should have done it when I first found out that he was responsible for the deaths of the Civil Rights leaders."

Candice placed a hand on Stone's shoulders. She gently massaged him.

"Stone, listen to me. There is nothing that you can do for her. From the looks of it, she has been dead for some time. At least twenty-four hours. The meeting is day after tomorrow. You promised Attorney Johnson that you were going to allow him to make the opening speech. The country needs for the meeting and the march to go off without a hitch. Otherwise, we will have total chaos. I know it is hard, but hold off on your anger until then. After the march begins, do whatever you want with Attorney Johnson. Just remember, the FBI is after you."

"No, you're right. It's just that, because of me, this lady is dead. I knew I should have persuaded her to go back to New York. If I had, she would be alive now. I should be the one lying there dead because I am the one that is stupid. Let's just get out of here."

Chapter 23

Reginald drove up into the driveway. He didn't bother to put the Mercedes in the garage. He was tired. His day had been exhausting. The meeting with the NAACP members had lasted for six hours. They had gone over everything imaginable. After that, a staff member from the President's office called. Reginald was on the phone with him for another hour and a half going over what role the President would play.

On the way home, Reginald had decided that he would rent a hotel room Downtown. This would allow him to relax and unwind on the eve of the meeting. Besides, there was not that much more preparation that he could personally do before the meeting. Now he had to leave the remaining tasks up to whatever committee that was charged with the responsibility of doing them.

Tonight he would pack his clothing, laptop computer and whatever else he needed for the meeting. He also had to get rid of the lifeless body of Shirley Whitaker. He had slept on the day bed the previous night, if one could call three hours sleeping. He wondered about where Stone was. He decided to look for him. He went to Stone's room, but it was empty. That was good. Maybe Stone had gotten lucky with that Secret Service agent. If so, he would be tied up literally for a while. Reginald headed back to his room. The door was closed. He opened it.

"Damn, Stone has been in here. Shirley's body has been moved. He knows. But when did he come back to the house? He is going to be pissed. He might try something. After all, I gave my word to that fool that no one else would die in exchange that he leave me alone until the national meeting was over. Surely, he had to know that I was going to do whatever was necessary to make sure the meeting went off without a hitch."

Reginald rolled Shirley's body up in the covers. He picked up the bundle and threw it over his shoulder. He went into the garage and laid the roll on the hood of the Range Rover, which was back in its spot. He unlocked the Rover and opened up the back. He placed the roll in the back and closed the door. He got in and pressed the garage door opener.

He drove to the same construction site where he had gotten rid of the other agents. He found a dumpster and threw the roll in it.

"I'll miss you, Shirley Whitaker. Just know that you gave your life for the good of the Black race. Sleep well."

Reginald said a small prayer for Shirley. Tears filled his eyes. He drove back to his house and waited for Stone. But Stone never showed. Stone was indeed tied up. He had cried for quite a while when he and Candice got back to the motel room. She cuddled him while he let it all out. Then they both went to sleep in each other's arms.

Reginald got up at his usual time. He did an abbreviated workout and got dressed. After breakfast, he loaded up the Range Rover and headed for Downtown. He checked into the Hyatt Hotel. He requested the same room that the Executive Director had stayed in. The hotel granted his request. When Reginald got into the room, he noticed that there was no way you could tell that a murder had taken place here. Reginald called his secretary and gave her the telephone number to his room. He instructed her to screen all of his calls, and under no circumstances was she to tell anyone where he was staying.

Agent Stone and Candice had breakfast in the restaurant of the motel.

Candice asked, "Why did you make an agreement with Attorney Johnson which allowed him to run free until the national meeting? You knew he was the murderer and that there was the potential that he would kill again."

"I know now that I made a mistake. I know that several innocent people died as a result of my blunders. At the time I made that agreement with Attorney Johnson, I was bound and helpless. He could have killed me right there on the spot, and no one would have been the wiser. For whatever reason, he chose to let me live. I was grateful and made the agreement."

"Do you know why he did the killings?"

"At first I thought that he was just another madman. But I have spent some time thinking about what he told me. He actually thinks that the current Civil Rights Leaders had to be totally eliminated or the race was going to die a slow death. According to him, he was going to provide a new direction for the Black race by taking over the NAACP. He intends to begin that new direction when he gives the opening speech at the national NAACP meeting. I really thought that no one else was going to die. No, I'm not being totally honest. I wanted to see history in the making. Don't you see, I was the first person, the only person until you, who had any idea of what was going on."

Candice sit up straight. "I don't agree with that philosophy at all. It takes all the things that have happened to us as a people for change to occur. I'm not all that religious and all, but I believe that God has a master plan. He will liberate us in his own way and in his own time. We have to remember that Blacks only got civil rights thirty years ago. It takes time."

"Candice I don't know who is right. All I know is that on tomorrow, Attorney Johnson will get his chance to make history. Only history will tell if he made a difference. Maybe he will live long enough to see if what he did was worth it. That is, assuming, of course, that he does not get the chair."

"I guess you are right. We will see. Listen, I have to get going. I have my meeting to discuss the security for the President in about an hour. Wait for me here at the motel until I return. I should get back here in about four hours. Maybe you could work out or something to pass the time."

"No, I've got to figure out how and when I'm going to effect the capture of Attorney Johnson. I also have to get in contact with Director Dixon. I don't want his goons to get to me while I'm trying to get to Attorney Johnson."

"I know where he is at. He is staying at the Hotel Nikko in Buckhead. I think calling him is a good idea. I don't want anything to happen to you. Oh, by the way, I'm going to help you capture Attorney Johnson. I believe getting him is going to be extremely difficult. Okay, see you later."

Stone read the morning paper in the motel lobby. Afterwards, he went up to his room. He dialed the number of the Hotel Nikko. He asked for C. J. Dixon's room. The hotel operator put him through.

"This is Director Dixon."

"Hi, Sir, this is Stone."

"Stone, where the hell are you. Why won't you turn yourself in. It would make things a whole lot easier. You know how this organization works. Don't be a fool."

"Sir, listen to me. I know who the murderer is. He will be at the NAACP meeting tomorrow. I'm going to need your help in apprehending him. You must trust me and call off those goons. Everything will be alright after tomorrow."

"Who is the murderer, Stone," the Director barked. "Tell me now or the deal is off."

Stone knew the Director was an impatient man. He would arrest Attorney Johnson on site. He would not wait until he gave his speech. Stone decided to make up something.

"Well, sir, I believe the murderer is a disgruntled NAACP member who was looked over time and time again when election time came. He will be there tomorrow and will be sitting in the VIP section at the dome. I will point him out to you."

"Alright Stone, you have a deal. I'll call my boys off and let you do your thing. But you had better be straight with me. If you are not, the consequences can and will be fatal. Do you get my drift?"

"Loud and clear, sir."

"Alright, Stone, I'm going to station my men all around the dome in strategic locations. You meet me at the Gate D at 8:00 o'clock tomorrow. At that time I will give you a radio set to a special frequency so that we can keep in contact with one another. Don't let me down, Stone. Goodbye."

Agent Stone felt better. At least now he could concentrate on Attorney Johnson without having to watch his own back. He also had help from a very capable agent in the name of Candice Reynolds. Stone spent the next few hours going over the specifics of how he was going to capture Attorney Johnson. He intended to work Johnson over for killing Shirley after they had made an agreement. Then he would turn him over to Director Dixon. He would be a hero again.

Reginald spent the day going over his speech. He wanted it to appear as though he was making it up as he went along. He practiced over and over again in the mirror until he could say most of the speech without looking at his notes.

At 6:00 o'clock in the evening he put everything away. He called room service and ordered a steak dinner with champagne. He intended to celebrate for the next two hours.

All had gone well considering the circumstances. Even with Stone in the picture and the death of Shirley, things could not have gone much smoother. Tomorrow was his big day. He thought about the Executive Director for a moment. It was too bad that he was not alive to hear his speech. But, that was the way it had to be.

Reginald wondered how all great men must have felt on the eve of their history making events. Did they have trouble keeping the butterflies in their stomachs from ripping their guts out? Did they know what impact their actions were going to make on the world in the months and years to come.

Reginald was not a man given to panic and uncertainty. But he had never faced anything of this magnitude before. There were the television cameras, the President of the United States would be there, anybody who was anybody would be there. The whole nation would be hanging on his every word. The stress began to build up inside of him. Doubts crept into his mind at all levels. He felt as though he was going to take off running and never stop. The weight of the world--no of a race was on his shoulders. It was a heavy weight.

There was a knock on the door. It was room service. This cleared his mind for the moment. He ate his food and drank the champagne. He got dressed for bed. He asked the hotel operator to hold all calls. Tonight he would get a good night's sleep.

Agent Stone went over his plan with Candice. She did not like it, but could not come up with a better one herself. It would have to do. They ordered a pizza and beer. They too decided that a good night's sleep was in order.

*   *   *   *   *   *

The first rays of sunshine hit the Georgia Dome. This was a magnificent structure. It was one of only few domes in the entire world, most of which were located in the United States.

Construction on the Georgia Dome was completed in the spring of 1993. The Dome has a seating capacity of 71,500. It rises to a height of 275 feet from the center of the playing field to the roof center, which makes it as tall as a twenty-seven story building.

The field of the Dome can be set up into various configurations for different types of sporting and entertainment events. It serves as home to the Atlanta Falcons Football Team. It also hosted the 1994 Superbowl, the USA Mobil Indoor Track and Field Events, and the Peach Bowl. It could also be configured to hold concerts and basketball games.

Today the Dome was configured for a concert. There was a large eight-foot high podium at the west end of the playing field. Two thousand chairs were placed on the field starting from the thirty yard line and heading toward the east goal post.

People began arriving at the Dome at 7:00 o'clock. Among them were hundreds of Secret Service agents. Many of the agents, along with Atlanta Police, formed a human barricade at the base of the podium.

Television and radio people began entering the press boxes like ants. Camera crews were all over the place hooking up wires and setting up lights.

Agent Stone and Candice approached the Dome on Northside Drive. The street was filled with barricades. No doubt the President was to take this route. They headed north on Northside Drive until Georgia Dome Drive. When they turned onto Georgia Dome Drive., they were stopped. Candice identified herself and Stone did the same. The place was crawling with Atlanta Police, Fulton County Sheriff's Deputies, Private Security People, FBI agents, and Secret Service Agents. Swat teams were stationed on the hills overlooking the Dome. Candice parked in the visitor parking area on the south side of the Dome in front of the box office. Stone got out and walked to Gate D. He and Candice had agreed that they would meet in Kicker's Sports Lounge in fifteen minutes.

When Stone got to Gate D, he saw the Director standing there with three of his goons.

"Good morning, Sir. How are you?"

"Glad to see that you made it, Stone. I was beginning to think that you might not."

"I'm not quite ready to be on the FBI's most wanted list just yet."

"Here is the radio, Stone. Don't let me down."

"I understand, Sir."

Stone took the radio and entered through Gate D. He looked out of the corner of his eye and saw one of the goons heading after him ever so subtly. Once inside, Stone headed straight for Kicker's Sports Bar. He walked as fast as he could without running.

By 9:30, the Dome was packed. Most of the people who had stood outside in the long lines were now inside. There had been long lines because the only people that were allowed in had to be people on the list that each security person had at each gate. The only way that you were on the list was that you were a member of the NAACP or an invited guest. Even if you weren't on the list, you could get in if one of the NAACP committee members standing at the gate approved you.

At 9:45, the President's motorcade arrived. The motorcade parked in the lot adjacent to the box office. The President and his entourage entered through gate D. They were ushered out onto the field and up on the podium.

At 10:00 o'clock, a local high school marching band began playing. They performed three selections. The crowd was revved up. When they finished performing, the loud speakers broadcast the official song of the NAACP, 'We Shall Overcome'. Everyone stood up and sang along.

When the song was over and people had taken their seats, the Master of Ceremonies walked up to the microphone on the podium. His name was Romles Gibbs. He was from Brooklyn, New York, and was active in the local politics there. He owned a chain of day care centers and had made a decent living from the business. He had often been the Master of Ceremonies for NAACP functions. He was very good at it. As usual, he was dressed impeccably.

"Ladies and gentlemen, honored guests, friends and foes, I welcome you to the National NAACP Meeting. The first order of business is to thank the God for our being here and to ask him to bless our meeting. So at this time, I would ask Reverend Anthony Hicks to come and give us the invocation."

Reverend Hicks gave a rousing prayer. He spoke about how God always has his plan. That perhaps the Civil Rights murders were just a way of bringing Whites and Blacks closer together in this country. Or it could be that Black people had forgotten that it was God who had brought them this far, and only God could continue to protect and strengthen them. Like most ministers, Reverend Hicks spoke about twice as long as his allotted time.

Mr. Gibbs walked back up to the microphone, "Thank you, Reverend Hicks, for such a heart warming prayer. Let us heed his words.

Now we will get into the program. As you can see, the first part of the program is open to the public. The second part of the meeting will be attended by NAACP delegates only. During that part of the meeting, we will elect our leaders for the next two years and conduct other internal organizational business. Now, we are going to hear from the President of the United States. Ladies and Gentlemen, I give you President Clinton!"

Everyone stood on their feet. They gave the President a standing ovation. The sound of 71,000 people clapping was deafening.

"Good morning, my fellow Americans. I am proud to be here today at perhaps the most important occasion since I began my Presidency. I am here today to give my support to one of the most, if not the most, important organizations in this country, the NAACP. It was this organization that has shouldered the burden of addressing the injustices that Black People have suffered in this country over the past decades. Recently, this organization has been befallen by some setbacks. As you know, some of its most hard working members have been murdered. But this organization has not been deterred from its purpose. For you see, the test of an individual and ultimately an organization's resolve is how it responds to adversity. The NAACP has responded. It has refused to be intimidated. It is working harder than ever before to protect the interest of its people. I salute the NAACP and all that it stands for. I am proud to be a part of this gathering. You have my support, one hundred percent. On tomorrow, I will continue to show my support by participating in what I believe will be the most historic of all marches. It is time that Blacks and Whites started working together in this country. I will take the lead."

The President waved his hand in the air. There were five minutes of clapping. Mr. Gibbs stood up. He raised his hands in the air and then slowly lowered them. The clapping stopped immediately.

"Let us thank the President, who has taken the time to be here to assist us in our cause. With his support, we cannot fail. We will continue to make a difference in this country for not only Black people, but all people. Next we will have the recognition of guests. This recognition will be given by Leola Jackson. I give you Ms. Jackson."

Ms. Jackson spent the next fifteen minutes recognizing all of the important dignitaries in attendance. The list read like a who's who in Civil Rights, the sports and entertainment world, and in the political arena.

"Thank you, Ms. Jackson. I noticed that you did not call my name, but that is okay. At least I get to talk. At this time, we will have the introduction for our keynote speaker. The speech that he will give is the customary opening speech for the NAACP. This speech sets the tone for the NAACP for the entire year. Giving this introduction will be Chavis Martin, the Committee Chair who is responsible for organizing the march that most of you will participate in tomorrow. Mr. Martin."

"Hello, fellow soldiers. Before I introduce our speaker, let's take a moment of silence to honor those slain Civil Rights leaders. I especially want to take this opportunity to remember our previous Executive Director, Mr. Harrison Weeks, whose life was snuffed out just days ago. So at this time, please bow your heads in a moment of silence.

"Now, ladies and gentlemen, let me introduce our speaker. He did his undergraduate work at Hampton University and attended law school at Howard Law School. He is one of the most successful attorneys in the nation. He has gotten some of the largest personal injury settlements in history. But all of that success and wealth has not caused him to forget the real riches in life. Those riches are the fulfillment you feel by working for the betterment of those who are less fortunate than you. This man believes in community service, not just a little work here and there, but the devotion of most, if not all, of his free time to such causes. The man I am referring to is none other than Reginald Johnson. This man stepped into the role of acting national spokesperson and then acting Executive Director at a time when most men would have succumbed to the worries of being killed for assuming such roles. Without this man, there might not have been a national meeting today. I present to you, Reginald Johnson."

Chapter 24

The Dome speakers began broadcasting "Amazing Grace". The audience joined in. The song brought many a tear to most of the eyes present.

Attorney Johnson stepped up to the microphone. It was as though he were in a trance. That trance had begun early this morning when he woke up. It had continued while he got dressed, ate breakfast and headed for the Dome. He was in such a trance that he hardly noticed the scuffles on the way to the Dome between Atlanta Police and protesters from the Ku Klux Klan whose assembly permits had been denied. When Reginald got to the Dome, he hardly said a word to any of the important people who tried to converse with him, including the President of the United States.

Reginald looked out over the crowd. About one third of the people in attendance were White. "Unbelievable," he thought. He looked above the playing field and saw the camera men stationed in their little booths all around the dome. He glanced behind him on the podium. There seated were both the King widows, the Mayor of Atlanta, Andrew Young, the President and a couple of Secret Service agents, Barbara Jordan, Clarence Thomas, of all people, the elite of the NAACP and some other people who Reginald did not even know.

On one of the monitors in the observation room, Candice and Agent Stone watched Attorney Johnson. Stone was secretly proud of the man. He thought to himself, "what balls this man has. What courage to try something like this. After all, this man was wealthy, he could have just enjoyed all that his wealth had to offer such as cars, women, and other material goods. But he believed in this ideal enough to risk everything."

Reginald just stood there at the microphone. The Dome became as quiet as a tomb. Everyone stopped moving about. Reginald's image could be seen on all the television screens not only in the Dome, but in every house in the

United States. There was even coverage in Europe and Japan. The world was waiting for him to speak. Still, he did not utter a word. The tension was mounting. At last Reginald spoke up, "THE TIME HAS COME....

"TO ALL BLACK PEOPLE, the message is clear, it is simple, you need only listen and heed these words, the time has come."

"THAT'S RIGHT, THE TIME HAS COME for us to thank God for all the many talents he has given us and to beg for his forgiveness for letting those talents waste away. For we are God's chosen people and he has allowed us to wallow in self-pity, poverty, ignorance, violent crime, and cultural suicide, all because we have failed to utilize our talents to help ourselves.

"NOW THE TIME HAS COME for us, Black people, to depend on ourselves, to work both individually and collectively to better ourselves. We don't need the government, white people, churches, and charitable organizations to provide the basic human needs that each of us should do for ourselves. It is time to stop buying what we want and begging for what we need.

"THE TIME HAS COME to realize that the Civil Rights Movement is dead, outdated and a waste of time. We have achieved the basic human rights such as voting, the right to own property, attend educational institutions, and basically enter through the front door. This was achieved 20 years ago. One hundred more years of the Civil Rights Movement will achieve no more in terms of human rights than we have now. For you see, basic human rights is all that any Civil Rights Movement can achieve. It cannot improve the individual. And it is the lack of individual achievement that collectively has led to a substandard race.

"FOR YOU SEE, THE TIME AS COME for all Black people to understand that there will always be a threshold level of racism as long as there is more than one race. Beyond that threshold level of racism, beyond those basic human rights, there is simply competition between the races, and, ultimately, among individuals. Each race competing with the other to achieve cultural and economic superiority. No one race has ever helped or should help another race to better itself. If you as Black people are looking for Whites to do it, then you will be waiting forever. The simple fact is that whenever Whites have come into contact with other races, be it the American Indians, Blacks, Hispanics, etc., they have conquered them, adapted from them the best that they had to offer such as land, minerals, certain phrases from their languages, cheap or slave labor, and then moved on to the next race.

"THE TIME HAS COME for Black people to stop trying to integrate, stop trying to be like White people. You don't have to integrate to get basic human rights. Blacks are the only race on earth that has tried to integrate with White people. No other race has tried it. Not the Japanese, the Chinese, the Arabs, the Jews, nor the Koreans. We are the only fools that have tried this idiotic endeavor for the last 200 years. Look at the results; housing projects, violent crime, minimum wage jobs, welfare, brothers begging at the corner for a quarter, laziness, distrust of other Blacks and a general lack of Black pride. Trying to integrate has caused cultural suicide.

"It is time to realize that yes, we were enslaved, but so were many other races and they didn't try to integrate. It is time to stop thinking that just because you are a minority, Whites owe you something because of what happened to you during and after slavery. Whites no longer believe this even if they once did. Look around you, affirmative action is also dead which is evidenced by a lack of hiring of Blacks just to fill quotas. It is time to realize that White people don't owe Black people anything, nothing. And until we stop believing that they do, we will not stand up and do things for ourselves.

"THE TIME HAS COME. The time has come for Black people to start trusting, respecting, and believing in each other. We have to realize that we are all Black. The days of being in a crowded room of Whites and not speaking to other Blacks must stop. How else can we network, make deals and help each other have a better quality of life unless we associate with each other. It is not wrong to talk to each other. It is time to understand that no Black person is an island. To build and have something of substance like office building etc., requires a team effort both in terms of labor and money.

"It is time to realize that all of us have equal worth. That's right, you high yellow Blacks, you dark skinned Blacks and all shades in between, you are all the same. No matter how much you suck up to Whites at lunch, or on the job, you are still viewed the same, as Black and inferior.

"It is time for Black people to take pride in loving and marrying one another, not become successful and then marry and give your money to them and be so proud of it.

"It is time to remember that it is not enough to run and get elected to political office, but you, as a Black person, must remember that you are Black and your political decisions must be geared toward making Black peoples' lives better, both economically and socially.

"It is time for us to hire each other, promote each other and to help each other make money rather than acting like crabs in a crab bucket. You know, if I can't lift myself up, then I'll do all I can do to make sure that I hold other Blacks down. Speaking of holding each other down, it is definitely time for us Black people to stop helping the system arrest, beat up, and prosecute our own Black boys. Stop working undercover in our own neighborhoods and putting our Black boys in jail. Have you ever seen an Oriental helping to arrest and prosecute another Oriental? Again, Black people are the only race that will assist another race to destroy itself. This was true during the time of slavery and it is definitely true during the era of crack cocaine and 9mm weapons. For ninety percent of the young Black boys in jail would not be there if it were not for other brainwashed Black police officers and Black judges helping to put them there rather than working to improve our youth. We must stop being the perfect enforcers for the system, all in the name of, 'I'm just doing my job'.

"THE TIME HAS COME. The time has come for us to improve ourselves. We must start by improving individually. Education is the key. All brains that are educated and trained the same, act the same. Black people must take responsibility for their own education. We know what is best for us. We cannot hold others responsible to educate us and our children. Why should they?

"It is time for Blacks to perform in the classroom and not accept that being Black means automatically that you can't make good grades just like everyone else. We can no longer afford to let our children go to college and waste most of their days in the student lounge playing cards and watching T.V. Black students must spend just as much time in the library as the students of other races. No one can make good grades without intensive study.

"It is time for Black people to understand that the purpose of an education is to learn a skill or trade in order to make money. Our students must be taught this from the start.

"It is time to teach our children discipline. That discipline should begin by requiring them to attend Church services regularly in order to develop good moral values, values that will teach our kids that you don't shoot someone for a starter jacket, for their car, or every time you get mad with them or disagree with them.

"It is time to require that our children read a book a week instead of being Nintendo heads for hours at a time. By reading, our kids can learn proper grammar instead of useless slang language. Technical manuals and computers are not based on slang language.

"We must stop letting our kids dress sloppily like the rappers with their clothes three sizes too big and hanging off of them. Speaking of rap, we must stop our children from listening to rap music all day because most kids who listen to that crap all day long usually never amount to anything except a jailbird.

"It is time to stop letting our youth put gold teeth in the front of their mouths. Mostly drug dealers have gold front teeth. Get rid of the earrings in the nose. Even if employers were generous enough to want to give a Black kid a job, who would want to hire someone with a ring in their nose to represent their company?

"It is simply time that we remember that we, the Black parents, must take back control of our children. We have to tell them what to do rather than asking or negotiating with them. Otherwise, they won't respect us. Either we take responsibility for parenting now or the police will do it for us later.

"We must stop rewarding our kids with $200 sneakers and they won't even attend school on a regular basis or do even the simplest of household chores like clean their room or wash the dishes. Then we wonder why they are so lazy.

"We must instill in our children that success for them means accomplishing more in their lifetimes than their parents did in theirs. We can't, as parents, simply let our children move back in with us the moment they encounter one of life's little roadblocks. If we let them move back in, they forever lose their ability to survive and prosper on their own.

"THE TIME HAS COME. The time has come for Black men to start being men. Stop blaming White men as the cause of your poverty, laziness, drug addiction and violence toward other Blacks and especially toward the Black women. It is time for Black men to stop welching off mother, grandmother, sister, spouse, and girlfriend. Our Black women were not meant to take care of you. It is time to stop having babies for other people to take care of. Any boy can have a baby, but only a man can raise a child.

"Black men must begin to respect Black women. Black women are not objects to be hit on, mistreated, and used. They are not sex objects. It is time to allow the hard working sisters to go their merry way down the sidewalk instead of you following them for two blocks and telling them how sexually gifted you are. And when you do work with Black women, treat them as professionals instead of trying all during the work day to get in bed with them. This is especially true when you are their supervisors. It is time for Black men to start taking care of Black women instead of the other way around. You Black men certainly take care of White women when you have them. You will even get two jobs if need be.

"It is time for Black men especially to get an education instead of going to jail. Black boys and men, you are not supposed to be in jail. That is not part of the natural order of things. In fact, you should never see the inside of a jail in your lifetime. It is time to stop using crack and carrying a gun. Stop hanging with the wrong crowd, being in the wrong place and doing the things that you know are against the law. For these things will surely land you in jail. It is time to stop spending you mother's and grandmother's hard earned money to make bond.

"Black men, unless you change your ways, the educational and financial gap between Black men and women will continue to widen. Most Black women will not have any mates, and the few that do will be living with Black men that can't complete a sentence and are unemployed, or the Black women will be living with a white male and be subjected to the overt racism of his family. It is time for Black men to take a bath, shave, get a haircut, wear clean and neat clothes and get a job. Do something, build something, stop begging for quarters on the corner.

"Stop using drugs and being high so that you don't have to face reality. It has been said that drugs, unemployment, and incarceration among Black men is by design of the White man. So what? Even if that's true, be a man, change it. Take those skills that you use to buy and sell drugs and start up and run legitimate businesses. Use the discipline that you use to practice basketball for hours and apply it to making money. Chase after money the same way you chase after women! Don't use your people skills to fit into the gang, use them to network with business people and make money. Damn it, it is time to stand up and be men!

"THE TIME HAS COME. The time has come for Black women to support Black men by demanding that they be men. You must require more of us Black men. Don't let Black men move in with you, drive your car, and spend your hard earned money. It is time to stop getting pregnant for Black men that you met at a club two weeks ago, then having to raise the child by yourself for the next 20 years."

"It is time to realize that you cannot date and marry Black men that are not your educational and financial equal. If you do, you will not be able to discuss current events, attend upscale social functions or even respect him over time. Don't let some Black brother make you feel guilty because you are not willing to wait for him time and time again while he is in jail doing time for crimes he committed.

"Black women, you must use your reason and logic rather than give into the passions of your heart when it comes to Black men. It is time for Black women to be as wise and discriminating when choosing their men as they are when buying a car or finding a place to stay. Black women, only accept the best, you deserve it."

"THE TIME HAS COME. The time has come for Black people to realize that we live in a technologically dependent, economic world. It is survival of the economic fittest. The only people that are going to survive in the future are the people with money. The only people that will have money are those who will have and use technology. Hardworking physical laborers will die a slow but sure economic death.

"It is time for Blacks to start being organized, to do their paperwork and file important documents away where they can find them when they need them. Stop having important papers and bills lying on a table or in a drawer someplace. If a Black person is poor, you can bet that their personal record keeping is a disaster.

"It is time for Blacks to produce something, something more than just the MVP of basketball, baseball, and football. We don't build anything, except churches, of course.

"It is time for us to be more than just consumers. You see, we make everyone else, Whites, Asians, Jews, and Arabs rich. Just put a business in our neighborhoods and we will patronize it as long as we know that it is other than Black owned. Never mind that the products and the services are atrocious; never mind that the prices are outrageous, we will buy from them. Yet, we demand perfection from Black owned businesses.

"Every day we spend countless millions of dollars on Chinese and Arab owned laundries, White owned movie rental stores and check cashing places, not to mention White owned restaurants, department stores, grocery stores, and service stations. It is time for us to stop servicing and making other races rich while we live in poverty. We can do more than just play sports, entertain, and operate barber and beauty salons. We must stop being the gullible consumer for the world!

"We must provide our own services and our own jobs. We are the only race that works for other races or depends on other races for our livelihood. When was the last time you saw an Asian working for a White man or vice-versa? It is time to understand that other races are not going to give you, a Black person, a job making as much or more money than they are. It does not matter how qualified you are in your chosen field. Other races simply take care of their own.

"No Black person would believe that Whites or Asians could play sports as well as Blacks. Well, it is time to start winning financially, too. The belief must stop that being Black means being poor. If we make money the same way we play sports, we will be the world's richest people. We must strive to provide the highest quality of products and services we offer in the same manner that we provide the best services in sports and entertainment.

"It is time to start thinking in the long term. Start accumulating wealth for our generations to come. Don't just buy an expensive car or shoes today and be happy; rather, plan for the economic future.

"It is time to realize that not all decisions are based on race; rather, most are based on the almighty dollar. To get the almighty dollar, Blacks must compete, that's right, both within and without the race. The best person wins, just like in sports.

"We must understand that wealth means power. Power means controlling your destiny. By controlling your destiny, you control your life and ultimately your quality of life. It is time to realize that Black people no longer need clean up after other races, be nannies for their children, or pick up their garbage. We no longer need front for other races so that other Blacks think that we are the owners. We can be the actual owners instead of renting and never accumulating equity. Blacks don't have to have Ph.Ds and can only find jobs washing dishes for $5.00 and hour. We no longer need be denied a good job so that we can't make money, pay our bills and have good credit.

"We can pool our money, not just to build churches, but to build restaurants, open banks, laundries, hospitals, office buildings, video shops and apartment buildings. We can then provide our own jobs. We will have enough jobs if we patronize our own businesses, which will then be able to expand and grow, and thus provide even more jobs. Of course, our Black businesses won't grow unless we, as Black people, pay our own people just as much for their services as we pay Whites for theirs. The days of having to go to the check cashing place rather than the bank can be over. We can own the bank!

"FINALLY, THE TIME HAS COME. The time has come to understand that there are inferior and superior races. This is just the simple fact of living on the planet. It is time for us Black people to stop being in the cellar and to take our rightful place at the top. It is time to put all that faith, church going, shouting and praying into action. And that action is using our talents, because we are the most talented people on earth.

"You can only use your talents through hard work. If any Black person truly took a good look at him or herself, then you would see that you are in the circumstances you are in because of hard work or the lack thereof. It is better to be a hard worker than it is to be talented. Hard work always wins out.

"When it is all said and done, the only people that are going to help improve the quality of life for Black people will be Black people themselves. This help starts with you, the individual, working to make yourself better right now. It is time to understand that if it is to be, it is up to us. If it is to be, it is up to me.

"YOU SEE, THE TIME HAS COME! THE TIME HAS COME! THE TIME HAS COME! THE TIME HAS COME! THE TIME HAS COME! THE TIME HAS COME!"

Reginald walked over to his seat and sat down. No one in the entire Dome said a word. This was not the kind of speech that they had expected.

Suddenly a man jumped to his feet and started clapping. Another one followed. Soon the entire place erupted with clapping and roaring shouts. It was indeed pandemonium.

People on the podium grabbed Reginald, they hugged him. Not all of the people in the audience were on their feet however. Most of the diehard Civil Rights leaders were still in their seats. They were in shock. They did not know what to do. This speech had been broadcast all over the world. The world had been told by the leader of the NAACP that the Civil Rights Movement was dead. To these older Civil Rights Leaders, the movement was their life. Many of them had not held a real job in twenty or more years.

Reginald looked back at the King widows. They looked totally disgusted. They gave him the look of," this is not over yet." Reginald gave them a cold stare.

Mr. Gibbs made his way back to the microphone. He let the audience revel in this moment for a while longer. Finally, he raised his hands. The audience obeyed and once again the Dome was quiet.

"Ladies and Gentlemen, I am speechless. This opening address is one of the greatest speeches of all time. This is a bold new approach for the NAACP, one that I don't think anyone expected, but no one can disagree with. Change is inevitable. The cards have been dealt, now let's play the hand."

There was more applause from the audience as they began to grasp the content of Reginald's speech in the depths of their minds.

"Now, Ladies and Gentlemen, the next speaker will be Chavis Martin. He will give you some of the details regarding tomorrow's planned march."

Before Chavis could get to the microphone, Reginald stood up. He raised his arms high. The crowd began to chant over and over again, "The Time Has Come! The Time Has Come! The Time Has Come!"

Suddenly Reginald walked to the Master of Ceremonies and handed him a note. Then he walked off of the Podium and onto the playing field. Candice and Agent Stone had worked their way down to the playing field during the speech. Reginald headed off the field at the northeast entrance next to the east goalpost. Candice and Agent Stone pushed their way through the security people and followed Attorney Johnson. Two of Director Dixon's goons were not far behind.

Reginald headed straight out the door through Receiving and Parcel pick up. He ran to the elevator located near Lower International Boulevard. He pressed the call button and the door opened. Once inside the elevator, he pressed plaza level. Out of the corner of his eye, he could see Agent Stone and Candice headed for the elevator. The doors closed and the elevator worked its way to the top.

Agent Stone and Candice took the stairs located by Receiving. By the time they got to the top, both of them were out of breath. They saw Attorney Johnson heading across the walkway to the Georgia World Congress Center. They ran after him. It did not dawn on either one of them that by the time they had gotten to the top of the stairs, Attorney Johnson should have been long gone. At this point, all they cared about was catching him. They saw him run down the side walk of the World Congress Center. He cut across the street and headed toward the Omni.

Both Candice and Agent Stone were feeling the effects of hypoxia, the lack of oxygen to the brain. They were beginning to get the headaches usually associated with this condition. Attorney Johnson ran toward the south end of the Omni and went around the building. He ran past the MARTA Station and into the McDonald's located by Gate A of the Omni.

Candice and Agent Stone entered the Mcdonald's. They looked around but did not see Attorney Johnson. Stone decided to go into the men's restroom. Candice said she was going into the ladies' room to catch her breath.

Candice walked into the restroom. She walked over to the sink and ran some water on her face. She washed her makeup off in the process. She reached into her handbag and pulled out her make up kit. She pulled out her eye shadow case and opened it. When she looked in the mirror, she saw Attorney Johnson just as he grabbed her by the neck with one hand and placed a razor to her throat with the other hand.

"So I see you and Stone are working together. I guess he got lucky after all. I hope it was good for you."

"What I do with my personal life is none of your damn business. And yes, I am working with Stone. You promised Stone that you would surrender yourself when you gave your speech or at the march or something to that effect."

"On the contrary, madam, it was Stone who said that he would take me into custody at that time. I never agreed to turn myself in willingly. Stone is a fool. He has been all along. How could he possibly think that after all the planning and preparations to change the course of history for Blacks in this country, that I was going to stop now?"

"Look, Attorney Johnson, we can work this out. Sooner or later, you have to turn yourself in."

Reginald was not listening to her. He flicked his wrist in a quick motion. Candice's throat was cut. She fell to the floor like a sack of potatoes.

Reginald came out of the bathroom. He could see Stone outside of the restaurant. He was struggling with two men, two very large men. Somehow Stone broke free momentarily. He turned and saw Attorney Johnson inside of McDonald's.

"Look, guys, there is the murderer. I told you that I followed him here. Now help me arrest him."

One of the goons answered Stone, "Yeah, sure, Stone, you and your little girlfriend tried to give us the slip. We did not see you chasing anybody. You broke your promise with the Director, and now you have to pay the piper."

"We are on the same team here. We work for the same agency. For God's sake, there is the murderer. Do something! Don't let him get away!"

The goon that had been talking to Stone reached for him. Stone stepped aside and he missed. Stone punched the other one solidly in the jaw and he stumbled backwards. Stone took off in full stride. He headed back in the direction of the MARTA Station. The two goons gave chase. Stone ran past

Gate B of the Omni and turned the corner and ran through the parking lot heading back toward the World Congress Center.

Reginald ran after them. When he turned the corner of the Omni Building, he saw one of the goons draw his weapon, take careful aim and fire. The bullet struck Stone in the back. He fell to the concrete.

The parking attendant yelled, "What is going on? You shot that man. Oh my God, I have to call the police."

The two goons ran past Stone and up the World Congress Center sidewalk. They then slowed to a walk as though they were merely out for a stroll.

Reginald watched as people gathered around the fallen body of Stone. He could not tell if he were alive or dead. An ambulance could be heard in the distance. A police officer ran from the direction of the World Congress Center to the scene.

Reginald buttoned his coat He walked up the stairs by the MARTA Station onto Techwood Avenue. He went down to International Plaza, turned right and walked to Upper Gate C of the Dome. He took the elevator back down to the field level and walked back in through the receiving area. He walked right into the Dome. He wondered how could this place be considered secure when there were ten to twenty security people on each gate and yet the receiving area was deserted. Anyone could walk right in just as he did.

Reginald identified himself to the myriad of security people as he entered onto the playing field. When the crowd saw him, they began to cheer. The Master of Ceremonies had read the note he had been handed and had announced to the crowd that Attorney Johnson had a family emergency.

This was the part of the meeting in which those who had made a significant contribution to the NAACP were being honored. Reginald had returned in time to hear Harrison Weeks being honored. He clapped his hands as people stood and clapped in memory of Mr. Weeks.

At 2:00 o'clock the public part of the meeting was over. The security people had everyone remain in their seats as the President and his entourage left the Dome. The President was scheduled to appear at a fundraiser for the AIDS Foundation at the Cobb County Civic Center that evening.

Then the Dome was cleared by security of all people who were not wearing NAACP delegate badges. After a brief meal, the business portion of the meeting began.

Most of the meeting centered around the march that was scheduled to take place on tomorrow. There were several attempts to critique Attorney Johnson's speech by some of the old time members, but Attorney Johnson kept the meeting moving in a positive direction. New officers were elected and ratified. Attorney Johnson was named as Executive Director by a unanimous vote. The next scheduled meeting was for March 15th in San Francisco. The meeting adjourned, followed by a reception held at the Hyatt Regency. Members of the NAACP partied their heads off. They had a new direction. At last there was something tangible to work towards. Something that they thought they could be a part of and make a difference in the lives of Black people.

Attorney Johnson shook hands until he thought his arms would fall off. He ran into the occasional diehard at the reception, but he was as gracious as could be. He agreed with whatever was said to him, knowing that he was going to do what he wanted to anyway.

Chapter 25

Reginald checked out of the Hyatt Hotel. He had decided that since the march was to kick off at 10:00 o'clock a.m., he might as well return to his house. He wanted to get his mail, do some cleaning and get some more belongings to take with him on the march.

Reginald was feeling good. He had done it. Now every Black person in the world had hope once again. No longer need Black people sugar coat everything concerning them while the race crumbled before their very eyes. Black people had a savior. That savior was Reginald Johnson.

As he stood on the curb, the valet returned with Reginald's Range Rover. Reginald was determined that he would break this cycle of subtle poverty. No longer would Black men work in jobs that are designed for college students.

But that was yet to come. For now, he had to concentrate on the march. After that, he was sure that there would be countless public appearances. He had better start now devising his strategies on how to handle the press. He did not want to come across like Malcolm X did, 'the angriest Black man in America.'

While Reginald agreed with most of Malcolm's philosophy, there was one major fundamental difference. Reginald did not blame Whites for the situation that Blacks found themselves in. Rather, he was thankful to Whites for all the things that they had done regarding Black people. For if it were not for Whites, the majority of Blacks might still be running around in the jungles of Africa even today. Some would argue that even if this were true, at least Blacks would be running around with dignity. But Reginald, like most wise men, worried about where they were now and how to get where they wanted to be rather than what might have been.

What Blacks failed to realize was that Whites do indeed have a lot of good qualities. They are a very organized race. They work for the common good of each other. They will not kill each other unless the economic stakes are very high. Where Blacks went wrong was, instead of trying to learn and use these qualities, they tried to immolate the skin color. Rather than place the qualities these people possessed in the high esteem that they deserved, Blacks placed the people themselves on a pedestal. Blacks did not try to be like Whites, they tried erroneously to be White, while shunning any and everything associated with Blackness. Of course, a people who didn't take time to learn about themselves, know their own history and take pride in who they were, are doomed to failure.

Reginald intended to teach Blacks how to be themselves and yet learn and adopt the best you can from other cultures. Blacks had to be taught that it was that ability that Whites possessed that keeps them on top, not their skin color.

Reginald headed up I-75. He happened to look at his gas gauge and noticed that it was low. He had a practice of always keeping more than half a tank of fuel. People running late, never seemed to make it most times because they always had to stop for gas.

He exited at the next off ramp and pulled into a B.P. station. He went inside and gave the attendant a twenty dollar bill and told him he intended to fill up. The Rover held fourteen dollars worth.

As Reginald placed the nozzle back in the slot on the pump, two young Black males approached him.

One of the youths said, "Hey, man, that's a bad ride you got there. Can I sit behind the wheel and see how it feels?"

"No, I don't think that would be a good idea, maybe some other time. I'm sort of in a hurry."

"Look, man, don't be dissing me."

Reginald started to walk back to the station building to get his change when he heard three shots ring out. The first shot hit him in the side. As he turned the other two hit him squarely in the chest. He fell to his knees. One of the young men ran over to him and grabbed the keys to the Rover out of his hand. Before he could run back to the Rover, Reginald grabbed him by the arm.

"You stupid little punk. Do you know what you have done? You have shot the one person who was probably going to make life better for all the millions of down and out Black youths like yourself. You asshole. By shooting me to get my sport utility, you have changed the course of history. You have sealed your doom and the doom of the Black Race."

Reginald began to lose consciousness. But before he did, he reached into his coat pocket and pulled out his razor. He handed it to the youth.

"Listen, you son-of-a-bitch. Take the Rover, but throw this razor away for me. That is the least that you can do."

Reginald passed out. As he did so, his hand opened and the boy was able free his arm from the vice-like grip. He took the razor, ran to the Rover and jumped in. He and his buddy drove off.

*   *   *   *   *   *

The patient in the wheel chair rolled himself down to the gift shop. He purchased the morning paper. He opened it up to the front page and looked at the headlines.

"EXECUTIVE DIRECTOR OF NAACP MURDERED IN CAR JACKING"

The man read the article that followed. It explained how Attorney Reginald Johnson had been murdered for his Range Rover on the eve of the historic march that was to begin today. The article chronicled the successful life of Attorney Johnson, including his rise to power in the NAACP.

The man began to cry. He was genuinely saddened by the article. He had known Attorney Johnson personally. He wondered what would happen to the NAACP. Just when it seemed like the NAACP had a leader capable of making the kinds of changes needed, his life was extinguished, just as the other Civil Rights leaders had been.

But more important than the NAACP, what would happen to Black people? Would there be another person with such vision that would rise to the occasion? Did people such as Attorney Johnson really only come along once in a lifetime?

Here was a man killed by the very thing that he was attempting to change. Life is so ironic some times. Just when you think that man is in charge, God shows us the folly of our ways.

The man wheeled himself back to his room. The nurse would be there any minute to take vitals, and he did not want to make her mad. He reached his room, number 211, and wheeled himself in. Not more than thirty seconds later, the nurse walked in.

"How are we today, Mr. Stone? You are the luckiest man I've ever seen. Most men who got shot the way you did, so close to the spine and all, would have surely died."

"I'm afraid that I, along with the Black race, may already be dead. For you see, I thought the time had come. But it has not come yet. I hope that I am alive when it does."

The young White nurse looked puzzled. She did not understand what he meant.

Stone wheeled himself to the window and looked out. He could see the marchers leaving the city of Atlanta. Once again they were heading down the same useless road. After the fanfare, after the media coverage ceased, Blacks would once again be in the same pathetic predicament that they have always been in. They would once again be taught by worthless leaders to be dependant on Whites.

Stone yelled out, "I love you, Reginald Johnson. If you can hear me, believe me, the time will come! The time will come! As of now, I dedicate my life to accomplishing your goals through any means necessary. The time will come! The time will come!"